THE SECRET ADVERSARY

Agatha Christie®

The Secret Adversary

HARPER

HARPER

HarperCollins *Publishers*
1 London Bridge Street
London SE1 9GF

www.harpercollins.co.uk

This paperback edition 2015

First published in Great Britain by
The Bodley Head Limited 1922

Agatha Christie® Tommy & Tuppence® The Secret Adversary™
copyright © 1922 Agatha Christie Limited. All rights reserved.
www.agathachristie.com

A catalogue record for this book is
available from the British Library

ISBN 978-0-00-759059-9

Set in Sabon by FMG using Atomik ePublisher from Easypress

Printed and bound in Great Britain by
Clays Ltd, St Ives plc

MIX
Paper from
responsible sources

FSC™ C007454

FSC is a non-profit international organisation established to promote
the responsible management of the world's forests. Products carrying the
FSC label are independently certified to assure consumers that they come
from forests that are managed to meet the social, economic and
ecological needs of present and future generations,
and other controlled sources.

Find out more about HarperCollins and the environment at
www.harpercollins.co.uk/green

To all those who lead monotonous lives in the hope that they may experience at second-hand the delights and dangers of adventure.

Agatha Christie

Contents

Prologue

It was 2 p.m. on the afternoon of May 7th, 1915. The *Lusitania* had been struck by two torpedoes in succession and was sinking rapidly, while the boats were being launched with all possible speed. The women and children were being lined up awaiting their turn. Some still clung desperately to husbands and fathers; others clutched their children closely to their breasts. One girl stood alone, slightly apart from the rest. She was quite young, not more than eighteen. She did not seem afraid, and her grave steadfast eyes looked straight ahead.

'I beg your pardon.'

A man's voice beside her made her start and turn. She had noticed the speaker more than once amongst the first-class passengers. There had been a hint of mystery about him which had appealed to her imagination. He spoke to no one. If anyone spoke to him he was quick to rebuff the overture. Also he had a nervous way of looking over his shoulder with a swift, suspicious glance.

She noticed now that he was greatly agitated. There were beads of perspiration on his brow. He was evidently in a state of overmastering fear. And yet he did not strike her as the kind of man who would be afraid to meet death!

1

'Yes?' Her grave eyes met his inquiringly.

He stood looking at her with a kind of desperate irresolution.

'It must be!' he muttered to himself. 'Yes—it is the only way.' Then aloud he said abruptly: 'You are an American?'

'Yes.'

'A patriotic one?'

The girl flushed.

'I guess you've no right to ask such a thing! Of course I am!'

'Don't be offended. You wouldn't be if you knew how much there was at stake. But I've got to trust someone—and it must be a woman.'

'Why?'

'Because of "women and children first."' He looked round and lowered his voice. 'I'm carrying papers—vitally important papers. They may make all the difference to the Allies in the war. You understand? These papers have *got* to be saved! They've more chance with you than with me. Will you take them?'

The girl held out her hand.

'Wait—I must warn you. There may be a risk—if I've been followed. I don't think I have, but one never knows. If so, there will be danger. Have you the nerve to go through with it?'

The girl smiled.

'I'll go through with it all right. And I'm real proud to be chosen! What am I to do with them afterwards?'

'Watch the newspapers! I'll advertise in the personal column of *The Times*, beginning "Shipmate." At the end of three days if there's nothing—well, you'll know I'm down and out. Then take the packet to the American Embassy, and deliver it into the Ambassador's own hands. Is that clear?'

'Quite clear.'

'Then be ready—I'm going to say goodbye.' He took her hand in his. 'Goodbye. Good luck to you,' he said in a louder tone.

Her hand closed on the oilskin packet that had lain in his palm.

The *Lusitania* settled with a more decided list to starboard. In answer to a quick command, the girl went forward to take her place in the boat.

CHAPTER 1

The Young Adventurers, Ltd.

'Tommy, old thing!'

'Tuppence, old bean!'

The two young people greeted each other affectionately, and momentarily blocked the Dover Street Tube exit in doing so. The adjective 'old' was misleading. Their united ages would certainly not have totalled forty-five.

'Not seen you for simply centuries,' continued the young man. 'Where are you off to? Come and chew a bun with me. We're getting a bit unpopular here—blocking the gangway as it were. Let's get out of it.'

The girl assenting, they started walking down Dover Street towards Piccadilly.

'Now then,' said Tommy, 'where shall we go?'

The very faint anxiety which underlay his tone did not escape the astute ears of Miss Prudence Cowley, known to her intimate friends for some mysterious reason as 'Tuppence.' She pounced at once.

'Tommy, you're stony!'

'Not a bit of it,' declared Tommy unconvincingly. 'Rolling in cash.'

'You always were a shocking liar,' said Tuppence severely, 'though you did once persuade Sister Greenbank that the doctor had ordered you beer as a tonic, but forgotten to write it on the chart. Do you remember?'

Tommy chuckled.

'I should think I did! Wasn't the old cat in a rage when she found out? Not that she was a bad sort really, old Mother Greenbank! Good old hospital—demobbed like everything else, I suppose?'

Tuppence sighed.

'Yes. You too?'

Tommy nodded.

'Two months ago.'

'Gratuity?' hinted Tuppence.

'Spent.'

'Oh, Tommy!'

'No, old thing, not in riotous dissipation. No such luck! The cost of living—ordinary plain, or garden living nowadays is, I assure you, if you do not know—'

'My dear child,' interrupted Tuppence, 'there is nothing I do *not* know about the cost of living. Here we are at Lyons', and we will each of us pay for our own. That's that!' And Tuppence led the way upstairs.

The place was full, and they wandered about looking for a table, catching odds and ends of conversation as they did so.

'And—do you know, she sat down and *cried* when I told

6

her she couldn't have the flat after all.' 'It was simply a *bargain*, my dear! Just like the one Mabel Lewis brought from Paris—'

'Funny scraps one does overhear,' murmured Tommy. 'I passed two Johnnies in the street today talking about someone called Jane Finn. Did you ever hear such a name?'

But at that moment two elderly ladies rose and collected parcels, and Tuppence deftly ensconced herself in one of the vacant seats.

Tommy ordered tea and buns. Tuppence ordered tea and buttered toast.

'And mind the tea comes in separate teapots,' she added severely.

Tommy sat down opposite her. His bared head revealed a shock of exquisitely slicked-back red hair. His face was pleasantly ugly—nondescript, yet unmistakably the face of a gentleman and a sportsman. His brown suit was well cut, but perilously near the end of its tether.

They were an essentially modern-looking couple as they sat there. Tuppence had no claim to beauty, but there was character and charm in the elfin lines of her little face, with its determined chin and large, wide-apart grey eyes that looked mistily out from under straight, black brows. She wore a small bright green toque over her black bobbed hair, and her extremely short and rather shabby skirt revealed a pair of uncommonly dainty ankles. Her appearance presented a valiant attempt at smartness.

The tea came at last, and Tuppence, rousing herself from a fit of meditation, poured it out.

'Now then,' said Tommy, taking a large bite of bun, 'lets's get up-to-date. Remember, I haven't seen you since that time in hospital in 1916.'

'Very well.' Tuppence helped herself liberally to buttered toast. 'Abridged biography of Miss Prudence Cowley, fifth daughter of Archdeacon Cowley of Little Missendell, Suffolk. Miss Cowley left the delights (and drudgeries) of her home life early in the war and came up to London, where she entered an officers' hospital. First month: Washed up six hundred and forty-eight plates every day. Second month: Promoted to drying aforesaid plates. Third month: Promoted to peeling potatoes. Fourth month: Promoted to cutting bread and butter. Fifth month: Promoted one floor up to duties of wardmaid with mop and pail. Sixth month: Promoted to waiting at table. Seventh month: Pleasing appearance and nice manners so striking that am promoted to waiting on the Sisters! Eighth month: Slight check in career. Sister Bond ate Sister Westhaven's egg! Grand row! Wardmaid clearly to blame! Inattention in such important matters cannot be too highly censured. Mop and pail again! How are the mighty fallen! Ninth month: Promoted to sweeping out wards, where I found a friend of my childhood in Lieutenant Thomas Beresford (bow, Tommy!), whom I had not seen for five long years. The meeting was affecting! Tenth month: Reproved by matron for visiting the pictures in company with one of the patients, namely: the aforementioned Lieutenant Thomas Beresford. Eleventh and twelfth months: Parlourmaid duties resumed with entire success. At the end of the year

8

left hospital in a blaze of glory. After that, the talented Miss Cowley drove successively a trade delivery van, a motor-lorry and a general. The last was the pleasantest. He was quite a young general!'

'What blighter was that?' inquired Tommy. 'Perfectly sickening the way those brass hats drove from the War Office to the Savoy, and from the Savoy to the War Office!'

'I've forgotten his name now,' confessed Tuppence. 'To resume, that was in a way the apex of my career. I next entered a Government office. We had several very enjoyable tea parties. I had intended to become a land girl, a postwoman, and a bus conductress by way of rounding off my career—but the Armistice intervened! I clung to the office with the true limpet touch for many long months, but, alas, I was combed out at last. Since then I've been looking for a job. Now then—your turn.'

'There's not so much promotion in mine,' said Tommy regretfully, 'and a great deal less variety. I went out to France again, as you know. Then they sent me to Mesopotamia, and I got wounded for the second time, and went into hospital out there. Then I got stuck in Egypt till the Armistice happened, kicked my heels there some time longer, and, as I told you, finally got demobbed. And, for ten long, weary months I've been job hunting! There aren't any jobs! And, if there were, they wouldn't give 'em to me. What good am I? What do I know about business? Nothing.'

Tuppence nodded gloomily.

'What about the colonies?' she suggested.

Tommy shook his head.

'I shouldn't like the colonies—and I'm perfectly certain they wouldn't like me!'

'Rich relations?'

Again Tommy shook his head.

'Oh, Tommy, not even a great-aunt?'

'I've got an old uncle who's more or less rolling, but he's no good.'

'Why not?'

'Wanted to adopt me once. I refused.'

'I think I remember hearing about it,' said Tuppence slowly. 'You refused because of your mother—'

Tommy flushed.

'Yes, it would have been a bit rough on the mater. As you know, I was all she had. Old boy hated her—wanted to get me away from her. Just a bit of spite.'

'Your mother's dead, isn't she?' said Tuppence gently.

Tommy nodded.

Tuppence's large grey eyes looked misty.

'You're a good sort, Tommy. I always knew it.'

'Rot!' said Tommy hastily. 'Well, that's my position. I'm just about desperate.'

'So am I! I've hung out as long as I could. I've touted round. I've answered advertisements. I've tried every mortal blessed thing. I've screwed and saved and pinched! But it's no good. I shall have to go home!'

'Don't you want to?'

'Of course I don't want to! What's the good of being sentimental? Father's a dear—I'm awfully fond of him—but you've no idea how I worry him! He has that delightful early Victorian view that short skirts and smoking are immoral. You can imagine what a thorn in the flesh I am to him! He just heaved a sigh of relief when the war took me off. You see, there are seven of us at home. It's awful! All housework and mothers' meetings! I have always been the changeling. I don't want to go back, but—oh, Tommy, what else is there to do?'

Tommy shook his head sadly. There was a silence, and then Tuppence burst out:

'Money, money, money! I think about money morning, noon and night! I dare say it's mercenary of me, but there it is!'

'Same here,' agreed Tommy with feeling.

'I've thought over every imaginable way of getting it too,' continued Tuppence. 'There are only three! To be left it, to marry it, or to make it. First is ruled out. I haven't got any rich elderly relatives. Any relatives I have are in homes for decayed gentlewomen! I always help old ladies over crossings, and pick up parcels for old gentlemen, in case they should turn out to be eccentric millionaires. But not one of them has ever asked me my name—and quite a lot never said "Thank you."'

There was a pause.

'Of course,' resumed Tuppence, 'marriage is my best chance. I made up my mind to marry money when I was quite young. Any thinking girl would! I'm not sentimental, you know.' She paused. 'Come now, you can't say I'm sentimental,' she added sharply.

'Certainly not,' agreed Tommy hastily. 'No one would ever think of sentiment in connexion with you.'

'That's not very polite,' replied Tuppence. 'But I dare say you mean it all right. Well, there it is! I'm ready and willing—but I never meet any rich men! All the boys I know are about as hard up as I am.'

'What about the general?' inquired Tommy.

'I fancy he keeps a bicycle shop in time of peace,' explained Tuppence. 'No, there it is! Now *you* could marry a rich girl.'

'I'm like you. I don't know any.'

'That doesn't matter. You can always get to know one. Now, if I see a man in a fur coat come out of the Ritz I can't rush up to him and say: "Look here, you're rich. I'd like to know you."'

'Do you suggest that I should do that to a similarly garbed female?'

'Don't be silly. You tread on her foot, or pick up her handkerchief, or something like that. If she thinks you want to know her she's flattered, and will manage it for you somehow.'

'You overrate my manly charms,' murmured Tommy.

'On the other hand,' proceeded Tuppence, 'my millionaire would probably run for his life! No—marriage is fraught with difficulties. Remains—to *make* money!'

'We've tried that, and failed,' Tommy reminded her.

'We've tried all the orthodox ways, yes. But suppose we try the unorthodox. Tommy, let's be adventurers!'

'Certainly,' replied Tommy cheerfully. 'How do we begin?'

'That's the difficulty. If we could make ourselves known, people might hire us to commit crimes for them.'

'Delightful,' commented Tommy. 'Especially coming from a clergyman's daughter!'

'The moral guilt,' Tuppence pointed out, 'would be theirs—not mine. You must admit that there's a difference between stealing a diamond necklace for yourself and being hired to steal it?'

'There wouldn't be the least difference if you were caught!'

'Perhaps not. But I shouldn't be caught. I'm so clever.'

'Modesty always was your besetting sin,' remarked Tommy.

'Don't rag. Look here, Tommy, shall we really? Shall we form a business partnership?'

'Form a company for the stealing of diamond necklaces?'

'That was only an illustration. Let's have a—what do you call it in book-keeping?'

'Don't know. Never did any.'

'I have—but I always got mixed up, and used to put credit entries on the debit side, and vice versa—so they fired me out. Oh, I know—a joint venture! It struck me as such a romantic phrase to come across in the middle of musty old figures. It's got an Elizabethan flavour about it—makes one think of galleons and doubloons. A joint venture!'

'Trading under the name of the Young Adventurers, Ltd.? Is that your idea, Tuppence?'

'It's all very well to laugh, but I feel there might be something in it.'

'How do you propose to get in touch with your would-be employers?'

'Advertisement,' replied Tuppence promptly. 'Have you got a bit of paper and a pencil? Men usually seem to have. Just like we have hairpins and powder-puffs.'

Tommy handed over a rather shabby green notebook, and Tuppence began writing busily.

'Shall we begin: "Young officer, twice wounded in the war—"'

'Certainly not.'

'Oh, very well, my dear boy. But I can assure you that that sort of thing might touch the heart of an elderly spinster, and she might adopt you, and then there would be no need for you to be a young adventurer at all.'

'I don't want to be adopted.'

'I forgot you had a prejudice against it. I was only ragging you! The papers are full up to the brim with that type of thing. Now listen—how's this? "Two young adventurers for hire. Willing to do anything, go anywhere. Pay must be good." (We might as well make that clear from the start.) Then we might add: "No reasonable offer refused"—like flats and furniture.'

'I should think any offer we get in answer to that would be a pretty *un*reasonable one!'

'Tommy! You're a genius! That's ever so much more chic. "No unreasonable offer refused—if pay is good." How's that?'

'I shouldn't mention pay again. It looks rather eager.'

'It couldn't look as eager as I feel! But perhaps you are right. Now I'll read it straight through. "Two young adventurers for hire. Willing to do anything, go anywhere. Pay must be good. No unreasonable offer refused." How would that strike you if you read it?'

'It would strike me as either being a hoax, or else written by a lunatic.'

'It's not half so insane as a thing I read this morning beginning "Petunia" and signed "Best Boy."' She tore out the leaf and handed it to Tommy. 'There you are. *The Times*, I think. Reply to Box so-and-so. I expect it will be about five shillings. Here's half a crown for my share.'

Tommy was holding the paper thoughtfully. His face burned a deeper red.

'Shall we really try it?' he said at last. 'Shall we, Tuppence? Just for the fun of the thing?'

'Tommy, you're a sport! I knew you would be! Let's drink to success.' She poured some cold dregs of tea into the two cups.

'Here's to our joint venture, and may it prosper!'

'The Young Adventurers, Ltd.!' responded Tommy.

They put down the cups and laughed rather uncertainly. Tuppence rose.

'I must return to my palatial suite at the hostel.'

'Perhaps it is time I strolled round to the Ritz,' agreed Tommy with a grin. 'Where shall we meet? And when?'

'Twelve o'clock tomorrow. Piccadilly Tube station. Will that suit you?'

'My time is my own,' replied Mr Beresford magnificently.

'So long, then.'

'Goodbye, old thing.'

The two young people went off in opposite directions. Tuppence's hostel was situated in what was charitably called Southern Belgravia. For reasons of economy she did not take a bus.

Agatha Christie

She was half-way across St James's Park, when a man's voice behind her made her start.

'Excuse me,' it said. 'But may I speak to you for a moment?'

16

CHAPTER 2

Mr Whittington's Offer

Tuppence turned sharply, but the words hovering on the tip of her tongue remained unspoken for the man's appearance and manner did not bear out her first and most natural assumption. She hesitated. As if he read her thoughts, the man said quickly:

'I can assure you I mean no disrespect.'

Tuppence believed him. Although she disliked and distrusted him instinctively, she was inclined to acquit him of the particular motive which she had at first attributed to him. She looked him up and down. He was a big man, clean shaven, with a heavy jowl. His eyes were small and cunning, and shifted their glance under her direct gaze.

'Well, what is it?' she asked.

The man smiled.

'I happened to overhear part of your conversation with the young gentleman in Lyons'.'

'Well—what of it?'

'Nothing—except that I think I may be of some use to you.'

Agatha Christie

Another inference forced itself into Tuppence's mind.

'You followed me here?'

'I took that liberty.'

'And in what way do you think you could be of use to me?'

The man took a card from his pocket and handed it to her with a bow.

Tuppence took it and scrutinized it carefully. It bore the inscription 'Mr Edward Whittington.' Below the name were the words 'Esthonia Glassware Co.,' and the address of a city office. Mr Whittington spoke again:

'If you will call upon me tomorrow morning at eleven o'clock, I will lay the details of my proposition before you.'

'At eleven o'clock?' said Tuppence doubtfully.

'At eleven o'clock.'

Tuppence made up her mind.

'Very well. I'll be there.'

'Thank you. Good evening.'

He raised his hat with a flourish, and walked away. Tuppence remained for some minutes gazing after him. Then she gave a curious movement of her shoulders, rather as a terrier shakes himself.

'The adventures have begun,' she murmured to herself. 'What does he want me to do, I wonder? There's something about you, Mr Whittington, that I don't like at all. But, on the other hand, I'm not the least bit afraid of you. And as I've said before, and shall doubtless say again, little Tuppence can look after herself, thank you!'

And with a short, sharp nod of her head she walked briskly onward. As a result of further meditations, however, she turned aside from the direct route and entered a post office. There she pondered for some moments, a telegraph form in her hand. The thought of a possible five shillings spent unnecessarily spurred her to action, and she decided to risk the waste of ninepence.

Disdaining the spiky pen and thick, black treacle which a beneficent Government had provided, Tuppence drew out Tommy's pencil which she had retained and wrote rapidly: 'Don't put in advertisement. Will explain tomorrow.' She addressed it to Tommy at his club, from which in one short month he would have to resign, unless a kindly fortune permitted him to renew his subscription.

'It may catch him,' she murmured. 'Anyway it's worth trying.'

After handing it over the counter she set out briskly for home, stopping at a baker's to buy three-pennyworth of new buns.

Later, in her tiny cubicle at the top of the house she munched buns and reflected on the future. What was the Esthonia Glassware Co., and what earthly need could it have for her services? A pleasurable thrill of excitement made Tuppence tingle. At any rate, the country vicarage had retreated into the background again. The morrow held possibilities.

It was a long time before Tuppence went to sleep that night, and, when at length she did, she dreamed that Mr Whittington had set her to washing up a pile of Esthonia Glassware, which bore an unaccountable resemblance to hospital plates!

Agatha Christie

It wanted some five minutes to eleven when Tuppence reached the block of buildings in which the offices of the Esthonia Glassware Co. were situated. To arrive before the time would look over-eager. So Tuppence decided to walk to the end of the street and back again. She did so. On the stroke of eleven she plunged into the recesses of the building. The Esthonia Glassware Co. was on the top floor. There was a lift, but Tuppence chose to walk up.

Slightly out of breath, she came to a halt outside the ground glass door with the legend painted across it: 'Esthonia Glassware Co.'

Tuppence knocked. In response to a voice from within, she turned the handle and walked into a small, rather dirty office.

A middle-aged clerk got down from a high stool at a desk near the window and came towards her inquiringly.

'I have an appointment with Mr Whittington,' said Tuppence.

'Will you come this way, please.' He crossed to a partition door with 'Private' on it, knocked, then opened the door and stood aside to let her pass in.

Mr Whittington was seated behind a large desk covered with papers. Tuppence felt her previous judgment confirmed. There was something wrong about Mr Whittington. The combination of his sleek prosperity and his shifty eye was not attractive.

He looked up and nodded.

'So you've turned up all right? That's good. Sit down, will you?'

Tuppence sat down on the chair facing him. She looked particularly small and demure this morning. She sat there meekly with downcast eyes whilst Mr Whittington sorted and rustled amongst his papers. Finally he pushed them away, and leaned over the desk.

'Now, my dear young lady, let us come to business.' His large face broadened into a smile. 'You want work? Well, I have work to offer you. What should you say now to £100 down, and all expenses paid?' Mr Whittington leaned back in his chair, and thrust his thumbs into the arm-holes of his waistcoat.

Tuppence eyed him warily.

'And the nature of the work?' she demanded.

'Nominal—purely nominal. A pleasant trip, that is all.'

'Where to?'

Mr Whittington smiled again.

'Paris.'

'Oh!' said Tuppence thoughtfully. To herself she said: 'Of course, if father heard that he would have a fit! But somehow I don't see Mr Whittington in the rôle of the gay deceiver.'

'Yes,' continued Whittington. 'What could be more delightful? To put the clock back a few years—a very few, I am sure—and re-enter one of those charming *pensionnats de jeunes filles* with which Paris abounds—'

Tuppence interrupted him.

'A *pensionnat*?'

'Exactly. Madame Colombier's in the Avenue de Neuilly.'

Tuppence knew the name well. Nothing could have been more select. She had had several American friends there. She was more than ever puzzled.

'You want me to go to Madame Colombier's? For how long?'

'That depends. Possibly three months.'

'And that is all? There are no other conditions?'

'None whatever. You would, of course, go in the character of my ward, and you would hold no communication with your friends. I should have to request absolute secrecy for the time being. By the way, you are English, are you not?'

'Yes.'

'Yet you speak with a slight American accent?'

'My great pal in hospital was a little American girl. I dare say I picked it up from her. I can soon get out of it again.'

'On the contrary, it might be simpler for you to pass as an American. Details about your past life in England might be more difficult to sustain. Yes, I think that would be decidedly better. Then—'

'One moment, Mr Whittington! You seem to be taking my consent for granted.'

Whittington looked surprised.

'Surely you are not thinking of refusing? I can assure you that Madame Colombier's is a most high-class and orthodox establishment. And the terms are most liberal.'

'Exactly,' said Tuppence. 'That's just it. The terms are almost too liberal, Mr Whittington. I cannot see any way in which I can be worth that amount of money to you.'

'No?' said Whittington softly. 'Well, I will tell you. I could doubtless obtain someone else for very much less. What I am willing to pay for is a young lady with sufficient intelligence and presence of mind to sustain her part well,

22

and also one who will have sufficient discretion not to ask too many questions.'

Tuppence smiled a little. She felt that Whittington had scored.

'There's another thing. So far there has been no mention of Mr Beresford. Where does he come in?'

'Mr Beresford?'

'My partner,' said Tuppence with dignity. 'You saw us together yesterday.'

'Ah, yes. But I'm afraid we shan't require his services.'

'Then it's off!' Tuppence rose. 'It's both or neither. Sorry—but that's how it is. Good morning, Mr Whittington.'

'Wait a minute. Let us see if something can't be managed. Sit down again, Miss—' He paused interrogatively.

Tuppence's conscience gave her a passing twinge as she remembered the archdeacon. She seized hurriedly on the first name that came into her head.

'Jane Finn,' she said hastily; and then paused open-mouthed at the effect of those two simple words.

All the geniality had faded out of Whittington's face. It was purple with rage, and the veins stood out on the forehead. And behind it all there lurked a sort of incredulous dismay. He leaned forward and hissed savagely:

'So that's your little game, is it?'

Tuppence, though utterly taken aback, nevertheless kept her head. She had not the faintest comprehension of his meaning, but she was naturally quick-witted, and felt it imperative to 'keep her end up' as she phrased it.

Whittington went on:

'Been playing with me, have you, all the time, like a cat and mouse? Knew all the time what I wanted you for, but kept up the comedy. Is that it, eh?' He was cooling down. The red colour was ebbing out of his face. He eyed her keenly. 'Who's been blabbing? Rita?'

Tuppence shook her head. She was doubtful as to how long she could sustain this illusion, but she realized the importance of not dragging an unknown Rita into it.

'No,' she replied with perfect truth. 'Rita knows nothing about me.'

His eyes still bored into her like gimlets.

'How much do you know?' he shot out.

'Very little indeed,' answered Tuppence, and was pleased to note that Whittington's uneasiness was augmented instead of allayed. To have boasted that she knew a lot might have raised doubts in his mind.

'Anyway,' snarled Whittington, 'you knew enough to come in here and plump out that name.'

'It might be my own name,' Tuppence pointed out.

'It's likely, isn't it, that there would be two girls with a name like that?'

'Or I might just have hit upon it by chance,' continued Tuppence, intoxicated with the success of truthfulness.

Mr Whittington brought his fist down upon the desk with a bang.

'Quit fooling! How much do you know? And how much do you want?'

The last five words took Tuppence's fancy mightily, especially after a meagre breakfast and a supper of buns the night before. Her present part was of the adventuress rather than the adventurous order, but she did not deny its possibilities. She sat up and smiled with the air of one who has the situation thoroughly well in hand.

'My dear Mr Whittington,' she said, 'let us by all means lay our cards upon the table. And pray do not be so angry. You heard me say yesterday that I proposed to live by my wits. It seems to me that I have now proved I have some wits to live by! I admit I have knowledge of a certain name, but perhaps my knowledge ends there.'

'Yes—and perhaps it doesn't,' snarled Whittington.

'You insist on misjudging me,' said Tuppence, and sighed gently.

'As I said once before,' said Whittington angrily, 'quit fooling, and come to the point. You can't play the innocent with me. You know a great deal more than you're willing to admit.'

Tuppence paused a moment to admire her own ingenuity, and then said softly:

'I shouldn't like to contradict you, Mr Whittington.'

'So we come to the usual question—how much?'

Tuppence was in a dilemma. So far she had fooled Whittington with complete success, but to mention a palpably impossible sum might awaken his suspicions. An idea flashed across her brain.

'Suppose we say a little something down, and a fuller discussion of the matter later?'

Whittington gave her an ugly glance.

'Blackmail, eh?'

Agatha Christie

Tuppence smiled sweetly.

'Oh no! Shall we say payment of services in advance?'

Whittington grunted.

'You see,' explained Tuppence sweetly, 'I'm not so very fond of money!'

'You're about the limit, that's what you are,' growled Whittington, with a sort of unwilling admiration. 'You took me in all right. Thought you were quite a meek little kid with just enough brains for my purpose.'

'Life,' moralized Tuppence, 'is full of surprises.'

'All the same,' continued Whittington, 'someone's been talking. You say it isn't Rita. Was it—? Oh, come in?'

The clerk followed his discreet knock into the room, and laid a paper at his master's elbow.

'Telephone message just come for you, sir.'

Whittington snatched it up and read it. A frown gathered on his brow.

'That'll do, Brown. You can go.'

The clerk withdrew, closing the door behind him. Whittington turned to Tuppence.

'Come tomorrow at the same time. I'm busy now. Here's fifty to go on with.'

He rapidly sorted out some notes, and pushed them across the table to Tuppence, then stood up, obviously impatient for her to go.

The girl counted the notes in a business-like manner, secured them in her handbag, and rose.

'Good morning, Mr Whittington,' she said politely. 'At least *au revoir*, I should say.'

26

'Exactly. *Au revoir*!' Whittington looked almost genial again, a reversion that aroused in Tuppence a faint misgiving. '*Au revoir*, my clever and charming young lady.'

Tuppence sped lightly down the stairs. A wild elation possessed her. A neighbouring clock showed the time to be five minutes to twelve.

'Let's give Tommy a surprise!' murmured Tuppence, and hailed a taxi.

The cab drew up outside the Tube station. Tommy was just within the entrance. His eyes opened to their fullest extent as he hurried forward to assist Tuppence to alight. She smiled at him affectionately, and remarked in a slightly affected voice:

'Pay the thing, will you, old bean? I've got nothing smaller than a five-pound note!'

CHAPTER 3

A Setback

The moment was not quite so triumphant as it ought to have been. To begin with, the resources of Tommy's pockets were somewhat limited. In the end the fare was managed, the lady recollecting a plebeian twopence, and the driver, still holding the varied assortment of coins in his hand, was prevailed upon to move on, which he did after one last hoarse demand as to what the gentleman thought he was giving him?

'I think you've given him too much, Tommy,' said Tuppence innocently. 'I fancy he wants to give some of it back.'

It was possibly this remark which induced the driver to move away.

'Well,' said Mr Beresford, at length able to relieve his feelings, 'what the—dickens, did you want to take a taxi for?'

'I was afraid I might be late and keep you waiting,' said Tuppence gently.

28

'Afraid—you—might—be—late! Oh, Lord, I give it up!' said Mr Beresford.

'And really and truly,' continued Tuppence, opening her eyes very wide, 'I haven't got anything smaller than a five-pound note.'

'You did that part of it very well, old bean, but all the same the fellow wasn't taken in—not for a moment!'

'No,' said Tuppence thoughtfully, 'he didn't believe it. That's the curious part about speaking the truth. No one does believe it. I found that out this morning. Now let's go to lunch. How about the Savoy?'

Tommy grinned.

'How about the Ritz?'

'On second thoughts, I prefer the Piccadilly. It's nearer. We shan't have to take another taxi. Come along.'

'Is this a new brand of humour? Or is your brain really unhinged?' inquired Tommy.

'Your last supposition is the correct one. I have come into money, and the shock has been too much for me! For that particular form of mental trouble an eminent physician recommends unlimited *hors d'oeuvre*, lobster *à l'américaine*, chicken Newberg, and *pêche Melba*! Let's go and get them!'

'Tuppence, old girl, what has really come over you?'

'Oh, unbelieving one!' Tuppence wrenched open her bag. 'Look here, and here, and here!'

'My dear girl, don't wave pound notes aloft like that!'

'They're not pound notes. They're five times better, and this one's ten times better!'

Tommy groaned.

'I must have been drinking unawares! Am I dreaming, Tuppence, or do I really behold a large quantity of five-pound notes being waved about in a dangerous fashion?'

'Even so, O King! *Now*, will you come and have lunch?'

'I'll come anywhere. But what have you been doing? Holding up a bank?'

'All in good time. What an awful place Piccadilly Circus is. There's a huge bus bearing down on us. It would be too terrible if they killed the five-pound notes!'

'Grill room?' inquired Tommy, as they reached the opposite pavement in safety.

'The other's more expensive,' demurred Tuppence.

'That's mere wicked wanton extravagance. Come on below.'

'Are you sure I can get all the things I want there?'

'That extremely unwholesome menu you were outlining just now? Of course you can—or as much as is good for you, anyway.'

'And now tell me,' said Tommy, unable to restrain his pent-up curiosity any longer, as they sat in state surrounded by the many *hors d'oeuvre* of Tuppence's dreams.

Miss Cowley told him.

'And the curious part of it is,' she ended, 'that I really did invent the name of Jane Finn! I didn't want to give my own because of poor father—in case I should get mixed up in anything shady.'

'Perhaps that's so,' said Tommy slowly. 'But you didn't invent it.'

'What?'

'No. *I* told it to you. Don't you remember, I said yesterday I'd overheard two people talking about a female called Jane Finn? That's what brought the name into your mind so pat.'

'So you did. I remember now. How extraordinary—' Tuppence tailed off into silence. Suddenly she roused herself. 'Tommy!'

'Yes?'

'What were they like, the two men you passed?'

Tommy frowned in an effort at remembrance.

'One was a big fat sort of chap. Clean shaven. I think— and dark.'

'That's him,' cried Tuppence, in an ungrammatical squeal. 'That's Whittington! What was the other man like?'

'I can't remember. I didn't notice him particularly. It was really the outlandish name that caught my attention.'

'And people say that coincidences don't happen!' Tuppence tackled her *pêche Melba* happily.

But Tommy had become serious.

'Look here, Tuppence, old girl, what is this going to lead to?'

'More money,' replied his companion.

'I know that. You've only got one idea in your head. What I mean is, what about the next step? How are you going to keep the game up?'

'Oh!' Tuppence laid down her spoon. 'You're right, Tommy, it is a bit of a poser.'

'After all, you know, you can't bluff him for ever. You're sure to slip up sooner or later. And, anyway, I'm not at all sure that it isn't actionable—blackmail, you know.'

'Nonsense. Blackmail is saying you'll tell unless you are given money. Now, there's nothing I could tell, because I don't really know anything.'

'H'm,' said Tommy doubtfully. 'Well, anyway, what *are* we going to do? Whittington was in a hurry to get rid of you this morning, but next time he'll want to know something more before he parts with his money. He'll want to know how much *you* know, and where you got your information from, and a lot of other things that you can't cope with. What are you going to do about it?'

Tuppence frowned severely.

'We must think. Order some Turkish coffee, Tommy. Stimulating to the brain. Oh, dear, what a lot I have eaten!'

'You have made rather a hog of yourself ! So have I for that matter, but I flatter myself that my choice of dishes was more judicious than yours. Two coffees.' (This was to the waiter.) 'One Turkish, one French.'

Tuppence sipped her coffee with a deeply reflective air, and snubbed Tommy when he spoke to her.

'Be quiet. I'm thinking.'

'Shades of Pelmanism!' said Tommy, and relapsed into silence.

'There!' said Tuppence at last. 'I've got a plan. Obviously what we've got to do is find out more about it all.'

Tommy applauded.

'Don't jeer. We can only find out through Whittington. We must discover where he lives, what he does—sleuth him, in fact! Now I can't do it, because he knows me, but he only saw you for a minute or two in Lyons'. He's not likely to recognize you. After all, one young man is much like another.'

'I repudiate that remark utterly. I'm sure my pleasing features and distinguished appearance would single me out from any crowd.'

'My plan is this,' Tuppence went on calmly. 'I'll go alone tomorrow. I'll put him off again like I did today. It doesn't matter if I don't get any more money at once. Fifty pounds ought to last us a few days.'

'Or even longer!'

'You'll hang about outside. When I come out I shan't speak to you in case he's watching. But I'll take up my stand somewhere near, and when he comes out of the building I'll drop a handkerchief or something, and off you go!'

'Off I go where?'

'Follow him, of course, silly! What do you think of the idea?'

'Sort of thing one reads about in books. I somehow feel that in real life one will feel a bit of an ass standing in the street for hours with nothing to do. People will wonder what I'm up to.'

'Not in the city. Everyone's in such a hurry. Probably no one will even notice you at all.'

'That's the second time you've made that sort of remark. Never mind, I forgive you. Anyway, it will be rather a lark. What are you doing this afternoon?'

'Well,' said Tuppence meditatively. 'I *had* thought of hats! Or perhaps silk stockings! Or perhaps—'

'Hold hard,' admonished Tommy. 'There's a limit to fifty pounds! But let's do dinner and a show tonight at all events.'

Agatha Christie

'Rather.'

The day passed pleasantly. The evening even more so. Two of the five-pound notes were now irretrievably dead.

They met by arrangement the following morning, and proceeded citywards. Tommy remained on the opposite side of the road while Tuppence plunged into the building.

Tommy strolled slowly down to the end of the street, then back again. Just as he came abreast of the buildings, Tuppence darted across the road.

'Tommy!'

'Yes. What's up?'

'The place is shut. I can't make anyone hear.'

'That's odd.'

'Isn't it? Come up with me, and let's try again.'

Tommy followed her. As they passed the third floor landing a young clerk came out of an office. He hesitated a moment, then addressed himself to Tuppence.

'Were you wanting the Esthonia Glassware?'

'Yes, please.'

'It's closed down. Since yesterday afternoon. Company being wound up, they say. Not that I've ever heard of it myself. But anyway the office is to let.'

'Th—thank you,' faltered Tuppence. 'I suppose you don't know Mr Whittington's address?'

'Afraid I don't. They left rather suddenly.'

'Thank you very much,' said Tommy. 'Come on, Tuppence.'

They descended to the street again where they gazed at one another blankly.

'That's torn it,' said Tommy at length.

'And I never suspected it,' wailed Tuppence.

'Cheer up, old thing, it can't be helped.'

'Can't it, though!' Tuppence's little chin shot out defiantly. 'Do you think this is the end? If so, you're wrong. It's just the beginning!'

'The beginning of what?'

'Of our adventure! Tommy, don't you see, if they are scared enough to run away like this, it shows that there must be a lot in this Jane Finn business! Well, we'll get to the bottom of it. We'll run them down! We'll be sleuths in earnest!'

'Yes, but there's no one left to sleuth.'

'No, that's why we'll have to start all over again. Lend me that bit of pencil. Thanks. Wait a minute—don't interrupt. There!' Tuppence handed back the pencil, and surveyed the piece of paper on which she had written with a satisfied eye.

'What's that?'

'Advertisement.'

'You're not going to put that thing in after all?'

'No, it's a different one.' She handed him the slip of paper. Tommy read the words on it aloud:

'WANTED, any information respecting Jane Finn. Apply Y. A.'

CHAPTER 4

Who is Jane Finn?

The next day passed slowly. It was necessary to curtail expenditure. Carefully husbanded, forty pounds will last a long time. Luckily the weather was fine, and 'walking is cheap,' dictated Tuppence. An outlying picture house provided them with recreation for the evening.

The day of disillusionment had been a Wednesday. On Thursday the advertisement had duly appeared. On Friday letters might be expected to arrive at Tommy's rooms.

He had been bound by an honourable promise not to open any such letters if they did arrive, but to repair to the National Gallery, where his colleague would meet him at ten o'clock.

Tuppence was first at the rendezvous. She ensconced herself on a red velvet seat, and gazed at the Turners with unseeing eyes until she saw the familiar figure enter the room.

'Well?'

'Well,' returned Mr Beresford provokingly. 'Which is your favourite picture?'

'Don't be a wretch. Aren't there *any* answers?'

Tommy shook his head with a deep and somewhat over-acted melancholy.

'I didn't want to disappoint you, old thing, by telling you right off. It's too bad. Good money wasted.' He sighed. 'Still, there it is. The advertisement has appeared, and—there are only two answers!'

'Tommy, you devil!' almost screamed Tuppence. 'Give them to me. How could you be so mean!'

'Your language, Tuppence, your language! They're very particular at the National Gallery. Government show, you know. And do remember, as I have pointed out to you before, that as a clergyman's daughter—'

'I ought to be on the stage!' finished Tuppence with a snap.

'That is not what I intended to say. But if you are sure that you have enjoyed to the full the reaction of joy after despair with which I have kindly provided you free of charge, let us get down to our mail, as the saying goes.'

Tuppence snatched the two precious envelopes from him unceremoniously, and scrutinized them carefully.

'Thick paper, this one. It looks rich. We'll keep it to the last and open the other first.'

'Right you are. One, two, three, go!'

Tuppence's little thumb ripped open the envelope, and she extracted the contents.

Dear Sir,

Referring to your advertisement in this morning's paper, I may be able to be of some use to you. Perhaps

*you could call and see me at the above address at eleven
o'clock tomorrow morning.*

    Yours truly,
    A. Carter

'27 Carshalton Terrace,' said Tuppence, referring to the
address. 'That's Gloucester Road way. Plenty of time to
get there if we Tube.'

'The following,' said Tommy, 'is the plan of campaign. It
is my turn to assume the offensive. Ushered into the presence of Mr Carter, he and I wish each other good morning
as is customary. He then says: "Please take a seat, Mr—
er?" To which I reply promptly and significantly: "Edward
Whittington!" whereupon Mr Carter turns purple in the
face and gasps out: "How much?" Pocketing the usual fee
of fifty pounds, I rejoin you in the road outside, and we
proceed to the next address and repeat the performance.'

'Don't be absurd, Tommy. Now for the other letter. Oh,
this is from the Ritz!'

'A hundred pounds instead of fifty!'

'I'll read it:

Dear Sir,

    *'Re your advertisement, I should be glad if you would
call round somewhere about lunch-time.*

    'Yours truly,

    'Julius P. Hersheimmer.'

*

'Ha!' said Tommy. 'Do I smell a Boche? Or only an American millionaire of unfortunate ancestry? At all events we'll call at lunch-time. It's a good time—frequently leads to free food for two.'

Tuppence nodded assent.

'Now for Carter. We'll have to hurry.'

Carshalton Terrace proved to be an unimpeachable row of what Tuppence called 'ladylike looking houses.' They rang the bell at No. 27, and a neat maid answered the door. She looked so respectable that Tuppence's heart sank. Upon Tommy's request for Mr Carter, she showed them into a small study on the ground floor, where she left them. Hardly a minute elapsed, however, before the door opened, and a tall man with a lean hawklike face and a tired manner entered the room.

'Mr Y.A.?' he said, and smiled. His smile was distinctly attractive. 'Do sit down, both of you.'

They obeyed. He himself took a chair opposite to Tuppence and smiled at her encouragingly. There was something in the quality of his smile that made the girl's usual readiness desert her.

As he did not seem inclined to open the conversation, Tuppence was forced to begin.

'We wanted to know—that is, would you be so kind as to tell us anything you know about Jane Finn?'

'Jane Finn? Ah!' Mr Carter appeared to reflect. 'Well, the question is, what do you know about her?'

Tuppence drew herself up.

'I don't see that that's got anything to do with it.'

'No? But it has, you know, really it has.' He smiled again in his tired way, and continued reflectively. 'So that brings us down to it again. What do *you* know about Jane Finn?'

'Come now,' he continued, as Tuppence remained silent. 'You must know *something* to have advertised as you did?' He leaned forward a little, his weary voice held a hint of persuasiveness. 'Suppose you tell me...'

There was something very magnetic about Mr Carter's personality. Tuppence seemed to shake herself free of it with an effort, as she said:

'We couldn't do that, could we, Tommy?'

But to her surprise, her companion did not back her up. His eyes were fixed on Mr Carter, and his tone when he spoke held an unusual note of deference.

'I dare say the little we know won't be any good to you, sir. But such as it is, you're welcome to it.'

'Tommy!' cried out Tuppence in surprise.

Mr Carter slewed round in his chair. His eyes asked a question.

Tommy nodded.

'Yes, sir, I recognized you at once. Saw you in France when I was with the Intelligence. As soon as you came into the room, I knew—'

Mr Carter held up his hand.

'No names, please. I'm known as Mr Carter here. It's my cousin's house, by the way. She's willing to lend it to me sometimes when it's a case of working on strictly unofficial lines. Well, now,'—he looked from one to the other—'who's going to tell me the story?'

'Fire ahead, Tuppence,' directed Tommy. 'It's your yarn.'

'Yes, little lady, out with it.'

And obediently Tuppence did out with it, telling the whole story from the forming of the Young Adventurers, Ltd., downwards.

Mr Carter listened in silence with a resumption of his tired manner. Now and then he passed his hand across his lips as though to hide a smile. When she had finished he nodded gravely.

'Not much. But suggestive. Quite suggestive. If you'll excuse me saying so, you're a curious young couple. I don't know—you might succeed where others have failed... I believe in luck, you know—always have...'

He paused a moment and then went on.

'Well, how about it? You're out for adventure. How would you like to work for me? All quite unofficial, you know. Expenses paid, and a moderate screw?'

Tuppence gazed at him, her lips parted, her eyes growing wider and wider.

'What should we have to do?' she breathed.

Mr Carter smiled.

'Just go on with what you're doing now. *Find Jane Finn.*'

'Yes, but—who *is* Jane Finn?'

Mr Carter nodded gravely.

'Yes, you're entitled to know that, I think.'

He leaned back in his chair, crossed his legs, brought the tips of his fingers together, and began in a low monotone:

'Secret diplomacy (which, by the way, is nearly always bad policy!) does not concern you. It will be sufficient to say

41

that in the early days of 1915 a certain document came into being. It was the draft of a secret agreement—treaty—call it what you like. It was drawn up ready for signature by the various representatives, and drawn up in America—at that time a neutral country. It was dispatched to England by a special messenger selected for that purpose, a young fellow called Danvers. It was hoped that the whole affair had been kept so secret that nothing would have leaked out. That kind of hope is usually disappointed. Somebody always talks!

'Danvers sailed for England on the *Lusitania*. He carried the precious papers in an oilskin packet which he wore next his skin. It was on that particular voyage that the *Lusitania* was torpedoed and sunk. Danvers was among the list of those missing. Eventually his body was washed ashore, and identified beyond any possible doubt. But the oilskin packet was missing!

'The question was, had it been taken from him, or had he himself passed it on into another's keeping? There were a few incidents that strengthened the possibility of the latter theory. After the torpedo struck the ship, in the few moments during the launching of the boats, Danvers was seen speaking to a young American girl. No one actually saw him pass anything to her, but he might have done so. It seems to me quite likely that he entrusted the papers to this girl, believing that she, as a woman, had a greater chance of bringing them safely to shore.

'But if so, where was the girl, and what had she done with the papers? By later advice from America it seemed likely that Danvers had been closely shadowed on the way

42

over. Was this girl in league with his enemies? Or had she, in her turn, been shadowed and either tricked or forced into handing over the precious packet?

'We set to work to trace her out. It proved unexpectedly difficult. Her name was Jane Finn, and it duly appeared among the list of the survivors, but the girl herself seemed to have vanished completely. Inquiries into her antecedents did little to help us. She was an orphan, and had been what we should call over here a pupil teacher in a small school out West. Her passport had been made out for Paris, where she was going to join the staff of a hospital. She had offered her services voluntarily, and after some correspondence they had been accepted. Having seen her name in the list of the saved from the *Lusitania*, the staff of the hospital were naturally very surprised at her not arriving to take up her billet, and at not hearing from her in any way.

'Well, every effort was made to trace the young lady—but all in vain. We tracked her across Ireland, but nothing could be heard of her after she set foot in England. No use was made of the draft treaty—as might very easily have been done—and we therefore came to the conclusion that Danvers had, after all, destroyed it. The war entered on another phase, the diplomatic aspect changed accordingly, and the treaty was never redrafted. Rumours as to its existence were emphatically denied. The disappearance of Jane Finn was forgotten and the whole affair was lost in oblivion.'

Mr Carter paused, and Tuppence broke in impatiently: 'But why has it all cropped up again? The war's over.'

A hint of alertness came into Mr Carter's manner.

'Because it seemed that the papers were not destroyed after all, and that they might be resurrected today with a new and deadly significance.'

Tuppence stared. Mr Carter nodded.

'Yes, five years ago, that draft treaty was a weapon in our hands; today it is a weapon against us. It was a gigantic blunder. If its terms were made public, it would mean disaster... It might possibly bring about another war—not with Germany this time! That is an extreme possibility, and I do not believe in its likelihood myself, but that document undoubtedly implicates a number of our statesmen whom we cannot afford to have discredited in any way at the present moment. As a party cry for Labour it would be irresistible, and a Labour Government at this juncture would, in my opinion, be a grave disability for British trade, but that is a mere nothing to the *real* danger.'

He paused, and then said quietly:

'You may perhaps have heard or read that there is Bolshevist influence at work behind the present labour unrest?'

Tuppence nodded.

'That is the truth, Bolshevist gold is pouring into this country for the specific purpose of procuring a Revolution. And there is a certain man, a man whose real name is unknown to us, who is working in the dark for his own ends. The Bolshevists are behind the labour unrest—but this man is *behind the Bolshevists*. Who is he? We do not know. He is always spoken of by the unassuming title of "Mr Brown." But one thing is certain, he is the master criminal of this age. He controls a marvellous organization. Most of

44

the peace propaganda during the war was originated and financed by him. His spies are everywhere.'

'A naturalized German?' asked Tommy.

'On the contrary, I have every reason to believe he is an Englishman. He was pro-German, as he would have been pro-Boer. What he seeks to attain we do not know—probably supreme power for himself, of a kind unique in history. We have no clue as to his real personality. It is reported that even his own followers are ignorant of it. Where we have come across his tracks, he has always played a secondary part. Somebody else assumes the chief rôle. But afterwards we always find that there had been some nonentity, a servant or a clerk, who had remained in the background unnoticed, and that the elusive Mr Brown has escaped us once more.'

'Oh!' Tuppence jumped. 'I wonder—'

'Yes?'

'I remember in Mr Whittington's office. The clerk—he called him Brown. You don't think—'

Carter nodded thoughtfully.

'Very likely. A curious point is that the name is usually mentioned. An idiosyncrasy of genius. Can you describe him at all?'

'I really didn't notice. He was quite ordinary—just like anyone else.'

Mr Carter sighed in his tired manner.

'That is the invariable description of Mr Brown! Brought a telephone message to the man Whittington, did he? Notice a telephone in the outer office?'

Tuppence thought.

'No, I don't think I did.'

'Exactly. That "message" was Mr Brown's way of giving an order to his subordinate. He overheard the whole conversation of course. Was it after that that Whittington handed you over the money, and told you to come the following day?'

Tuppence nodded.

'Yes, undoubtedly the hand of Mr Brown!' Mr Carter paused. 'Well, there it is, you see what you are pitting yourself against? Possibly the finest criminal brain of the age. I don't quite like it, you know. You're such young things, both of you. I shouldn't like anything to happen to you.'

'It won't,' Tuppence assured him positively.

'I'll look after her, sir,' said Tommy.

'And *I'll* look after *you*,' retorted Tuppence, resenting the manly assertion.

'Well, then, look after each other,' said Mr Carter, smiling. 'Now let's get back to business. There's something mysterious about this draft treaty that we haven't fathomed yet. We've been threatened with it—in plain and unmistakable terms. The Revolutionary elements as good as declared that it's in their hands, and that they intend to produce it at a given moment. On the other hand, they are clearly at fault about many of its provisions. The Government consider it as mere bluff on their part, and, rightly or wrongly, have stuck to the policy of absolute denial. I'm not so sure. There have been hints, indiscreet allusions, that seem to indicate that the menace is a real one. The position is much as though they had got hold of an incriminating document, but couldn't read it because it was in cipher—but we know that the draft treaty wasn't in cipher—couldn't be in the nature of things—so that won't wash. But there's *something*. Of course, Jane Finn may be dead for all we know—but I don't think so. The curious thing is that *they're trying to get information about the girl from us.*'

'What?'

'Yes. One or two little things have cropped up. And your story, little lady, confirms my idea. They know we're looking for Jane Finn. Well, they'll produce a Jane Finn of their own—say at a *pensionnat* in Paris.' Tuppence gasped, and Mr Carter smiled. 'No one knows in the least what she looks like, so that's all right. She's primed with a trumped-up tale, and her real business is to get as much information as possible out of us. See the idea?'

'Then you think'—Tuppence paused to grasp the supposition fully—'that it *was* as Jane Finn that they wanted me to go to Paris?'

Mr Carter smiled more wearily than ever.

'I believe in coincidences, you know,' he said.

CHAPTER 5

Mr Julius P. Hersheimmer

'Well,' said Tuppence, recovering herself, 'it really seems as though it were meant to be.'

Carter nodded.

'I know what you mean. I'm superstitious myself. Luck, and all that sort of thing. Fate seems to have chosen you out to be mixed up in this.'

Tommy indulged in a chuckle.

'My word! I don't wonder Whittington got the wind up when Tuppence plumped out that name! I should have myself. But look here, sir, we're taking up an awful lot of your time. Have you any tips to give us before we clear out?'

'I think not. My experts, working in stereotyped ways, have failed. You will bring imagination and an open mind to the task. Don't be discouraged if that too does not succeed. For one thing there is a likelihood of the pace being forced.'

Tuppence frowned uncomprehendingly.

'When you had that interview with Whittington, they had time before them. I have information that the big *coup* was planned for early in the new year. But the Government is contemplating legislative action which will deal effectually with the strike menace. They'll get wind of it soon, if they haven't already, and it's possible that they may bring things to a head. I hope it will myself. The less time they have to mature their plans the better. I'm just warning you that you haven't much time before you, and that you needn't be cast down if you fail. It's not an easy proposition anyway. That's all.'

Tuppence rose.

'I think we ought to be business-like. What exactly can we count upon you for, Mr Carter?'

Mr Carter's lips twitched slightly, but he replied succinctly:

'Funds within reason, detailed information on any point, and *no official recognition*. I mean that if you get yourselves into trouble with the police, I can't officially help you out of it. You're on your own.'

Tuppence nodded sagely.

'I quite understand that. I'll write out a list of the things I want to know when I've had time to think. Now—about money—'

'Yes, Miss Tuppence. Do you want to say how much?'

'Not exactly. We've got plenty to go on with for the present, but when we want more—'

'It will be waiting for you.'

'Yes, but—I'm sure I don't want to be rude about the Government if you've got anything to do with it, but you know one really has the devil of a time getting anything out of it! And if we have to fill up a blue form and send it in, and then, after three months, they send us a green one, and so on—well, that won't be much use, will it?'

Mr Carter laughed outright.

'Don't worry, Miss Tuppence. You will send a personal demand to me here, and the money, in notes, shall be sent by return of post. As to salary, shall we say at the rate of three hundred a year? And an equal sum for Mr Beresford, of course.'

Tuppence beamed upon him.

'How lovely. You are kind. I do love money! I'll keep beautiful accounts of our expenses—all debit and credit, and the balance on the right side, and a red line drawn sideways with the totals the same at the bottom. I really know how to do it when I think.'

'I'm sure you do. Well, goodbye, and good luck to you both.'

He shook hands with them and in another minute they were descending the steps of 27 Carshalton Terrace with their heads in a whirl.

'Tommy! Tell me at once, who is "Mr Carter"?'

Tommy murmured a name in her ear.

'Oh!' said Tuppence, impressed.

'And I can tell you, old bean, he's IT!'

'Oh!' said Tuppence again. Then she added reflectively: 'I like him, don't you? He looks so awfully tired and bored, and yet you feel that underneath he's just like steel, all keen and flashing. Oh!' She gave a skip. 'Pinch me, Tommy, do pinch me. I can't believe it's real!'

Mr Beresford obliged.

'Ow! That's enough! Yes, we're not dreaming. We've got a job!'

'And what a job! The joint venture has really begun.'

'It's more respectable than I thought it would be,' said Tuppence thoughtfully.

'Luckily I haven't got your craving for crime! What time is it? Let's have lunch—oh!'

The same thought sprang to the minds of each. Tommy voiced it first.

'Julius P. Hersheimmer!'

'We never told Mr Carter about hearing from him.'

'Well, there wasn't much to tell—not till we've seen him. Come on, we'd better take a taxi.'

'Now who's being extravagant?'

'All expenses paid, remember. Hop in.'

'At any rate, we shall make a better effect arriving this way,' said Tuppence, leaning back luxuriously. 'I'm sure blackmailers never arrive in buses!'

'We've ceased being blackmailers,' Tommy pointed out.

'I'm not sure I have,' said Tuppence darkly.

On inquiring for Mr Hersheimmer, they were at once taken up to his suite. An impatient voice cried 'Come in' in answer to the page-boy's knock, and the lad stood aside to let them pass in.

Mr Julius P. Hersheimmer was a great deal younger than either Tommy or Tuppence had pictured him. The girl put him down as thirty-five. He was of middle height, and squarely built to match his jaw. His face was pugnacious but pleasant. No one could have mistaken him for anything but an American, though he spoke with very little accent.

'Get my note?' Sit down and tell me right away all you know about my cousin.'

'Your cousin?'

'Sure thing. Jane Finn.'

'Is she your cousin?'

'My father and her mother were brother and sister,' explained Mr Hersheimmer meticulously.

'Oh!' cried Tuppence. 'Then you know where she is?'

'No!' Mr Hersheimmer brought down his fist with a bang on the table. 'I'm darned if I do! Don't you?'

'We advertised to receive information, not to give it,' said Tuppence severely.

'I guess I know that. I can read. But I thought maybe it was her back history you were after, and that you'd know where she was now?'

'Well, we wouldn't mind hearing her back history,' said Tuppence guardedly.

But Mr Hersheimmer seemed to grow suddenly suspicious.

'See here,' he declared. 'This isn't Sicily! No demanding ransom or threatening to crop her ears if I refuse. These are the British Isles, so quit the funny business, or I'll just sing out for that beautiful big British policeman I see out there in Piccadilly.'

Tommy hastened to explain.

'We haven't kidnapped your cousin. On the contrary, we're trying to find her. We're employed to do so.'

Mr Hersheimmer leant back in his chair.

'Put me wise,' he said succinctly.

Tommy fell in with this demand in so far as he gave him a guarded version of the disappearance of Jane Finn, and of the possibility of her having been mixed up unawares in 'some political show.' He alluded to Tuppence and himself as 'private inquiry agents' commissioned to find her, and added that they would therefore be glad of any details Mr Hersheimmer could give them.

That gentleman nodded approval.

'I guess that's all right. I was just a mite hasty. But London gets my goat! I only know little old New York. Just trot out your questions and I'll answer.'

For the moment this paralysed the Young Adventurers, but Tuppence, recovering herself, plunged boldly into the breach with a reminiscence culled from detective fiction.

'When did you last see the dece—your cousin, I mean?'

'Never seen her,' responded Mr Hersheimmer.

'What?' demanded Tommy astonished.

Hersheimmer turned to him.

'No, sir. As I said before, my father and her mother were brother and sister, just as you might be'—Tommy did not correct this view of their relationship—'but they didn't always get on together. And when my aunt made up her mind to marry Amos Finn, who was a poor school teacher out West, my father was just mad! Said if he made his pile, as he seemed in a fair way to do, she'd never see a cent of it. Well, the upshot was that Aunt Jane went out West and we never heard from her again.

'The old man *did* pile it up. He went into oil, and he went into steel, and he played a bit with railroads, and I can tell you he made Wall Street sit up!' He paused. 'Then he died—last fall—and I got the dollars. Well, would you believe it, my conscience got busy! Kept knocking me up and saying: What about your Aunt Jane, way out West? It worried me some. You see, I figured it out that Amos Finn would never make good. He wasn't the sort. End of it was, I hired a man to hunt her down. Result, she was dead, and Amos Finn was dead, but they'd left a daughter—Jane—who'd been torpedoed in the *Lusitania* on her way to Paris. She was saved all right, but they didn't seem able to hear of her over this side. I guessed they weren't hustling any, so I thought I'd come along over, and speed things up. I phoned Scotland Yard and the Admiralty first thing. The Admiralty rather choked me off, but Scotland Yard were very civil—said they would make inquiries, even sent a man round this morning to get her photograph. I'm off to Paris tomorrow, just to see what the Prefecture is doing. I guess if I go to and fro hustling them, they ought to get busy!'

The energy of Mr Hersheimmer was tremendous. They bowed before it.

'But say now,' he ended, 'you're not after her for anything? Contempt of court, or something British? A proud-spirited young American girl might find your rules and regulations in wartime rather irksome, and get up against it. If that's the case, and there's such a thing as graft in this country, I'll buy her off.'

Tuppence reassured him.

'That's good. Then we can work together. What about some lunch? Shall we have it up here, or go down to the restaurant?'

Tuppence expressed a preference for the latter, and Julius bowed to her decision.

Oysters had just given place to Sole Colbert when a card was brought to Hersheimmer.

'Inspector Japp, C.I.D. Scotland Yard again. Another man this time. What does he expect I can tell him that I didn't tell the first chap? I hope they haven't lost that photograph. That Western photographer's place was burned down and all his negatives destroyed—this is the only copy in existence. I got it from the principal of the college there.'

An unformulated dread swept over Tuppence.

'You—you don't know the name of the man who came this morning?'

'Yes, I do. No, I don't. Half a second. It was on his card. Oh, I know! Inspector Brown. Quiet unassuming sort of chap.'

CHAPTER 6

A Plan of Campaign

A veil might with profit be drawn over the events of the next half-hour. Suffice it to say that no such person as 'Inspector Brown' was known to Scotland Yard. The photograph of Jane Finn, which would have been of the utmost value to the police in tracing her, was lost beyond recovery. Once again 'Mr Brown' had triumphed.

The immediate result of this set-back was to effect a *rapprochement* between Julius Hersheimmer and the Young Adventurers. All barriers went down with a crash, and Tommy and Tuppence felt they had known the young American all their lives. They abandoned the discreet reticence of 'private inquiry agents,' and revealed to him the whole history of the joint venture, whereat the young man declared himself 'tickled to death.'

He turned to Tuppence at the close of the narration. 'I've always had a kind of idea that English girls were just a mite moss-grown. Old-fashioned and sweet, you know, but scared to move round without a footman or a maiden aunt. I guess I'm a bit behind the times!'

The upshot of these confidential relations was that Tommy and Tuppence took up their abode forthwith at the Ritz, in order, as Tuppence put it, to keep in touch with Jane Finn's only living relation. 'And put like that,' she added confidentially to Tommy, 'nobody could boggle at the expense!'

Nobody did, which was the great thing.

'And now,' said the young lady on the morning after their installation, 'to work!'

Mr Beresford put down the *Daily Mail*, which he was reading, and applauded with somewhat unnecessary vigour. He was politely requested by his colleague not to be an ass.

'Dash it all, Tommy, we've got to *do* something for our money.'

Tommy sighed.

'Yes, I fear even the dear old Government will not support us at the Ritz in idleness for ever.'

'Therefore, as I said before, we must *do* something.'

'Well,' said Tommy, picking up the *Daily Mail* again, '*do* it. I shan't stop you.'

'You see,' continued Tuppence. 'I've been thinking—'

She was interrupted by a fresh bout of applause.

'It's all very well for you to sit there being funny, Tommy. It would do you no harm to do a little brain work too.'

'My union, Tuppence, my union! It does not permit me to work before 11 a.m.'

'Tommy, do you want something thrown at you? It is absolutely essential that we should without delay map out a plan of campaign.'

'Hear, hear!'

'Well, let's do it.'

Tommy laid his paper finally aside. 'There's something of the simplicity of the truly great mind about you, Tuppence. Fire ahead. I'm listening.'

'To begin with,' said Tuppence, 'what have we to go upon?'

'Absolutely nothing,' said Tommy cheerily.

'Wrong!' Tuppence wagged an energetic finger. 'We have two distinct clues.'

'What are they?'

'First clue, we know one of the gang.'

'Whittington?'

'Yes. I'd recognize him anywhere.'

'Hum,' said Tommy doubtfully. 'I don't call that much of a clue. You don't know where to look for him, and it's about a thousand to one against your running against him by accident.'

'I'm not so sure about that,' replied Tuppence thoughtfully. 'I've often noticed that once coincidences start happening they go on happening in the most extraordinary way. I dare say it's some natural law that we haven't found out. Still, as you say, we can't rely on that. But there *are* places in London where simply everyone is bound to turn up sooner or later. Piccadilly Circus, for instance. One of my ideas was to take up my stand there every day with a tray of flags.'

'What about meals?' inquired the practical Tommy.

'How like a man! What does mere food matter?'

'That's all very well. You've just had a thundering good breakfast. No one's got a better appetite than you have, Tuppence, and by tea-time you'd be eating the flags, pins and all. But, honestly, I don't think much of the idea. Whittington mayn't be in London at all.'

'That's true. Anyway, I think clue No. 2 is more promising.'

'Let's hear it.'

'It's nothing much. Only a Christian name—Rita. Whittington mentioned it that day.'

'Are you proposing a third advertisement: Wanted, female crook, answering to the name of Rita?'

'I am not. I propose to reason in a logical manner. That man, Danvers, was shadowed on the way over, wasn't he? And it's more likely to have been a woman than a man—'

'I don't see that at all.'

'I am absolutely certain that it would be a woman, and a good-looking one,' replied Tuppence calmly.

'On these technical points I bow to your decision,' murmured Mr Beresford.

'Now, obviously, this woman, whoever she was, was saved.'

'How do you make that out?'

'If she wasn't, how would they have known Jane Finn had got the papers?'

'Correct. Proceed, O Sherlock!'

'Now there's just a chance, I admit it's only a chance, that this woman may have been "Rita".'

'And if so?'

'If so, we've got to hunt through the survivors of the *Lusitania* till we find her.'

'Then the first thing is to get a list of the survivors.'

'I've got it. I wrote a long list of things I wanted to know, and sent it to Mr Carter. I got his reply this morning, and among other things it encloses the official statement of those saved from the *Lusitania*. How's that for clever little Tuppence?'

'Full marks for industry, zero for modesty. But the great point is, is there a "Rita" on the list?'

'That's just what I don't know,' confessed Tuppence.

'Don't know?'

'Yes, look here.' Together they bent over the list. 'You see, very few Christian names are given. They're nearly all Mrs or Miss.'

Tommy nodded.

'That complicates matters,' he murmured thoughtfully.

Tuppence gave her characteristic 'terrier' shake.

'Well, we've just got to get down to it, that's all. We'll start with the London area. Just note down the addresses of any of the females who live in London or roundabout, while I put on my hat.'

Five minutes later the young couple emerged into Piccadilly, and a few seconds later a taxi was bearing them to The Laurels, Glendower Road, N.7., the residence of Mrs Edgar Keith, whose name figured first in a list of seven reposing in Tommy's pocket-book.

The Laurels was a dilapidated house, standing back from the road with a few grimy bushes to support the fiction of a front garden. Tommy paid off the taxi, and accompanied Tuppence to the front door bell. As she was about to ring it, he arrested her hand.

'What are you going to say?'

'What am I going to say? Why, I shall say—Oh dear, I don't know. It's very awkward.'

'I thought as much,' said Tommy with satisfaction. 'How like a woman! No foresight! Now just stand aside, and see how easily the mere male deals with the situation.' He pressed the bell. Tuppence withdrew to a suitable spot.

A slatternly-looking servant, with an extremely dirty face and a pair of eyes that did not match, answered the door.

Tommy had produced a notebook and pencil.

'Good morning,' he said briskly and cheerfully. 'From the Hampstead Borough Council. The New Voting Register. Mrs Edgar Keith lives here, does she not?'

'Yaas,' said the servant.

'Christian name?' asked Tommy, his pencil poised.

'Missus's? Eleanor Jane.'

'Eleanor,' spelt Tommy. 'Any sons or daughters over twenty-one?'

'Naow.'

'Thank you.' Tommy closed the notebook with a brisk snap. 'Good morning.'

The servant volunteered her first remark:

'I thought perhaps as you'd come about the gas,' she observed cryptically, and shut the door.

Tommy rejoined his accomplice.

'You see, Tuppence,' he observed. 'Child's play to the masculine mind.'

'I don't mind admitting that for once you've scored handsomely. I should never have thought of that.'

'Good wheeze, wasn't it? And we can repeat it *ad lib*.'

Lunch-time found the young couple attacking steak and chips in an obscure hostelry with avidity. They had collected

61

a Gladys Mary and a Marjorie, been baffled by one change of address, and had been forced to listen to a long lecture on universal suffrage from a vivacious American lady whose Christian name had proved to be Sadie.

'Ah!' said Tommy, imbibing a long draught of beer, 'I feel better. Where's the next draw?'

The notebook lay on the table between them. Tuppence picked it up.

'Mrs Vandemeyer,' she read, '20 South Audley Mansions. Miss Wheeler, 43 Clapington Road, Battersea. She's a lady's maid, as far as I remember, so probably won't be there, and, anyway, she's not likely.'

'Then the Mayfair lady is clearly indicated as the first port of call.'

'Tommy, I'm getting discouraged.'

'Buck up, old bean. We always knew it was an outside chance. And, anyway, we're only starting. If we draw a blank in London, there's a fine tour of England, Ireland and Scotland before us.'

'True,' said Tuppence, her flagging spirits reviving. 'And all expenses paid! But, oh, Tommy, I do like things to happen quickly. So far, adventure has succeeded adventure, but this morning has been dull as dull.'

'You must stifle this longing for vulgar sensation, Tuppence. Remember that if Mr Brown is all he is reported to be, it's a wonder that he has not ere now done us to death. That's a good sentence, quite a literary flavour about it.'

'You're really more conceited than I am—with less excuse! Ahem! But it certainly is queer that Mr Brown has not yet wreaked vengeance upon us. (You see, I can do it too.) We pass on our way unscathed.'

'Perhaps he doesn't think us worth bothering about,' suggested the young man simply.

Tuppence received the remark with great disfavour.

'How horrid you are, Tommy. Just as though we didn't count.'

'Sorry, Tuppence. What I meant was that we work like moles in the dark, and that he has no suspicion of our nefarious schemes. Ha ha!'

'Ha ha!' echoed Tuppence approvingly, as she rose.

South Audley Mansions was an imposing looking block of flats just off Park Lane. No. 20 was on the second floor.

Tommy had by this time the glibness born of practice. He rattled off the formula to the elderly woman, looking more like a housekeeper than a servant, who opened the door to him.

'Christian name?'

'Margaret.'

Tommy spelt it, but the other interrupted him.

'No, *gue*.'

'Oh, Marguerite; French way, I see.' He paused then plunged boldly. 'We had her down as Rita Vandemeyer, but I suppose that's correct?'

'She's mostly called that, sir, but Marguerite's her name.'

'Thank you. That's all. Good morning.'

Hardly able to contain his excitement, Tommy hurried down the stairs. Tuppence was waiting at the angle of the turn.

'You heard?'

'Yes. Oh, *Tommy*!'

Tommy squeezed her arm sympathetically.

'I know, old thing. I feel the same.'

'It's—it's so lovely to think of things—and then for them really to happen!' cried Tuppence enthusiastically.

Her hand was still in Tommy's. They had reached the entrance hall. There were footsteps on the stairs above them, and voices.

Suddenly, to Tommy's complete surprise, Tuppence dragged him into the little space by the side of the lift where the shadow was deepest.

'What the—'

'Hush!'

Two men came down the stairs and passed out through the entrance. Tuppence's hand closed tighter on Tommy's arm.

'Quick—follow them. I daren't. He might recognize me. I don't know who the other man is, but the bigger of the two was Whittington.'

CHAPTER 7

The House in Soho

Whittington and his companion were walking at a good pace. Tommy started in pursuit at once, and was in time to see them turn the corner of the street. His vigorous strides soon enabled him to gain upon them, and by the time he, in his turn, reached the corner the distance between them was sensibly lessened. The small Mayfair streets were comparatively deserted, and he judged it wise to content himself with keeping them in sight.

The sport was a new one to him. Though familiar with the technicalities from a course of novel reading, he had never before attempted to 'follow' anyone, and it appeared to him at once that, in actual practice, the proceeding was fraught with difficulties. Supposing, for instance, that they should suddenly hail a taxi? In books, you simply leapt into another, promised the driver a sovereign—or its modern equivalent—and there you were. In actual fact, Tommy foresaw that it was extremely likely there would be no second taxi. Therefore he would have to run. What happened in actual fact to a young man who ran incessantly and persistently through the London streets? In a main road he might hope to create the illusion that he was merely running for a bus. But in these obscure aristocratic byways he could not but feel that an officious policeman might stop him to explain matters.

At this juncture in his thoughts a taxi with flag erect turned the corner of the street ahead. Tommy held his breath. Would they hail it?

He drew a sigh of relief as they allowed it to pass unchallenged. Their course was a zigzag one designed to bring them as quickly as possible to Oxford Street. When at length they turned into it, proceeding in an easterly direction, Tommy slightly increased his pace. Little by little he gained upon them. On the crowded pavement there was little chance of his attracting their notice, and he was anxious if possible to catch a word or two of their conversation. In this he was completely foiled: they spoke low and the din of the traffic drowned their voices effectually.

Just before the Bond Street Tube station they crossed the road, Tommy, unperceived, faithfully at their heels, and entered the big Lyons'. There they went up to the first floor, and sat at a small table in the window. It was late, and the place was thinning out. Tommy took a seat at the table next to them sitting directly behind Whittington in case of recognition. On the other hand, he had a full view of the second man and studied him attentively. He was fair, with a weak, unpleasant face, and Tommy put him down as being either a Russian or a Pole. He was probably about fifty years of age, his shoulders cringed a little as he talked, and his eyes, small and crafty, shifted unceasingly.

Having already lunched heartily, Tommy contented himself with ordering a Welsh rarebit and a cup of coffee. Whittington ordered a substantial lunch for himself and his companion; then, as the waitress withdrew, he moved his chair a little closer to the table and began to talk earnestly in a low voice. The other man joined in. Listen as he would, Tommy could only catch a word here and there; but the gist of it seemed to be some directions or orders which the big man was impressing on his companion, and with which the latter seemed from time to time to disagree. Whittington addressed the other as Boris.

Tommy caught the word 'Ireland' several times, also 'propaganda,' but of Jane Finn there was no mention. Suddenly, in a lull in the clatter of the room, he got one phrase entire. Whittington was speaking. 'Ah, but you don't know Flossie. She's a marvel. An archbishop would swear she was his own mother. She gets the voice right every time, and that's really the principal thing.'

Tommy did not hear Boris's reply, but in response to it Whittington said something that sounded like: 'of course— only in an emergency...'

Then he lost the thread again. But presently the phrases became distinct again, whether because the other two had insensibly raised their voices, or because Tommy's ears were getting more attuned, he could not tell. But two words certainly had a most stimulating effect upon the listener. They were uttered by Boris and they were: 'Mr Brown.'

Whittington seemed to remonstrate with him, but he merely laughed.

'Why not, my friend? It is a name most respectable—most common. Did he not choose it for that reason? Ah, I should like to meet him—Mr Brown.'

There was a steely ring in Whittington's voice as he replied:

'Who knows? You may have met him already.'

'Bah!' retorted the other. 'That is children's talk—a fable for the police. Do you know what I say to myself sometimes? That he is a fable invented by the Inner Ring, a bogy to frighten us with. It might be so.'

'And it might not.'

'I wonder... or is it indeed true that he is with us and amongst us, unknown to all but a chosen few? If so, he keeps his secret well. And the idea is a good one, yes. We never know. We look at each other—*one of us is Mr Brown*—which? He commands—but also he serves. Among us—in the midst of us. And no one knows which he is...'

With an effort the Russian shook off the vagary of his fancy. He looked at his watch.

'Yes,' said Whittington. 'We might as well go.'

He called the waitress and asked for his bill. Tommy did likewise, and a few moments later was following the two men down the stairs.

Outside, Whittington hailed a taxi, and directed the driver to Waterloo.

Taxis were plentiful here, and before Whittington's had driven off another was drawing up to the curb in obedience to Tommy's peremptory hand.

'Follow that other taxi,' directed the young man. 'Don't lose it.'

The elderly chauffeur showed no interest. He merely grunted and jerked down his flag. The drive was uneventful. Tommy's taxi came to rest at the departure platform just after Whittington's. Tommy was behind him at the booking-office. He took a first-class single to Bournemouth, Tommy did the same. As he emerged, Boris remarked, glancing up at the clock: 'You are early. You have nearly half an hour.'

Boris's words had aroused a new train of thought in Tommy's mind. Clearly Whittington was making the journey alone, while the other remained in London. Therefore he was left with a choice as to which he would follow. Obviously, he could not follow both of them unless—Like Boris, he glanced up at the clock, and then to the announcement board of the trains. The Bournemouth train left at 3.30. It was now ten past. Whittington and Boris were walking up and down by the bookstall. He gave one doubtful look at them, then hurried into an adjacent telephone box. He dared not waste time in trying to get hold of Tuppence. In all probability she was still in the neighbourhood of South Audley Mansions. But there remained another ally. He rang up the Ritz and asked for Julius Hersheimmer. There was a click and a buzz. Oh, if only the young American was in his room! There was another click, and then 'Hello' in unmistakable accents came over the wire.

'That you, Hersheimmer? Beresford speaking. I'm at Waterloo. I've followed Whittington and another man here. No time to explain. Whittington's off to Bournemouth by the 3.30. Can you get here by then?'

The reply was reassuring.

'Sure. I'll hustle.'

The telephone rang off. Tommy put back the receiver with a sigh of relief. His opinion of Julius's power of hustling was high. He felt instinctively that the American would arrive in time.

Whittington and Boris were still where he had left them. If Boris remained to see his friend off, all was well. Then Tommy fingered his pocket thoughtfully. In spite of the carte blanche assured to him, he had not yet acquired the habit of going about with any considerable sum of money on him. The taking of the first-class ticket to Bournemouth had left him with only a few shillings in his pocket. It was to be hoped that Julius would arrive better provided.

In the meantime, the minutes were creeping by: 3.15, 3.20, 3.25, 3.27. Supposing Julius did not get there in time. 3.29.... Doors were banging. Tommy felt cold waves of despair pass over him. Then a hand fell on his shoulder.

'Here I am, son. Your British traffic beats description! Put me wise to the crooks right away.'

'That's Whittington—there, getting in now, that big dark man. The other is the foreign chap he's talking to.'

'I'm on to them. Which of the two is my bird?'

Tommy had thought out this question.

'Got any money with you?'

Julius shook his head, and Tommy's face fell.

'I guess I haven't more than three or four hundred dollars with me at the moment,' explained the American.

Tommy gave a faint whoop of relief.

'Oh, Lord, you millionaires! You don't talk the same language! Climb aboard the lugger. Here's your ticket. Whittington's your man.'

'Me for Whittington!' said Julius darkly. The train was just starting as he swung himself aboard. 'So long, Tommy.' The train slid out of the station.

Tommy drew a deep breath. The man Boris was coming along the platform towards him. Tommy allowed him to pass and then took up the chase once more.

From Waterloo Boris took the Tube as far as Piccadilly Circus. Then he walked up Shaftesbury Avenue, finally turning off into the maze of mean streets round Soho. Tommy followed him at a judicious distance.

They reached at length a small dilapidated square. The houses there had a sinister air in the midst of their dirt and decay. Boris looked round, and Tommy drew back into the shelter of a friendly porch. The place was almost deserted. It was a cul-de-sac, and consequently no traffic passed that way. The stealthy way the other had looked round stimulated Tommy's imagination. From the shelter of the doorway he watched him go up the steps of a particularly evil-looking house and rap sharply, with a peculiar rhythm, on the door. It was opened promptly, he said a word or two to the doorkeeper, then passed inside. The door was shut to again.

It was at this juncture that Tommy lost his head. What he ought to have done, what any sane man would have done, was to remain patiently where he was and wait for his man to come out again. What he did do was entirely foreign to the sober common sense which was, as a rule, his leading characteristic. Something, as he expressed it, seemed to snap in his brain. Without a moment's pause for reflection he, too, went up the steps, and reproduced as far as he was able the peculiar knock.

The door swung open with the same promptness as before. A villainous-faced man with close-cropped hair stood in the doorway.

'Well?' he grunted.

It was at that moment that the full realization of his folly began to come home to Tommy. But he dared not hesitate. He seized at the first words that came into his mind.

'Mr Brown?' he said.

To his surprise the man stood aside.

'Upstairs,' he said, jerking his thumb over his shoulder, 'second door on your left.'

CHAPTER 8

The Adventures of Tommy

Taken aback though he was by the man's words, Tommy did not hesitate. If audacity had successfully carried him so far, it was to be hoped it would carry him yet farther. He quietly passed into the house and mounted the ramshackle staircase. Everything in the house was filthy beyond words. The grimy paper, of a pattern now indistinguishable, hung in loose festoons from the wall. In every angle was a grey mass of cobweb.

Tommy proceeded leisurely. By the time he reached the bend of the staircase, he had heard the man below disappear into a back room. Clearly no suspicion attached to him as yet. To come to the house and ask for 'Mr Brown' appeared indeed to be a reasonable and natural proceeding.

At the top of the stairs Tommy halted to consider his next move. In front of him ran a narrow passage, with doors opening on either side of it. From the one nearest him on the left came a low murmur of voices. It was this room which he had been directed to enter. But what held his glance fascinated was a small recess immediately on his right, half concealed by a torn velvet curtain. It was directly opposite the left-hand door and, owing to its angle, it also commanded a good view of the upper part of the staircase. As a hiding-place for one or, at a pinch, two men, it was ideal, being about two feet deep and three feet wide. It attracted Tommy mightily. He thought things over in his usual slow and steady way, deciding that the mention of 'Mr Brown' was not a request for an individual, but in all probability a password used by the gang. His lucky use of it had gained him admission. So far he had aroused no suspicion. But he must decide quickly on his next step.

Suppose he were boldly to enter the room on the left of the passage. Would the mere fact of his having been admitted to the house be sufficient? Perhaps a further password would be required, or, at any rate, some proof of identity. The doorkeeper clearly did not know all the members of the gang by sight, but it might be different upstairs. On the whole it seemed to him that luck had served him very well so far, but that there was such a thing as trusting it too far. To enter that room was a colossal risk. He could not hope to sustain his part indefinitely; sooner or later he was almost bound to betray himself, and then he would have thrown away a vital chance in mere foolhardiness.

A repetition of the signal sounded on the door below, and Tommy, his mind made up, slipped quickly into the recess, and cautiously drew the curtain farther across so that it shielded him completely from sight. There were several rents and slits in the ancient material which afforded him a good view. He would watch events, and any time he chose could, after all, join the assembly, modelling his behaviour on that of the new arrival.

The man who came up the staircase with a furtive, soft-footed tread was quite unknown to Tommy. He was obviously of the very dregs of society. The low beetling brows, and the criminal jaw, the bestiality of the whole countenance were new to the young man, though he was of a type that Scotland Yard would have recognized at a glance.

The man passed the recess, breathing heavily as he went. He stopped at the door opposite, and gave a repetition of the signal knock. A voice inside called out something, and the man opened the door and passed in, affording Tommy a momentary glimpse of the room inside. He thought there must be about four or five people seated round a long table that took up most of the space, but his attention was caught and held by a tall man with close-cropped hair and a short, pointed, naval-looking beard, who sat at the head of the table with papers in front of him. As the newcomer entered he glanced up, and with a correct, but curiously precise enunciation, which attracted Tommy's notice, he asked: 'Your number, comrade?'

'Fourteen, guv'nor,' replied the other hoarsely.

'Correct.'

The door shut again.

'If that isn't a Hun, I'm a Dutchman!' said Tommy to himself. 'And running the show darned systematically, too—as they always do. Lucky I didn't roll in. I'd have given the wrong number, and there would have been the deuce to pay. No, this is the place for me. Hullo, here's another knock.'

This visitor proved to be of an entirely different type to the last. Tommy recognized in him an Irish Sinn Feiner. Certainly Mr Brown's organization was a far-reaching concern. The common criminal, the well-bred Irish gentleman, the pale Russian, and the efficient German master of the ceremonies! Truly a strange and sinister gathering! Who was this man who held in his fingers these curiously variegated links of an unknown chain?

In this case, the procedure was exactly the same. The signal knock, the demand for a number, and the reply 'Correct.'

Two knocks followed in quick succession on the door below. The first man was quite unknown to Tommy, who put him down as a city clerk. A quiet, intelligent-looking man, rather shabbily dressed. The second was of the working classes, and his face was vaguely familiar to the young man.

Three minutes later came another, a man of commanding appearance, exquisitely dressed, and evidently well born. His face, again, was not unknown to the watcher, though he could not for the moment put a name to it.

After his arrival there was a long wait. In fact, Tommy concluded that the gathering was now complete, and was just cautiously creeping out from his hiding-place, when another knock sent him scuttling back to cover.

This last-comer came up the stairs so quietly that he was almost abreast of Tommy before the young man had realized his presence.

He was a small man, very pale, with a gentle almost womanish air. The angle of the cheek-bones hinted at his Slavonic ancestry, otherwise there was nothing to indicate his nationality. As he passed the recess, he turned his head slowly. The strange light eyes seemed to burn through the curtain; Tommy could hardly believe that the man did not know he was there and in spite of himself he shivered. He was no more fanciful than the majority of young Englishmen, but he could not rid himself of the impression that some unusually potent force emanated from the man. The creature reminded him of a venomous snake.

A moment later his impression was proved correct. The new-comer knocked on the door as all had done, but his reception was very different. The bearded man rose to his feet, and all the others followed suit. The German came forward and shook hands. His heels clicked together.

'We are honoured,' he said. 'We are greatly honoured. I much feared that it would be impossible.'

The other answered in a low voice that had a kind of hiss in it:

'There were difficulties. It will not be possible again, I fear. But one meeting is essential—to define my policy. I can do nothing without—Mr Brown. He is here?'

The change in the German's air was audible as he replied with slight hesitation:

'We have received a message. It is impossible for him to be present in person.' He stopped, giving a curious impression of having left the sentence unfinished.

A very slow smile overspread the face of the other. He looked round at a circle of uneasy faces.

'Ah! I understand. I have read of his methods. He works in the dark and trusts no one. But, all the same, it is possible that he is among us now...' He looked round him again, and again that expression of fear swept over the group. Each man seemed eyeing his neighbour doubtfully.

The Russian tapped his cheek.

'So be it. Let us proceed.'

The German seemed to pull himself together. He indicated the place he had been occupying at the head of the table. The Russian demurred, but the other insisted.

'It is the only possible place,' he said, 'for—Number One. Perhaps Number Fourteen will shut the door!'

In another moment Tommy was once more confronting bare wooden panels, and the voices within had sunk once more to a mere undistinguishable murmur. Tommy became restive. The conversation he had overheard had stimulated his curiosity. He felt that, by hook or by crook, he must hear more.

There was no sound from below, and it did not seem likely that the door-keeper would come upstairs. After listening intently for a minute or two, he put his head round the curtain. The passage was deserted. Tommy bent down and removed his shoes, then, leaving them behind the curtain, he walked gingerly out on his stockinged feet, and kneeling down by the closed door he laid his ear cautiously to the crack. To his intense annoyance he could distinguish little more; just a chance word here and there if a voice was raised, which merely served to whet his curiosity still farther.

He eyed the handle of the door tentatively. Could he turn it by degrees so gently and imperceptibly that those

78

in the room would notice nothing? He decided that with great care it could be done. Very slowly, a fraction of an inch at a time, he moved it round, holding his breath in his excessive care. A little more—a little more still—would it never be finished? Ah! at last it would turn no farther.

He stayed so for a minute or two, then drew a deep breath, and pressed it ever so slightly inward. The door did not budge. Tommy was annoyed. If he had to use too much force, it would almost certainly creak. He waited until the voices rose a little, then he tried again. Still nothing happened. He increased the pressure. Had the beastly thing stuck? Finally, in desperation, he pushed with all his might. But the door remained firm, and at last the truth dawned upon him. It was locked or bolted on the inside.

For a moment or two Tommy's indignation got the better of him.

'Well, I'm damned!' he said. 'What a dirty trick!'

As his indignation cooled, he prepared to face the situation. Clearly the first thing to be done was to restore the handle to its original position. If he let it go suddenly, the men inside would be almost certain to notice it, so with the same infinite pains he reversed his former tactics. All went well, and with a sigh of relief the young man rose to his feet. There was a certain bulldog tenacity about Tommy that made him slow to admit defeat. Checkmated for the moment, he was far from abandoning the conflict. He still intended to hear what was going on in the locked room. As one plan had failed, he must hunt about for another.

Agatha Christie

He looked round him. A little farther along the passage on the left was a second door. He slipped silently along to it. He listened for a moment or two, then tried the handle. It yielded, and he slipped inside.

The room, which was untenanted, was furnished as a bedroom. Like everything else in the house, the furniture was falling to pieces, and the dirt was, if anything, more abundant.

But what interested Tommy was the thing he had hoped to find, a communicating door between the two rooms, up on the left by the window. Carefully closing the door into the passage behind him, he stepped across to the other and examined it closely. The bolt was shot across it. It was very rusty, and had clearly not been used for some time. By gently wriggling it to and fro, Tommy managed to draw it back without making too much noise. Then he repeated his former manœuvres with the handle—this time with complete success. The door swung open—a crack, a mere fraction, but enough for Tommy to hear what went on. There was a velvet *portière* on the inside of this door which prevented him from seeing, but he was able to recognize the voices with a reasonable amount of accuracy.

The Sinn Feiner was speaking. His rich Irish voice was unmistakable:

'That's all very well. But more money is essential. No money—no results!'

Another voice which Tommy rather thought was that of Boris replied:

'Will you guarantee that there *are* results?'

'In a month from now—sooner or later as you wish—I will guarantee you such a reign of terror in Ireland as shall shake the British Empire to its foundations.'

There was a pause, and then came the soft, sibilant accents of Number One:

'Good! You shall have the money. Boris, you will see to that.'

Boris asked a question:

'Via the Irish Americans, and Mr Potter as usual?'

'I guess that'll be all right!' said a new voice, with a transatlantic intonation, 'though I'd like to point out, here and now, that things are getting a mite difficult. There's not the sympathy there was, and a growing disposition to let the Irish settle their own affairs without interference from America.'

Tommy felt that Boris had shrugged his shoulders as he answered:

'Does that matter, since the money only nominally comes from the States?'

'The chief difficulty is the landing of the ammunition,' said the Sinn Feiner. 'The money is conveyed in easily enough—thanks to our colleague here.'

Another voice, which Tommy fancied was that of the tall, commanding-looking man whose face had seemed familiar to him, said:

'Think of the feelings of Belfast if they could hear you!'

'That is settled, then,' said the sibilant tones. 'Now, in the matter of the loan to an English newspaper, you have arranged the details satisfactorily, Boris?'

'I think so.'

'That is good. An official denial from Moscow will be forthcoming if necessary.'

There was a pause, and then the clear voice of the German broke the silence:

'I am directed by—Mr Brown, to place the summaries of the reports from the different unions before you. That of the miners is most satisfactory. We must hold back the railways. There may be trouble with the A.S.E.'

For a long time there was a silence, broken only by the rustle of papers and an occasional word of explanation from the German. Then Tommy heard the light tap-tap of fingers drumming on the table.

'And—the date, my friend?' said Number One.

'The 29th.'

The Russian seemed to consider.

'That is rather soon.'

'I know. But it was settled by the principal Labour leaders, and we cannot seem to interfere too much. They must believe it to be entirely their own show.'

The Russian laughed softly, as though amused.

'Yes, yes,' he said. 'That is true. They must have no inkling that we are using them for our own ends. They are honest men—and that is their value to us. It is curious—but you cannot make a revolution without honest men. The instinct of the populace is infallible.' He paused, and then repeated, as though the phrase pleased him: 'Every revolution has had its honest men. They are soon disposed of afterwards.'

There was a sinister note in his voice.

The German resumed:

'Clymes must go. He is too far-seeing. Number Fourteen will see to that.'

There was a hoarse murmur.

'That's all right, guv'nor.' And then after a moment or two: 'Suppose I'm nabbed.'

'You will have the best legal talent to defend you,' replied the German quietly. 'But in any case you will wear gloves fitted with the finger-prints of a notorious housebreaker. You have little to fear.'

'Oh, I ain't afraid, guv'nor. All for the good of the cause. The streets is going to run with blood, so they say.' He spoke with a grim relish. 'Dreams of it, sometimes, I does. And diamonds and pearls rolling about in the gutter for anyone to pick up!'

Tommy heard a chair shifted. Then Number One spoke:

'Then all is arranged. We are assured of success?'

'I—think so.' But the German spoke with less than his usual confidence.

Number One's voice held suddenly a dangerous quality:

'What has gone wrong?'

'Nothing; but—'

'But what?'

'The labour leaders. Without them, as you say, we can do nothing. If they do not declare a general strike on the 29th—'

'Why should they not?'

'As you've said, they're honest. And, in spite of everything we've done to discredit the Government in their eyes, I'm not sure that they haven't got a sneaking faith and belief in it.'

'But—'

'I know. They abuse it unceasingly. But, on the whole, public opinion swings to the side of the Government. They will not go against it.'

Again the Russian's fingers drummed on the table.

'To the point, my friend. I was given to understand that there was a certain document in existence which assured success.'

'That is so. If that document were placed before the leaders, the result would be immediate. They would publish it broadcast throughout England, and declare for the revolution without a moment's hesitation. The Government would be broken finally and completely.'

'Then what more do you want?'

'The document itself,' said the German bluntly.

'Ah! It is not in your possession? But you know where it is?'

'No.'

'Does anyone know where it is?'

'One person—perhaps. And we are not sure of that even.'

'Who is this person?'

'A girl.'

Tommy held his breath.

'A girl?' The Russian's voice rose contemptuously. 'And you have not made her speak? In Russia we have ways of making a girl talk.'

'This case is different,' said the German sullenly.

'How—different?' He paused a moment, then went on: 'Where is the girl now?'

'The girl?'

'Yes.'

'She is—'

But Tommy heard no more. A crashing blow descended on his head, and all was darkness.

CHAPTER 9

Tuppence Enters Domestic Service

When Tommy set forth on the trail of the two men, it took all Tuppence's self-command to refrain from accompanying him. However, she contained herself as best she might, consoled by the reflection that her reasoning had been justified by events. The two men had undoubtedly come from the second floor flat, and that one slender thread of the name 'Rita' had set the Young Adventurers once more upon the track of the abductors of Jane Finn.

The question was what to do next? Tuppence hated letting the grass grow under her feet. Tommy was amply employed, and debarred from joining him in the chase, the girl felt at a loose end. She retraced her steps to the entrance hall of the mansions. It was now tenanted by a small lift-boy, who was polishing brass fittings, and whistling the latest air with a good deal of vigour and a reasonable amount of accuracy.

He glanced round at Tuppence's entry. There was a certain amount of the gamin element in the girl, at all events she invariably got on well with small boys. A sympathetic bond seemed instantly to be formed. She reflected that an ally in the enemy's camp, so to speak, was not to be despised.

'Well, William,' she remarked cheerfully, in the best approved hospital-early-morning style, 'getting a good shine up?'

The boy grinned responsively.

'Albert, miss,' he corrected.

'Albert be it,' said Tuppence. She glanced mysteriously round the hall. The effect was purposely a broad one in case Albert should miss it. She leaned towards the boy and dropped her voice: 'I want a word with you, Albert.'

Albert ceased operations on the fittings and opened his mouth slightly.

'Look! Do you know what this is?' With dramatic gesture she flung back the left side of her coat and exposed a small enamelled badge. It was extremely unlikely that Albert would have any knowledge of it—indeed, it would have been fatal for Tuppence's plans, since the badge in question was the device of a local training corps originated by the archdeacon in the early days of the war. Its presence in Tuppence's coat was due to the fact that she had used it for pinning in some flowers a day or two before. But Tuppence had sharp eyes, and had noted the corner of a threepenny detective novel protruding from Albert's pocket, and the immediate enlargement of his eyes told her that her tactics were good, and that the fish would rise to the bait.

'American Detective Force!' she hissed.

Albert fell for it.

'Lord!' he murmured ecstatically.

Tuppence nodded at him with the air of one who has established a thorough understanding.

'Know who I'm after?' she inquired genially.

Albert, still round-eyed, demanded breathlessly:

'One of the flats?'

Tuppence nodded and jerked a thumb up the stairs.

'No. 20. Calls herself Vandemeyer. Vandemeyer! Ha! ha!'

Albert's hand stole to his pocket.

'A crook?' he queried eagerly.

'A crook? I should say so. Ready Rita they call her in the States.'

'Ready Rita,' repeated Albert deliriously. 'Oh, ain't it just like the pictures!'

It was. Tuppence was a great frequenter of the cinema.

'Annie always said as how she was a bad lot,' continued the boy.

'Who's Annie?' inquired Tuppence idly.

''Ouse-parlourmaid. She's leaving today. Many's the time Annie's said to me: "Mark my words, Albert, I wouldn't wonder if the police was to come after her one of these days." Just like that. But she's a stunner to look at, ain't she?'

'She's some peach,' allowed Tuppence carefully. 'Finds it useful in her lay-out, you bet. Has she been wearing any of the emeralds, by the way?'

'Emeralds? Them's the green stones, isn't they?'

Tuppence nodded.

'That's what we're after her for. You know old man Rysdale?'

Albert shook his head.

'Peter B. Rysdale, the oil king?'

'It seems sort of familiar to me.'

'The sparklers belonged to him. Finest collection of emeralds in the world. Worth a million dollars!'

'Lumme!' came ecstatically from Albert. 'It sounds more like the pictures every minute.'

Tuppence smiled, gratified at the success of her efforts.

'We haven't exactly proved it yet. But we're after her. And'—she produced a long drawn-out wink—'I guess she won't get away with the goods this time.'

Albert uttered another ejaculation indicative of delight.

'Mind you, sonny, not a word of this,' said Tuppence suddenly. 'I guess I oughtn't to have put you wise, but in the States we know a real smart lad when we see one.'

'I'll not breathe a word,' protested Albert eagerly. 'Ain't there anything I could do? A bit of shadowing, maybe, or suchlike?'

Tuppence affected to consider, then shook her head.

'Not at the moment, but I'll bear you in mind, son. What's this about the girl you say is leaving?'

'Annie? Regular turn up, they 'ad. As Annie said, servants is someone nowadays, and to be treated accordingly, and, what with her passing the word round, she won't find it so easy to get another.'

'Won't she?' said Tuppence thoughtfully. 'I wonder—'

An idea was dawning in her brain. She thought a minute or two, then tapped Albert on the shoulder.

'See here, son, my brain's got busy. How would it be if you mentioned that you'd got a young cousin, or a friend of yours had, that might suit the place. You get me?'

'I'm there,' said Albert instantly. 'You leave it to me, miss, and I'll fix the whole thing up in two ticks.'

'Some lad!' commented Tuppence, with a nod of approval. 'You might say that the young woman could come right away. You let me know, and if it's O.K. I'll be round tomorrow at eleven o'clock.'

'Where am I to let you know to?'

'Ritz,' replied Tuppence laconically. 'Name of Cowley.'

Albert eyed her enviously.

'It must be a good job, this tec business.'

'It sure is,' drawled Tuppence, 'especially when old man Rysdale backs the bill. But don't fret, son. If this goes well, you shall come in on the ground floor.'

With which promise she took leave of her new ally, and walked briskly away from South Audley Mansions, well pleased with her morning's work.

But there was no time to be lost. She went straight back to the Ritz and wrote a few brief words to Mr Carter. Having dispatched this, and Tommy not having yet returned—which did not surprise her—she started off on a shopping expedition which, with an interval for tea and assorted creamy cakes, occupied her until well after six o'clock, and she returned to the hotel jaded, but satisfied with her purchases. Starting with a cheap clothing store, and passing through one or two second-hand establishments, she had finished the day at a well-known hairdresser's. Now, in the seclusion of her bedroom, she unwrapped that final purchase. Five minutes later she smiled contentedly at her reflection in the glass. With an actress's pencil she had slightly altered the line of her eyebrows, and that, taken in conjunction with the new luxuriant growth of fair hair above, so changed her appearance that she felt confident that even if she came face to face with Whittington he would not recognize her. She would wear elevators in her shoes, and the cap and apron would be an even more valuable disguise. From hospital experience she knew only too well that a nurse out of uniform is frequently unrecognized by her patients.

'Yes,' said Tuppence aloud, nodding at the pert reflection in the glass, 'you'll do.' She then resumed her normal appearance.

Dinner was a solitary meal. Tuppence was rather surprised at Tommy's non-return. Julius, too, was absent—but that to the girl's mind was more easily explained. His 'hustling' activities were not confined to London, and his abrupt appearances and disappearances were fully accepted by the Young Adventurers as part of the day's work. It was quite on the cards that Julius P. Hersheimmer had left for Constantinople at a moment's notice if he fancied that a clue to his cousin's disappearance was to be found there. The energetic young man had succeeded in making the lives of several Scotland Yard men unbearable to them, and the telephone girls at the Admiralty had learned to know and dread the familiar 'Hullo!' He had spent three hours in Paris hustling the Prefecture, and had returned from there imbued with the idea, possibly inspired by a weary French official, that the true clue to the mystery was to be found in Ireland.

'I dare say he's dashed off there now,' thought Tuppence. 'All very well, but this is very dull for *me*! Here I am bursting with news, and absolutely no one to tell it to!

Tommy might have wired, or something. I wonder where he is. Anyway, he can't have "lost the trail" as they say. That reminds me—' And Miss Cowley broke off in her meditations, and summoned a small boy.

Ten minutes later the lady was ensconced comfortably on her bed, smoking cigarettes and deep in the perusal of *Garnaby Williams, the Boy Detective*, which, with other threepenny works of lurid fiction, she had sent out to purchase. She felt, and rightly, that before the strain of attempting further intercourse with Albert, it would be as well to fortify herself with a good supply of local colour.

The morning brought a note from Mr Carter:

Dear Miss Tuppence

You have made a splendid start, and I congratulate you. I feel, though, that I should like to point out to you once more the risks you are running, especially if you pursue the course you indicate. Those people are absolutely desperate and incapable of either mercy or pity. I feel that you probably underestimate the danger, and therefore warn you again that I can promise you no protection. You have given us valuable information, and if you choose to withdraw now no one could blame you. At any rate, think the matter over well before you decide.

If, in spite of my warnings, you make up your mind to go through with it, you will find everything arranged. You have lived for two years with Miss Dufferin, the Parsonage, Llanelly, and Mrs Vandemeyer can apply to her for a reference.

May I be permitted a word or two of advice? Stick as near to the truth as possible—it minimizes the danger of 'slips'. I suggest that you should represent yourself to be what you are, a former V.A.D., who has chosen domestic service as a profession. There are many such at the present time. That explains away any incongruities of voice or manner which otherwise might awaken suspicion.

Whichever way you decide, good luck to you.

Your sincere friend,

Mr Carter

Tuppence's spirits rose mercurially. Mr Carter's warnings passed unheeded. The young lady had far too much confidence in herself to pay any heed to them.

With some reluctance she abandoned the interesting part she had sketched out for herself. Although she had no doubts of her own powers to sustain a rôle indefinitely, she had too much common sense not to recognize the force of Mr Carter's arguments.

There was still no word or message from Tommy, but the morning post brought a somewhat dirty postcard with the words: 'It's O.K.' scrawled upon it.

At 10.30 Tuppence surveyed with pride a slightly battered tin trunk containing her new possessions. It was artistically corded. It was with a slight blush that she rang the bell and ordered it to be placed in a taxi. She drove to Paddington, and left the box in the cloak room. She then repaired with a handbag to the fastnesses of the ladies' waiting-room. Ten minutes later a metamorphosed Tuppence walked demurely out of the station and entered a bus.

It was a few minutes past eleven when Tuppence again entered the hall of South Audley Mansions. Albert was on the look-out, attending to his duties in a somewhat desultory fashion. He did not immediately recognize Tuppence. When he did, his admiration was unbounded.

'Blest if I'd have known you! That rig-out's top-hole.'

'Glad you like it, Albert,' replied Tuppence modestly. 'By the way, am I your cousin, or am I not?'

'Your voice too,' cried the delighted boy. 'It's as English as anything! No, I said as a friend of mine knew a young gal. Annie wasn't best pleased. She stopped on till today—to oblige, *she* said, but really it's so as to put you against the place.'

'Nice girl,' said Tuppence.

Albert suspected no irony.

'She's style about her, and keeps her silver a treat—but, my word, ain't she got a temper. Are you going up now, miss? Step inside the lift. No. 20 did you say?' And he winked.

Tuppence quelled him with a stern glance, and stepped inside.

As she rang the bell of No. 20 she was conscious of Albert's eyes descending beneath the level of the floor.

A smart young woman opened the door.

'I've come about the place,' said Tuppence.

'It's a rotten place,' said the young woman without hesitation. 'Regular old cat—always interfering. Accused me of tampering with her letters. Me! The flap was half undone anyway. There's never anything in the waste-paper basket—she burns everything. She's a wrong 'un, that's what she is. Swell clothes but no class. Cook knows something about her—but she won't tell—scared to death of her. And suspicious! She's on to you in a minute if you as much as speak to a fellow. I can tell you—'

But what more Annie could tell, Tuppence was never destined to learn, for at that moment a clear voice with a peculiarly steely ring to it called:

'Annie!'

The smart young woman jumped as if she had been shot.

'Yes, ma'am?'

'Who are you talking to?'

'It's a young woman about the situation, ma'am.'

'Show her in then. At once.'

'Yes, ma'am.'

Tuppence was ushered into a room on the right of the long passage. A woman was standing by the fire-place. She was no longer in her first youth, and the beauty she undeniably possessed was hardened and coarsened. In her youth she must have been dazzling. Her pale gold hair, owing a slight assistance to art, was coiled low on her neck, her eyes, of a piercing electric blue, seemed to possess a faculty of boring into the very soul of the person she was looking at. Her exquisite figure was enhanced by a wonderful gown of indigo charmeuse. And yet, despite her swaying grace, and the almost ethereal beauty of her face, you felt instinctively the presence of something hard and menacing, a kind of metallic strength that found expression in the tones of her voice and in that gimlet-like quality of her eyes.

For the first time Tuppence felt afraid. She had not feared Whittington, but this woman was different. As if fascinated, she watched the long cruel line of the red curving mouth, and again she felt that sensation of panic pass over her. Her usual self-confidence deserted her. Vaguely she felt that deceiving this woman would be very different to deceiving Whittington. Mr Carter's warning recurred to her mind. Here, indeed, she might expect no mercy.

Fighting down that instinct of panic which urged her to turn tail and run without further delay, Tuppence returned the lady's gaze firmly and respectfully.

As though that first scrutiny had been satisfactory, Mrs Vandemeyer motioned to a chair.

'You can sit down. How did you hear I wanted a house-parlourmaid?'

'Through a friend who knows the lift boy here. He thought the place might suit me.'

Again that basilisk glance seemed to pierce her through.

'You speak like an educated girl?'

Glibly enough, Tuppence ran through her imaginary career on the lines suggested by Mr Carter. It seemed to her, as she did so, that the tension of Mrs Vandemeyer's attitude relaxed.

'I see,' she remarked at length. 'Is there anyone I can write to for a reference?'

'I lived last with a Miss Dufferin, The Parsonage, Llanelly. I was with her two years.'

'And then you thought you would get more money by coming to London, I suppose? Well, it doesn't matter to me. I will give you £50–£60—whatever you want. You can come at once?'

'Yes, ma'am. Today, if you like. My box is at Paddington.'

'Go and fetch it by taxi, then. It's an easy place. I am out a good deal. By the way, what's your name?'

'Prudence Cooper, ma'am.'

'Very well, Prudence. Go away and fetch your box. I shall be out to lunch. The cook will show you where everything is.'

'Thank you, ma'am.'

Tuppence withdrew. The smart Annie was not in evidence. In the hall below a magnificent hall porter had relegated Albert to the background. Tuppence did not even glance at him as she passed meekly out.

The adventure had begun, but she felt less elated than she had done earlier in the morning. It crossed her mind that if the unknown Jane Finn had fallen into the hands of Mrs Vandemeyer, it was likely to have gone hard with her.

CHAPTER 10

Enter Sir James Peel Edgerton

Tuppence betrayed no awkwardness in her new duties. The daughters of the archdeacon were well grounded in household tasks. They were also experts in training a 'raw girl,' the inevitable result being that the raw girl, once trained, departed somewhere where her newly-acquired knowledge commanded a more substantial remuneration than the archdeacon's meagre purse allowed.

Tuppence had therefore very little fear of proving inefficient. Mrs Vandemeyer's cook puzzled her. She evidently went in deadly terror of her mistress. The girl thought it probable that the other woman had some hold over her. For the rest, she cooked like a *chef*, as Tuppence had an opportunity of judging that evening. Mrs Vandemeyer was expecting a guest to dinner, and Tuppence accordingly laid the beautifully polished table for two. She was a little exercised in her own mind as to this visitor. It was highly possible that it might prove to be Whittington. Although she felt fairly confident that he would not recognize her, yet she would have been better pleased had the guest proved to be a total stranger. However, there was nothing for it but to hope for the best.

At a few minutes past eight the front door bell rang, and Tuppence went to answer it with some inward trepidation. She was relieved to see that the visitor was the second of the two men whom Tommy had taken upon himself to follow.

He gave his name as Count Stepanov. Tuppence announced him, and Mrs Vandemeyer rose from her seat on a low divan with a quick murmur of pleasure.

'It is delightful to see you, Boris Ivanovitch,' she said.

'And you, madame!' He bowed low over her hand.

Tuppence returned to the kitchen.

'Count Stepanov, or some such,' she remarked, and affecting a frank and unvarnished curiosity: 'Who's he?'

'A Russian gentleman, I believe.'

'Come here much?'

'Once in a while. What d'you want to know for?'

'Fancied he might be sweet on the missus, that's all,' explained the girl, adding with an appearance of sulkiness: 'How you do take one up!'

'I'm not quite easy in my mind about the *soufflé*,' explained the other.

'You know something,' thought Tuppence to herself, but aloud she only said: 'Going to dish up now? Right-o.'

Whilst waiting at table, Tuppence listened closely to all that was said. She remembered that this was one of the men Tommy was shadowing when she had last seen him. Already, although she would hardly admit it, she was becoming uneasy about her partner. Where was he? Why had no word of any kind come from him? She had arranged before leaving the Ritz to have all letters or messages sent on at once by special messenger to a small stationer's shop near at hand where Albert was to call in frequently. True, it was only yesterday morning that she had parted from Tommy, and she told herself that any anxiety on his behalf would be absurd. Still, it was strange he had sent no word of any kind.

But, listen as she might, the conversation presented no clue. Boris and Mrs Vandemeyer talked on purely indifferent subjects: plays they had seen, new dances, and the latest society gossip. After dinner they repaired to the small boudoir where Mrs Vandemeyer, stretched on the divan, looked more wickedly beautiful than ever. Tuppence brought in the coffee and liqueurs and unwillingly retired. As she did so, she heard Boris say:

'New, isn't she?'

'She came in today. The other was a fiend. This girl seems all right. She waits well.'

Tuppence lingered a moment longer by the door which she had carefully neglected to close, and heard him say:

'Quite safe, I suppose?'

'Really, Boris, you are absurdly suspicious. I believe she's the cousin of the hall porter, or something of the kind. And nobody even dreams that I have any connexion with our—mutual friend, Mr Brown.'

'For Heaven's sake, be careful, Rita. That door isn't shut.'

'Well, shut it then,' laughed the woman.

Tuppence removed herself speedily.

She dared not absent herself longer from the back premises, but she cleared away and washed up with a breathless speed acquired in hospital. Then she slipped quietly back to the boudoir door. The cook, more leisurely, was still busy in the kitchen and, if she missed the other, would only suppose her to be turning down the beds.

Alas! The conversation inside was being carried on in too low a tone to permit of her hearing anything of it. She dared not reopen the door, however gently. Mrs Vandemeyer was sitting almost facing it, and Tuppence respected her mistress's lynx-eyed powers of observation.

Nevertheless, she felt she would give a good deal to overhear what was going on. Possibly, if anything unforeseen had happened, she might get news of Tommy. For some moments she reflected desperately, then her face brightened. She went quickly along the passage to Mrs Vandemeyer's bedroom, which had long French windows leading on to a balcony that ran the length of the flat. Slipping quickly through the window, Tuppence crept noiselessly along till she reached the boudoir window. As she had thought it stood a little ajar, and the voices within were plainly audible.

Tuppence listened attentively, but there was no mention of anything that could be twisted to apply to Tommy. Mrs Vandemeyer and the Russian seemed to be at variance over some matter, and finally the latter exclaimed bitterly:

'With your persistent recklessness, you will end by ruining us!'

'Bah!' laughed the woman. 'Notoriety of the right kind is the best way of disarming suspicion. You will realize that one of these days—perhaps sooner than you think!'

'In the meantime, you are going about everywhere with Peel Edgerton. Not only is he, perhaps, the most celebrated K. C. in England, but his special hobby is criminology! It is madness!'

'I know that his eloquence has saved untold men from the gallows,' said Mrs Vandemeyer calmly. 'What of it? I may need his assistance in that line myself some day. If so, how fortunate to have such a friend at court—or perhaps it would be more to the point to say *in* court.'

Boris got up and began striding up and down. He was very excited.

'You are a clever woman, Rita; but you are also a fool! Be guided by me, and give up Peel Edgerton.'

Mrs Vandemeyer shook her head gently.

'I think not.'

'You refuse?' There was an ugly ring in the Russian's voice.

'I do.'

'Then, by Heaven,' snarled the Russian, 'we will see—'

But Mrs Vandemeyer also rose to her feet, her eyes flashing.

'You forget, Boris,' she said. 'I am accountable to no one. I take my orders only from—Mr Brown.'

The other threw up his hands in despair.

'You are impossible,' he muttered. 'Impossible! Already it may be too late. They say Peel Edgerton can *smell* a criminal! How do we know what is at the bottom of his sudden interest in you? Perhaps even now his suspicions are aroused. He guesses—'

Mrs Vandemeyer eyed him scornfully.

'Reassure yourself, my dear Boris. He suspects nothing. With less than your usual chivalry, you seem to forget that I am commonly accounted a beautiful woman. I assure you that is all that interests Peel Edgerton.'

Boris shook his head doubtfully.

'He has studied crime as no other man in this kingdom has studied it. Do you fancy that you can deceive him?'

Mrs Vandemeyer's eyes narrowed.

'If he is all that you say—it would amuse me to try!'

'Good heavens, Rita—'

'Besides,' added Mrs Vandemeyer, 'he is extremely rich. I am not one who despises money. The "sinews of war" you know, Boris!'

'Money—money! That is always the danger with you, Rita. I believe you would sell your soul for money. I believe—' He paused, then in a low, sinister voice he said slowly: 'Sometimes I believe that you would sell—*us*!'

Mrs Vandemeyer smiled and shrugged her shoulders.

'The price, at any rate, would have to be enormous,' she said lightly. 'It would be beyond the power of anyone but a millionaire to pay.'

'Ah!' snarled the Russian. 'You see, I was right.'

'My dear Boris, can you not take a joke?'

'Was it a joke?'

'Of course.'

'Then all I can say is that your ideas of humour are peculiar, my dear Rita.'

Mrs Vandemeyer smiled.

'Let us not quarrel, Boris. Touch the bell. We will have some drinks.'

Tuppence beat a hasty retreat. She paused a moment to survey herself in Mrs Vandemeyer's long glass, and be sure that nothing was amiss with her appearance. Then she answered the bell demurely.

The conversation that she had overheard, although interesting in that it proved beyond doubt the complicity of both Rita and Boris, threw very little light on the present preoccupations. The name of Jane Finn had not even been mentioned.

The following morning a few brief words with Albert informed her that nothing was waiting for her at the stationer's. It seemed incredible that Tommy, if all was well with him, should not send any word to her. A cold hand seemed to close round her heart... Supposing... She choked her fears down bravely. It was no good worrying. But she leapt at a chance offered her by Mrs Vandemeyer.

'What day do you usually go out, Prudence?'

'Friday's my usual day, ma'am.'

Mrs Vandemeyer lifted her eyebrows.

'And today is Friday! But I suppose you hardly wish to go out today, as you only came yesterday.'

'I was thinking of asking you if I might, ma'am.'

Mrs Vandemeyer looked at her a minute longer, and then smiled.

'I wish Count Stepanov could hear you. He made a suggestion about you last night.' Her smile broadened, cat-like. 'Your request is very—typical. I am satisfied. You do not understand all this—but you can go out today. It makes no difference to me, as I shall not be dining at home.'

'Thank you, ma'am.'

Tuppence felt a sensation of relief once she was out of the other's presence. Once again she admitted to herself that she was afraid, horribly afraid, of the beautiful woman with the cruel eyes.

In the midst of a final desultory polishing of her silver, Tuppence was disturbed by the ringing of the front door bell, and went to answer it. This time the visitor was neither Whittington nor Boris, but a man of striking appearance.

Just a shade over average height, he nevertheless conveyed the impression of a big man. His face, clean-shaven and exquisitely mobile, was stamped with an expression of power and force far beyond the ordinary. Magnetism seemed to radiate from him.

Tuppence was undecided for the moment whether to put him down as an actor or a lawyer, but her doubts were soon solved as he gave her his name: Sir James Peel Edgerton.

She looked at him with renewed interest. This, then, was the famous K. C. whose name was familiar all over England. She had heard it said that he might one day be Prime Minister. He was known to have refused office in the interests of his profession, preferring to remain a simple Member for a Scotch constituency.

Tuppence went back to her pantry thoughtfully. The great man had impressed her. She understood Boris's agitation. Peel Edgerton would not be an easy man to deceive.

In about a quarter of an hour the bell rang, and Tuppence repaired to the hall to show the visitor out. He had given her a piercing glance before. Now, as she handed him his hat and stick, she was conscious of his eyes raking her through. As she opened the door and stood aside to let him pass out, he stopped in the doorway.

'Not been doing this long, eh?'

Tuppence raised her eyes, astonished. She read in his glance kindliness, and something else more difficult to fathom.

He nodded as though she had answered.

'V.A.D. and hard up, I suppose?'

'Did Mrs Vandemeyer tell you that?' asked Tuppence suspiciously.

'No, child. The look of you told me. Good place here?'

'Very good, thank you, sir.'

'Ah, but there are plenty of good places nowadays. And a change does no harm sometimes.'

'Do you mean—?' began Tuppence.

But Sir James was already on the topmost stair. He looked back with his kindly, shrewd glance.

'Just a hint,' he said. 'That's all.'

Tuppence went back to the pantry more thoughtful than ever.

CHAPTER 11

Julius Tells a Story

Dressed appropriately, Tuppence duly sallied forth for her 'afternoon out'. Albert was in temporary abeyance, but Tuppence went herself to the stationer's to make quite sure that nothing had come for her. Satisfied on this point, she made her way to the Ritz. On inquiry she learnt that Tommy had not yet returned. It was the answer she had expected, but it was another nail in the coffin of her hopes. She resolved to appeal to Mr Carter, telling him when and where Tommy had started on his quest, and asking him to do something to trace him. The prospect of his aid revived her mercurial spirits, and she next inquired for Julius Hersheimmer. The reply she got was to the effect that he had returned about half an hour ago, but had gone out immediately.

Tuppence's spirits revived still more. It would be something to see Julius. Perhaps he could devise some plan for finding out what had become of Tommy. She wrote her note to Mr Carter in Julius's sitting-room, and was just addressing the envelope when the door burst open.

Agatha Christie

'What the hell—' began Julius, but checked himself abruptly. 'I beg your pardon, Miss Tuppence. Those fools down at the office would have it that Beresford wasn't here any longer—hadn't been here since Wednesday. Is that so?'

Tuppence nodded.

'You don't know where he is?' she asked faintly.

'I? How should I know? I haven't had one darned word from him, though I wired him yesterday morning.'

'I expect your wire's at the office unopened.'

'But where is he?'

'I don't know. I hoped you might.'

'I tell you I haven't had one darned word from him since we parted at the depot on Wednesday.'

'What depot?'

'Waterloo. Your London and South Western road.'

'Waterloo?' frowned Tuppence.

'Why, yes. Didn't he tell you?'

'I haven't seen him either,' replied Tuppence impatiently. 'Go on about Waterloo. What were you doing there?'

'He gave me a call. Over the phone. Told me to get a move on, and hustle. Said he was trailing two crooks.'

'Oh!' said Tuppence, her eyes opening. 'I see. Go on.'

'I hurried along right away. Beresford was there. He pointed out the crooks. The big one was mine, the guy you bluffed. Tommy shoved a ticket into my hand and told me to get aboard the cars. He was going to sleuth the other crook.' Julius paused. 'I thought for sure you'd know all this.'

108

'Julius,' said Tuppence firmly, 'stop walking up and down. It makes me giddy. Sit down in that arm-chair, and tell me the whole story with as few fancy turns of speech as possible.'

Mr Hersheimmer obeyed.

'Sure,' he said. 'Where shall I begin?'

'Where you left off. At Waterloo.'

'Well,' began Julius, 'I got into one of your dear old-fashioned first-class British compartments. The train was just off. First thing I knew a guard came along and informed me mightily politely that I wasn't in a smoking-carriage. I handed him out half a dollar, and that settled that. I did a bit of prospecting along the corridor to the next coach. Whittington was there right enough. When I saw the skunk, with his big sleek fat face, and thought of poor little Jane in his clutches, I felt real mad that I hadn't got a gun with me. I'd have tickled him up some.

'We got to Bournemouth all right. Whittington took a cab and gave the name of an hotel. I did likewise, and we drove up within three minutes of each other. He hired a room, and I hired one too. So far it was all plain sailing. He hadn't the remotest notion that anyone was on to him. Well, he just sat around in the hotel lounge, reading the papers and so on, till it was time for dinner. He didn't hurry any over that either.

'I began to think that there was nothing doing, that he'd just come on the trip for his health, but I remembered that he hadn't changed for dinner, though it was by way of being a slap-up hotel, so it seemed likely enough that he'd be going out on his real business afterwards.

'Sure enough, about nine o'clock, so he did. Took a car across the town—mighty pretty place by the way, I guess I'll take Jane there for a spell when I find her—and then paid it off and struck out along those pine-woods on the top of the cliff. I was there too, you understand. We walked, maybe, for half an hour. There's a lot of villas all the way along, but by degrees they seemed to get more and more thinned out, and in the end we got to one that seemed the last of the bunch. Big house it was, with a lot of piny grounds around it.

'It was a pretty black night, and the carriage drive up to the house was dark as pitch. I could hear him ahead, though I couldn't see him. I had to walk carefully in case he might get on to it that he was being followed. I turned a curve and I was just in time to see him ring the bell and get admitted to the house. I just stopped where I was. It was beginning to rain, and I was soon pretty near soaked through. Also, it was almighty cold.

'Whittington didn't come out again, and by and by I got kind of restive, and began to mooch around. All the ground floor windows were shuttered tight, but upstairs, on the first floor (it was a two-storied house) I noticed a window with a light burning and the curtains not drawn.

'Now, just opposite to that window, there was a tree growing. It was about thirty foot away from the house, maybe, and I sort of got it into my head that, if I climbed up that tree, I'd very likely be able to see into that room. Of course, I knew there was no reason why Whittington should be in that room rather than in any other—less

110

reason, in fact, for the betting would be on his being in one of the reception-rooms downstairs. But I guess I'd got the hump from standing so long in the rain, and anything seemed better than going on doing nothing. So I started up.

'It wasn't so easy, by a long chalk! The rain had made the boughs mighty slippery, and it was all I could do to keep a foothold, but bit by bit I managed it, until at last there I was level with the window.

'But then I was disappointed. I was too far to the left. I could only see sideways into the room. A bit of curtain, and a yard of wall-paper was all I could command. Well, that wasn't any manner of good to me, but just as I was going to give it up, and climb down ignominiously, someone inside moved and threw his shadow on my little bit of wall—and, by gum, it was Whittington!

'After that, my blood was up. I'd just *got* to get a look into that room. It was up to me to figure out how. I noticed that there was a long branch running out from the tree in the right direction. If I could only swarm about half-way along it, the proposition would be solved. But it was mighty uncertain whether it would bear my weight. I decided I'd just got to risk that, and I started. Very cautiously, inch by inch, I crawled along. The bough creaked and swayed in a nasty fashion, and it didn't do to think of the drop below, but at last I got safely to where I wanted to be.

'The room was medium-sized, furnished in a kind of bare hygienic way. There was a table with a lamp on it in the middle of the room, and sitting at that table, facing towards me, was Whittington right enough. He was talking to a woman dressed as a hospital nurse. She was sitting with her back to me, so I couldn't see her face. Although the blinds were up, the window itself was shut, so I couldn't catch a word of what they said. Whittington seemed to be doing all the talking, and the nurse just listened. Now and then she nodded, and sometimes she'd shake her head, as though she were answering questions. He seemed very emphatic—once or twice he beat with his fist on the table. The rain had stopped now, and the sky was clearing in that sudden way it does.

'Presently, he seemed to get to the end of what he was saying. He got up, and so did she. He looked towards the window and asked something—I guess it was whether it was raining. Anyway, she came right across and looked out. Just then the moon came out from behind the clouds. I was scared the woman would catch sight of me, for I was full in the moonlight. I tried to move back a bit. The jerk I gave was too much for that rotten old branch. With an almighty crash, down it came, and Julius P. Hersheimmer with it!'

'Oh, Julius,' breathed Tuppence, 'how exciting! Go on.'

'Well, luckily for me, I pitched down into a good soft bed of earth—but it put me out of action for the time, sure enough. The next thing I knew, I was lying in bed with a hospital nurse (not Whittington's one) on one side of me, and a little black-bearded man with gold glasses, and medical man written all over him, on the other. He rubbed his hands together, and raised his eyebrows as I stared at him. "Ah!" he said. "So our young friend is coming round again. Capital. Capital."

'I did the usual stunt. Said: "What's happened?" And "Where am I?" But I knew the answer to the last well enough. There's no moss growing on my brain. "I think that'll do for the present, sister," said the little man, and the nurse left the room in a sort of brisk well-trained way. But I caught her handing me out a look of deep curiosity as she passed through the door.

'That look of hers gave me an idea. "Now then, doc," I said, and tried to sit up in bed, but my right foot gave me a nasty twinge as I did so. "A slight sprain," explained the doctor. "Nothing serious. You'll be about again in a couple of days."

'I noticed you walked lame,' interpolated Tuppence.

Julius nodded, and continued:

'"How did it happen?" I asked again. He replied dryly. "You fell, with a considerable portion of one of my trees, into one of my newly-planted flower-beds."

'I liked the man. He seemed to have a sense of humour. I felt sure that he, at least, was plumb straight. "Sure, doc," I said, "I'm sorry about the tree, and I guess the new bulbs will be on me. But perhaps you'd like to know what I was doing in your garden?" "I think the facts do call for an explanation," he replied. "Well, to begin with, I wasn't after the spoons."

'He smiled. "My first theory. But I soon altered my mind. By the way, you are an American, are you not?" I told him my name. "And you?" "I am Dr Hall, and this, as you doubtless know, is my private nursing home."

'I didn't know, but wasn't going to put him wise. I was just thankful for the information. I liked the man, and I felt he was straight, but I wasn't going to give him the whole story. For one thing he probably wouldn't have believed it.

'I made up my mind in a flash. "Why, doctor," I said, "I guess I feel an almighty fool, but I owe it to you to let you know that it wasn't the Bill Sikes business I was up to." Then I went on and mumbled out something about a girl. I trotted out the stern guardian business, and a nervous breakdown, and finally explained that I had fancied I recognized her among the patients at the home, hence my nocturnal adventures.

'I guess it was just the kind of story he was expecting. "Quite a romance," he said genially, when I'd finished. "Now, doc," I went on, "will you be frank with me? Have you here now, or have you had here at any time, a young girl called Jane Finn?" He repeated the name thoughtfully. "Jane Finn?" he said. "No."

'I was chagrined, and I guess I showed it. "You are sure?" "Quite sure, Mr Hersheimmer. It is an uncommon name, and I should not have been likely to forget it."

'Well, that was flat. It laid me out for a space. I'd kind of hoped my search was at an end. "That's that," I said at last. "Now, there's another matter. When I was hugging that darned branch I thought I recognized an old friend of mine talking to one of your nurses." I purposely didn't mention any name because, of course, Whittington might be calling himself something quite different down here, but the doctor answered at once. "Mr Whittington, perhaps?" "That's the fellow," I replied. "What's he doing down here? Don't tell me *his* nerves are out of order?"

114

'Dr Hall laughed. "No. He came down to see one of my nurses, Nurse Edith, who is a niece of his." "Why, fancy that!" I exclaimed, "Is he still here?" "No, he went back to town almost immediately." "What a pity!" I ejaculated. "But perhaps I could speak to his niece—Nurse Edith, did you say her name was?"

'But the doctor shook his head. "I'm afraid that, too, is impossible. Nurse Edith left with a patient tonight also." "I seem to be real unlucky," I remarked. "Have you Mr Whittington's address in town? I guess I'd like to look him up when I get back." "I don't know his address. I can write to Nurse Edith for it if you like." I thanked him. "Don't say who it is wants it. I'd like to give him a little surprise."

'That was about all I could do for the moment. Of course, if the girl was really Whittington's niece, she might be too cute to fall into the trap, but it was worth trying. Next thing I did was to write out a wire to Beresford saying where I was, and that I was laid up with a sprained foot, and telling him to come down if he wasn't busy. I had to be guarded in what I said. However, I didn't hear from him, and my foot soon got all right. It was only ricked, not really sprained, so today I said goodbye to the little doctor chap, asked him to send me word if he heard from Nurse Edith, and came right away back to town. Say, Miss Tuppence, you're looking mighty pale?'

'It's Tommy,' said Tuppence. 'What can have happened to him?'

'Buck up, I guess he's all right really. Why shouldn't he be? See here, it was a foreign-looking guy he went off after. Maybe they've gone abroad—to Poland, or something like that?'

Tuppence shook her head.

'He couldn't without passports and things. Besides I've seen that man, Boris Something, since. He dined with Mrs Vandemeyer last night.'

'Mrs Who?'

'I forgot. Of course you don't know all that.'

'I'm listening,' said Julius, and gave vent to his favourite expression. 'Put me wise.'

Tuppence thereupon related the events of the last two days. Julius's astonishment and admiration were unbounded.

'Bully for you! Fancy you a menial. It just tickles me to death!' Then he added seriously: 'But say now, I don't like it, Miss Tuppence, I sure don't. You're just as plucky as they make 'em, but I wish you'd keep right out of this. These crooks we're up against would as soon croak a girl as a man any day.'

'Do you think I'm afraid?' said Tuppence indignantly, valiantly repressing memories of the steely glitter in Mrs Vandemeyer's eyes.

'I said before you were darned plucky. But that doesn't alter facts.'

'Oh, bother *me*!' said Tuppence impatiently. 'Let's think about what can have happened to Tommy. I've written to Mr Carter about it,' she added, and told him the gist of her letter.

Julius nodded gravely.

'I guess that's good as far as it goes. But it's for us to get busy and do something.'

'What can we do?' asked Tuppence, her spirits rising.

'I guess we'd better get on the track of Boris. You say he's been to your place. Is he likely to come again?'

'He might. I really don't know.'

'I see. Well, I guess I'd better buy a car, a slap-up one, dress as a chauffeur and hang about outside. Then if Boris comes, you could make some kind of signal, and I'd trail him. How's that?'

'Splendid, but he mightn't come for weeks.'

'We'll have to chance that. I'm glad you like the plan.' He rose.

'Where are you going?'

'To buy the car, of course,' replied Julius, surprised. 'What make do you like? I guess you'll do some riding in it before we've finished.'

'Oh,' said Tuppence faintly. 'I *like* Rolls-Royces, but—'

'Sure,' agreed Julius. 'What you say goes. I'll get one.'

'But you can't at once,' cried Tuppence. 'People wait ages sometimes.'

'Little Julius doesn't,' affirmed Mr Hersheimmer. 'Don't you worry any. I'll be round in the car in half an hour.'

Tuppence got up.

'You're awfully good, Julius. But I can't help feeling that it's rather a forlorn hope. I'm really pinning my faith to Mr Carter.'

'Then I shouldn't.'

'Why?'

'Just an idea of mine.'

'Oh, but he must do something. There's no one else. By the way, I forgot to tell you of a queer thing that happened this morning.'

And she narrated her encounter with Sir James Peel Edgerton. Julius was interested.

'What did the guy mean, do you think?' he asked.

'I don't quite know,' said Tuppence meditatively. 'But I think that, in an ambiguous, legal, without prejudicish lawyer's way, he was trying to warn me.'

'Why should he?'

'I don't know,' confessed Tuppence. 'But he looked kind, and simply awfully clever. I wouldn't mind going to him and telling him everything.'

Somewhat to her surprise, Julius negatived the idea sharply.

'See here,' he said, 'we don't want any lawyers mixed up in this. That guy couldn't help us any.'

'Well, I believe he could,' reiterated Tuppence obstinately.

'Don't you think it. So long. I'll be back in half an hour.'

Thirty-five minutes had elapsed when Julius returned. He took Tuppence by the arm, and walked her to the window.

'There she is.'

'Oh!' said Tuppence with a note of reverence in her voice, as she gazed down at the enormous car.

'She's some pace-maker, I can tell you,' said Julius complacently.

'How did you get it?' gasped Tuppence.

'She was just being sent home to some bigwig.'

'Well?'

'I went round to his house,' said Julius. 'I said that I reckoned a car like that was worth every penny of twenty

118

thousand dollars. Then I told him that it was worth just about fifty thousand dollars to me if he'd get out.'

'Well?' said Tuppence, intoxicated.

'Well,' returned Julius, 'he got out, that's all.'

CHAPTER 12

A Friend in Need

Friday and Saturday passed uneventfully. Tuppence had received a brief answer to her appeal from Mr Carter. In it he pointed out that the Young Adventurers had undertaken the work at their own risk, and had been fully warned of the dangers. If anything had happened to Tommy he regretted it deeply, but he could do nothing.

This was cold comfort. Somehow, without Tommy, all the savour went out of the adventure, and, for the first time, Tuppence felt doubtful of success. While they had been together she had never questioned it for a minute. Although she was accustomed to take the lead, and to pride herself on her quick-wittedness, in reality she had relied upon Tommy more than she realized at the time. There was something so eminently sober and clear-headed about him, his common sense and soundness of vision were so unvarying, that without him Tuppence felt much like a rudderless ship. It was curious that Julius, who was undoubtedly much cleverer than Tommy, did not give her the same feeling of support.

She had accused Tommy of being a pessimist, and it is certain that he always saw the disadvantages and difficulties which she herself was optimistically given to overlooking, but nevertheless she had really relied a good deal on his judgment. He might be slow, but he was very sure.

It seemed to the girl that, for the first time, she realized the sinister character of the mission they had undertaken so light-heartedly. It had begun like a page of romance. Now, shorn of its glamour, it seemed to be turning to grim reality. Tommy—that was all that mattered. Many times in the day Tuppence blinked the tears out of her eyes resolutely. 'Little fool,' she would apostrophize herself, 'don't snivel. Of course you're fond of him. You've known him all your life. But there's no need to be sentimental about it.'

In the meantime, nothing more was seen of Boris. He did not come to the flat, and Julius and the car waited in vain. Tuppence gave herself over to new meditations. Whilst admitting the truth of Julius's objections, she had nevertheless not entirely relinquished the idea of appealing to Sir James Peel Edgerton. Indeed, she had gone so far as to look up his address in the *Red Book*. Had he meant to warn her that day? If so, why? Surely she was at least entitled to demand an explanation. He had looked at her so kindly. Perhaps he might tell them something concerning Mrs Vandemeyer which might lead to a clue to Tommy's whereabouts.

Anyway, Tuppence decided, with her usual shake of the shoulders, it was worth trying, and try it she would. Sunday was her afternoon out. She would meet Julius, persuade him to her point of view, and they would beard the lion in his den.

Agatha Christie

When the day arrived Julius needed a considerable amount of persuading, but Tuppence held firm. 'It can do no harm,' was what she always came back to. In the end Julius gave in, and they proceeded in the car to Carlton House Terrace.

The door was opened by an irreproachable butler. Tuppence felt a little nervous. After all, perhaps it *was* colossal cheek on her part. She had decided not to ask if Sir James was 'at home,' but to adopt a more personal attitude.

'Will you ask Sir James if I can see him for a few minutes? I have an important message for him.'

The butler retired, returning a moment or two later.

'Sir James will see you. Will you step this way?'

He ushered them into a room at the back of the house, furnished as a library. The collection of books was a magnificent one, and Tuppence noticed that all one wall was devoted to works on crime and criminology. There were several deep-padded leather armchairs, and an old-fashioned open hearth. In the window was a big roll-top desk strewn with papers at which the master of the house was sitting.

He rose as they entered.

'You have a message for me? Ah'—he recognized Tuppence with a smile—'it's you, is it? Brought a message from Mrs Vandemeyer, I suppose?'

'Not exactly,' said Tuppence. 'In fact, I'm afraid I only said that to be quite sure of getting in. Oh, by the way, this is Mr Hersheimmer, Sir James Peel Edgerton.'

'Pleased to meet you,' said the American, shooting out a hand.

'Won't you both sit down?' asked Sir James. He drew forward two chairs.

'Sir James,' said Tuppence, plunging boldly, 'I dare say you will think it is the most awful cheek of me coming here like this. Because, of course, it's nothing whatever to do with you, and then you're a very important person, and of course Tommy and I are very unimportant.' She paused for breath.

'Tommy?' queried Sir James, looking across at the American.

'No, that's Julius,' explained Tuppence. 'I'm rather nervous, and that makes me tell it badly. What I really want to know is what you meant by what you said to me the other day? Did you mean to warn me against Mrs Vandemeyer? You did, didn't you?'

'My dear young lady, as far as I recollect I only mentioned that there were equally good situations to be obtained elsewhere.'

'Yes, I know. But it was a hint, wasn't it?'

'Well, perhaps it was,' admitted Sir James gravely.

'Well, I want to know more. I want to know just *why* you gave me a hint.'

Sir James smiled at her earnestness.

'Suppose the lady brings a libel action against me for defamation of character?'

'Of course,' said Tuppence. 'I know lawyers are always dreadfully careful. But can't we say "without prejudice" first, and then say just what we want to.'

'Well,' said Sir James, still smiling, 'without prejudice, then, if I had a young sister forced to earn her living, I should not like to see her in Mrs Vandemeyer's service. I felt

Agatha Christie

it incumbent on me just to give you a hint. It is no place for a young and inexperienced girl. That is all I can tell you.'

'I see,' said Tuppence thoughtfully. 'Thank you very much. But I'm not *really* inexperienced, you know. I knew perfectly that she was a bad lot when I went there—as a matter of fact that's *why* I went—' She broke off, seeing some bewilderment on the lawyer's face, and went on: 'I think perhaps I'd better tell you the whole story, Sir James. I've a sort of feeling that you'd know in a minute if I didn't tell the truth, and so you might as well know all about it from the beginning. What do you think, Julius?'

'As you're bent on it, I'd go right ahead with the facts,' replied the American, who had so far sat in silence.

'Yes, tell me all about it,' said Sir James. 'I want to know who Tommy is.'

Thus encouraged Tuppence plunged into her tale, and the lawyer listened with close attention.

'Very interesting,' he said, when she finished. 'A great deal of what you tell me, child, is already known to me. I've had certain theories of my own about this Jane Finn. You've done extraordinarily well so far, but it's rather too bad of—what do you know him as?—Mr Carter to pitchfork you two young things into an affair of this kind. By the way, where did Mr Hersheimmer come in originally? You didn't make that clear?'

Julius answered for himself.

'I'm Jane's first cousin,' he explained, returning the lawyer's keen gaze.

'Ah!'

124

The Secret Adversary

'Oh, Sir James,' broke out Tuppence, 'what do you think has become of Tommy?'

'H'm.' The lawyer rose, and paced slowly up and down. 'When you arrived, young lady, I was just packing up my traps. Going to Scotland by the night train for a few days' fishing. But there are different kinds of fishing. I've a good mind to stay, and see if we can't get on the track of that young chap.'

'Oh!' Tuppence clasped her hands ecstatically.

'All the same, as I said before, it's too bad of—of Carter to set you two babies on a job like this. Now, don't get offended, Miss—er—'

'Cowley. Prudence Cowley. But my friends call me Tuppence.'

'Well, Miss Tuppence, then, as I'm certainly going to be a friend. Don't be offended because I think you're young. Youth is a failing only too easily outgrown. Now, about this young Tommy of yours—'

'Yes.' Tuppence clasped her hands.

'Frankly, things look bad for him. He's been butting in somewhere where he wasn't wanted. Not a doubt of it. But don't give up hope.'

'And you really will help us? There, Julius! He didn't want me to come,' she added by way of explanation.

'H'm,' said the lawyer, favouring Julius with another keen glance. 'And why was that?'

'I reckoned it would be no good worrying you with a petty little business like this.'

'I see.' He paused a moment. 'This petty little business, as you call it, bears directly on a very big business, bigger perhaps than either of you or Miss Tuppence know. If this boy is alive, he may have very valuable information to give us. Therefore, we must find him.'

'Yes, but how?' cried Tuppence. 'I've tried to think of everything.'

Sir James smiled.

'And yet there's one person quite near at hand who in all probability knows where he is, or at all events where he is likely to be.'

'Who is that?' asked Tuppence, puzzled.

'Mrs Vandemeyer.'

'Yes, but she'd never tell us.'

'Ah, that is where I come in. I think it quite likely that I shall be able to make Mrs Vandemeyer tell me what I want to know.'

'How?' demanded Tuppence, opening her eyes very wide.

'Oh, just by asking her questions,' replied Sir James easily. 'That's the way we do it, you know.'

He tapped with his fingers on the table, and Tuppence felt again the intense power that radiated from the man.

'And if she won't tell?' asked Julius suddenly.

'I think she will. I have one or two powerful levers. Still, in that unlikely event, there is always the possibility of bribery.'

'Sure. And that's where I come in!' cried Julius, bringing his fist down on the table with a bang. 'You can count on me, if necessary, for one million dollars. Yes, sir, one million dollars!'

Sir James sat down and subjected Julius to a long scrutiny.

'Mr Hersheimmer,' he said at last, 'that is a very large sum.'

'I guess it'll have to be. These aren't the kind of folk to offer sixpence to.'

'At the present rate of exchange it amounts to considerably over two hundred and fifty thousand pounds.'

'That's so. Maybe you think I'm talking through my hat, but I can deliver the goods all right, with enough over to spare for your fee.'

Sir James flushed slightly.

'There is no question of a fee, Mr Hersheimmer. I am not a private detective.'

'Sorry. I guess I was just a mite hasty, but I've been feeling bad about this money question. I wanted to offer a big reward for news of Jane some days ago, but your crusted institution of Scotland Yard advised me against it. Said it was undesirable.'

'They were probably right,' said Sir James dryly.

'But it's all O.K. about Julius,' put in Tuppence. 'He's not pulling your leg. He's got simply pots of money.'

'The old man piled it up in style,' explained Julius. 'Now, let's get down to it. What's your idea?'

Sir James considered for a moment or two.

'There is no time to be lost. The sooner we strike the better.' He turned to Tuppence. 'Is Mrs Vandemeyer dining out tonight, do you know?'

'Yes, I think so, but she will not be out late. Otherwise, she would have taken the latchkey.'

'Good. I will call upon her about ten o'clock. What time are you supposed to return?'

'About nine-thirty or ten, but I could go back earlier.'

'You must not do that on any account. It might arouse suspicion if you did not stay out till the usual time. Be back by nine-thirty. I will arrive at ten. Mr Hersheimmer will wait below in a taxi perhaps.'

'He's got a new Rolls-Royce car,' said Tuppence with vicarious pride.

'Even better. If I succeed in obtaining the address from her, we can go there at once, taking Mrs Vandemeyer with us if necessary. You understand?'

'Yes.' Tuppence rose to her feet with a skip of delight. 'Oh, I feel so much better!'

'Don't build on it too much, Miss Tuppence. Go easy.'

Julius turned to the lawyer.

'Say, then, I'll call for you in the car round about nine-thirty. Is that right?'

'Perhaps that will be the best plan. It would be unnecessary to have two cars waiting about. Now, Miss Tuppence, my advice to you is to go and have a good dinner, a *really* good one, mind. And don't think ahead more than you can help.'

He shook hands with them both, and a moment later they were outside.

'Isn't he a duck?' inquired Tuppence ecstatically, as she skipped down the steps. 'Oh, Julius, isn't he just a duck?'

'Well, I allow he seems to be the goods all right. And I was wrong about its being useless to go to him. Say, shall we go right away back to the Ritz?'

'I must walk a bit, I think. I feel so excited. Drop me in the Park, will you? Unless you'd like to come too?'

Julius shook his head.

'I want to get some petrol,' he explained. 'And send off a cable or two.'

'All right. I'll meet you at the Ritz at seven. We'll have to dine upstairs. I can't show myself in these glad rags.'

'Sure. I'll get Felix to help me choose the menu. He's some head waiter, that. So long.'

Tuppence walked briskly along towards the Serpentine, first glancing at her watch. It was nearly six o'clock. She remembered that she had had no tea, but felt too excited to be conscious of hunger. She walked as far as Kensington Gardens and then slowly retraced her steps, feeling infinitely better for the fresh air and exercise. It was not so easy to follow Sir James's advice and put the possible events of the evening out of her head. As she drew nearer and nearer to Hyde Park Corner, the temptation to return to South Audley Mansions was almost irresistible.

At any rate, she decided, it would do no harm just to go and *look* at the building. Perhaps, then, she could resign herself to waiting patiently for ten o'clock.

South Audley Mansions looked exactly the same as usual. What Tuppence had expected she hardly knew, but the sight of its red brick solidity slightly assuaged the growing and entirely unreasonable uneasiness that possessed her. She was just turning away when she heard a piercing whistle, and the faithful Albert came running from the building to join her.

Tuppence frowned. It was no part of the programme to have attention called to her presence in the neighbourhood, but Albert was purple with suppressed excitement.

'I say, miss, she's a-going!'

'Who's going?' demanded Tuppence sharply.

'The crook. Ready Rita. Mrs Vandemeyer. She's a-packing up, and she's just sent down word for me to get her a taxi.'

'What?' Tuppence clutched his arm.

'It's the truth, miss. I thought maybe as you didn't know about it.'

'Albert,' cried Tuppence, 'you're a brick. If it hadn't been for you we'd have lost her.'

Albert flushed with pleasure at this tribute.

'There's no time to lose,' said Tuppence, crossing the road. 'I've got to stop her. At all costs I must keep her here until—' She broke off. 'Albert, there's a telephone here, isn't there?'

The boy shook his head.

'The flats mostly have their own, miss. But there's a box just round the corner.'

'Go to it then, at once, and ring up the Ritz Hotel. Ask for Mr Hersheimmer, and when you get him tell him to get Sir James and come at once, as Mrs Vandemeyer is trying to hook it. If you can't get him, ring up Sir James Peel Edgerton, you'll find his number in the book, and tell him what's happening. You won't forget the names, will you?'

Albert repeated them glibly. 'You trust to me, miss, it'll be all right. But what about you? Aren't you afraid to trust yourself with her?'

'No, no, that's all right. *But go and telephone*. Be quick.'

Drawing a long breath, Tuppence entered the Mansions and ran up to the door of No. 20. How she was to detain Mrs Vandemeyer until the two men arrived, she did not know, but somehow or other it had to be done, and she must accomplish the task single-handed. What had occasioned this precipitate departure? Did Mrs Vandemeyer suspect her?

Speculations were idle. Tuppence pressed the bell firmly. She might learn something from the cook.

Nothing happened and, after waiting some minutes, Tuppence pressed the bell again, keeping her finger on the button for some little while. At last she heard footsteps inside, and a moment later Mrs Vandemeyer herself opened the door. She lifted her eyebrows at the sight of the girl.

'You?'

'I had a touch of toothache, ma'am,' said Tuppence glibly. 'So thought it better to come home and have a quiet evening.'

Mrs Vandemeyer said nothing, but she drew back and let Tuppence pass into the hall.

'How unfortunate for you,' she said coldly. 'You had better go to bed.'

'Oh, I shall be all right in the kitchen, ma'am. Cook will—'

'Cook is out,' said Mrs Vandemeyer, in a rather disagreeable tone. 'I sent her out. So you see you had better go to bed.'

Suddenly Tuppence felt afraid. There was a ring in Mrs Vandemeyer's voice that she did not like at all. Also, the other woman was slowly edging her up the passage. Tuppence turned at bay.

'I don't want—'

Then, in a flash, a rim of cold steel touched her temple, and Mrs Vandemeyer's voice rose cold and menacing:

'You damned little fool! Do you think I don't know? No, don't answer. If you struggle or cry out, I'll shoot you like a dog.'

The rim of steel pressed a little harder against the girl's temple.

'Now then, march,' went on Mrs Vandemeyer. 'This way—into my room. In a minute, when I've done with you, you'll go to bed as I told you to. And you'll sleep—oh yes, my little spy, you'll sleep all right!'

There was a sort of hideous geniality in the last words which Tuppence did not at all like. For the moment there was nothing to be done, and she walked obediently into Mrs Vandemeyer's bedroom. The pistol never left her forehead. The room was in a state of wild disorder, clothes were flung about right and left, a suit-case and a hat box, half-packed, stood in the middle of the floor.

Tuppence pulled herself together with an effort. Her voice shook a little, but she spoke out bravely.

'Come now,' she said, 'this is nonsense. You can't shoot me. Why, everyone in the building would hear the report.'

'I'd risk that,' said Mrs Vandemeyer cheerfully. 'But, as long as you don't sing out for help, you're all right—and I don't think you will. You're a clever girl. You deceived *me* all right. I hadn't a suspicion of you! So I've no doubt that you understand perfectly well that this is where I'm on top and you're underneath. Now then—sit on the bed. Put your hands above your head, and if you value your life don't move them.'

Tuppence obeyed passively. Her good sense told her that there was nothing else to do but accept the situation. If she shrieked for help there was very little chance of anyone hearing her, whereas there was probably quite a good chance of Mrs Vandemeyer's shooting her. In the meantime, every minute of delay gained was valuable.

Mrs Vandemeyer laid down the revolver on the edge of the wash-stand within reach of her hand, and, still eyeing Tuppence like a lynx in case the girl should attempt to move, she took a little stoppered bottle from its place on the marble and poured some of its contents into a glass which she filled up with water.

'What's that?' asked Tuppence sharply.

'Something to make you sleep soundly.'

Tuppence paled a little.

'Are you going to poison me?' she asked in a whisper.

'Perhaps,' said Mrs Vandemeyer, smiling agreeably.

'Then I shan't drink it,' said Tuppence firmly. 'I'd much rather be shot. At any rate that would make a row, and someone might hear it. But I won't be killed off quietly like a lamb.'

Mrs Vandemeyer stamped her foot.

'Don't be a little fool! Do you really think I want a hue and cry for murder out after me? If you've any sense at all, you'll realize that poisoning you wouldn't suit my book at all. It's a sleeping-draught, that's all. You'll wake up tomorrow morning none the worse. I simply don't want the bother of tying you up and gagging you. That's the alternative—and you won't like it, I can tell you! I can be very rough if I choose. So drink this down like a good girl, and you'll be none the worse for it.'

In her heart of hearts Tuppence believed her. The arguments she had adduced rang true. It was a simple and effective method of getting her out of the way for the time being. Nevertheless, the girl did not take kindly to the idea of being tamely put to sleep without as much as one bid for freedom. She felt that once Mrs Vandemeyer gave them the slip, the last hope of finding Tommy would be gone.

Tuppence was quick in her mental processes. All these reflections passed through her mind in a flash, and she saw where a chance, a very problematic chance, lay, and she determined to risk all in one supreme effort.

Accordingly, she lurched suddenly off the bed and fell on her knees before Mrs Vandemeyer, clutching her skirts frantically.

'I don't believe it,' she moaned. 'It's poison—I know it's poison. Oh, don't make me drink it'—her voice rose to a shriek—'don't make me drink it!'

Mrs Vandemeyer, glass in hand, looked down with a curling lip at this sudden collapse.

'Get up, you little idiot! Don't go on drivelling there. How you ever had the nerve to play your part as you did I can't think.' She stamped her foot. 'Get up, I say.'

But Tuppence continued to cling and sob, interjecting her sobs with incoherent appeals for mercy. Every minute gained was to the good. Moreover, as she grovelled, she moved imperceptibly nearer to her objective.

Mrs Vandemeyer gave a sharp impatient exclamation, and jerked the girl to her knees.

'Drink it at once!' Imperiously she pressed the glass to the girl's lips.

Tuppence gave one last despairing moan.

'You swear it won't hurt me?' she temporized.

'Of course it won't hurt you. Don't be a fool.'

'Will you swear it?'

'Yes, yes,' said the other impatiently. 'I swear it.'

Tuppence raised a trembling left hand to the glass.

'Very well.' Her mouth opened meekly.

Mrs Vandemeyer gave a sigh of relief, off her guard for the moment. Then, quick as a flash, Tuppence jerked the glass upward as hard as she could. The fluid in it splashed into Mrs Vandemeyer's face, and during her momentary gasp, Tuppence's right hand shot out and grasped the revolver where it lay on the edge of the wash-stand. The next moment she had sprung back a pace, and the revolver pointed straight at Mrs Vandemeyer's heart, with no unsteadiness in the hand that held it.

In the moment of victory, Tuppence betrayed a somewhat unsportsman-like triumph.

'Now who's on top and who's underneath?' she crowed.

The other's face was convulsed with rage. For a minute Tuppence thought she was going to spring upon her, which would have placed the girl in an unpleasant dilemma, since she meant to draw the line at actually letting off the revolver. However, with an effort, Mrs Vandemeyer controlled herself, and at last a slow evil smile crept over her face.

'Not a fool then, after all! You did that well, girl. But you shall pay for it—oh, yes, you shall pay for it! I have a long memory!'

'I'm surprised you should have been gulled so easily,' said Tuppence scornfully. 'Did you really think I was the kind of girl to roll about on the floor and whine for mercy?'

'You may do—some day!' said the other significantly.

The cold malignity of her manner sent an unpleasant chill down Tuppence's spine, but she was not going to give in to it.

'Supposing we sit down,' she said pleasantly. 'Our present attitude is a little melodramatic. No—not on the bed. Draw a chair up to the table, that's right. Now I'll sit opposite you with the revolver in front of me—just in case of accidents. Splendid. Now, let's talk.'

'What about?' said Mrs Vandemeyer sullenly.

Tuppence eyed her thoughtfully for a minute. She was remembering several things. Boris's words, 'I believe you would sell—*us*!' and her answer, 'The price would have to be enormous,' given lightly, it was true, yet might not there be a substratum of truth in it? Long ago, had not Whittington asked: 'Who's been blabbing? Rita?' Would Rita Vandemeyer prove to be the weak spot in the armour of Mr Brown?

Keeping her eyes fixed steadily on the other's face, Tuppence replied quietly:

'Money—'

Mrs Vandemeyer started. Clearly, the reply was unexpected.

'What do you mean?'

'I'll tell you. You said just now that you had a long memory. A long memory isn't half as useful as a long purse!

136

I dare say it relieves your feelings a good deal to plan out all sorts of dreadful things to do to me, but is that *practical*? Revenge is very unsatisfactory. Everyone always says so. But money'—Tuppence warmed to her pet creed—'well, there's nothing unsatisfactory about money, is there?'

'Do you think,' said Mrs Vandemeyer scornfully, 'that I am the kind of woman to sell my friends?'

'Yes,' said Tuppence promptly, 'if the price was big enough.'

'A paltry hundred pounds or so!'

'No,' said Tuppence. 'I should suggest—a hundred thousand!'

Her economical spirit did not permit her to mention the whole million dollars suggested by Julius.

A flush crept over Mrs Vandemeyer's face.

'What did you say?' she asked, her fingers playing nervously with a brooch on her breast. In that moment Tuppence knew that the fish was hooked, and for the first time she felt a horror of her own money-loving spirit. It gave her a dreadful sense of kinship to the woman fronting her.

'A hundred thousand pounds,' repeated Tuppence.

The light died out of Mrs Vandemeyer's eyes. She leaned back in her chair.

'Bah!' she said. 'You haven't got it.'

'No,' admitted Tuppence, 'I haven't—but I know someone who has.'

'Who?'

'A friend of mine.'

'Must be a millionaire,' remarked Mrs Vandemeyer unbelievingly.

137

'As a matter of fact he is. He's an American. He'll pay you that without a murmur. You can take it from me that it's a perfectly genuine proposition.'

Mrs Vandemeyer sat up again.

'I'm inclined to believe you,' she said slowly.

There was silence between them for some time, then Mrs Vandemeyer looked up.

'What does he want to know, this friend of yours?'

Tuppence went through a momentary struggle, but it was Julius's money, and his interests must come first.

'He wants to know where Jane Finn is,' she said boldly.

Mrs Vandemeyer showed no surprise.

'I'm not sure where she is at the present moment,' she replied.

'But you could find out?'

'Oh, yes,' returned Mrs Vandemeyer carelessly. 'There would be no difficulty about that.'

'Then'—Tuppence's voice shook a little—'there's a boy, a friend of mine. I'm afraid something's happened to him, through your pal, Boris.'

'What's his name?'

'Tommy Beresford.'

'Never heard of him. But I'll ask Boris. He'll tell me anything he knows.'

'Thank you.' Tuppence felt a terrific rise in her spirits. It impelled her to more audacious efforts. 'There's one thing more.'

'Well?'

Tuppence leaned forward and lowered her voice.

'*Who is Mr Brown?*'

Her quick eyes saw the sudden paling of the beautiful face. With an effort Mrs Vandemeyer pulled herself together and tried to resume her former manner. But the attempt was a mere parody.

She shrugged her shoulders.

'You can't have learnt much about us if you don't know that *nobody knows who Mr Brown is...*'

'You do,' said Tuppence quietly.

Again the colour deserted the other's face.

'What makes you think that?'

'I don't know,' said the girl truthfully. 'But I'm sure.'

Mrs Vandemeyer stared in front of her for a long time.

'Yes,' she said hoarsely, at last, '*I* know. I was beautiful, you see—very beautiful—'

'You are still,' said Tuppence with admiration.

Mrs Vandemeyer shook her head. There was a strange gleam in her electric-blue eyes.

'Not beautiful enough,' she said in a soft dangerous voice. 'Not—beautiful—enough! And sometimes, lately, I've been afraid... It's dangerous to know too much!' She leaned forward across the table. 'Swear that my name shan't be brought into it—that no one shall ever know.'

'I swear it. And, once he's caught, you'll be out of danger.'

A terrified look swept across Mrs Vandemeyer's face.

'Shall I? Shall I ever be?' She clutched Tuppence's arm. 'You're sure about the money?'

'Quite sure.'

'When shall I have it? There must be no delay.'

'This friend of mine will be here presently. He may have to send cables, or something like that. But there won't be any delay—he's a terrific hustler.'

A resolute look settled on Mrs Vandemeyer's face.

'I'll do it. It's a great sum of money, and besides'—she gave a curious smile—'it is not—wise to throw over a woman like me!'

For a moment or two, she remained smiling, and lightly tapping her fingers on the table. Suddenly she started, and her face blanched.

'What was that?'

'I heard nothing.'

Mrs Vandemeyer gazed round her fearfully.

'If there should be someone listening—'

'Nonsense. Who could there be?'

'Even the walls might have ears,' whispered the other. 'I tell you I'm frightened. You don't know him!'

'Think of the hundred thousand pounds,' said Tuppence soothingly.

Mrs Vandemeyer passed her tongue over her dried lips.

'You don't know him,' she reiterated hoarsely. 'He's—ah!'

With a shriek of terror she sprang to her feet. Her outstretched hand pointed over Tuppence's head. Then she swayed to the ground in a dead faint.

Tuppence looked round to see what had startled her.

In the doorway were Sir James Peel Edgerton and Julius Hersheimmer.

CHAPTER 13

The Vigil

Sir James brushed past Julius and hurriedly bent over the fallen woman.

'Heart,' he said sharply. 'Seeing us so suddenly must have given her a shock. Brandy—and quickly, or she'll slip through our fingers.'

Julius hurried to the wash-stand.

'Not here,' said Tuppence over her shoulder. 'In the tantalus in the dining-room. Second door down the passage.'

Between them Sir James and Tuppence lifted Mrs Vandemeyer and carried her to the bed. There they dashed water on her face, but with no result. The lawyer fingered her pulse.

'Touch and go,' he muttered. 'I wish that young fellow would hurry up with the brandy.'

At that moment Julius re-entered the room, carrying a glass half full of the spirit which he handed to Sir James. While Tuppence lifted her head the lawyer tried to force a little of the spirit between her closed lips. Finally the woman opened her eyes feebly. Tuppence held the glass to her lips.

'Drink this.'

Mrs Vandemeyer complied. The brandy brought the colour back to her white cheeks, and revived her in a marvellous fashion. She tried to sit up—then fell back with a groan, her hand to her side.

'It's my heart,' she whispered. 'I mustn't talk.'

She lay back with closed eyes.

Sir James kept his finger on her wrist a minute longer, then withdrew it with a nod.

'She'll do now.'

All three moved away, and stood together talking in low voices. One and all were conscious of a certain feeling of anticlimax. Clearly any scheme for cross-questioning the lady was out of the question for the moment. For the time being they were baffled, and could do nothing.

Tuppence related how Mrs Vandemeyer had declared herself willing to disclose the identity of Mr Brown, and how she had consented to discover and reveal to them the whereabouts of Jane Finn. Julius was congratulatory.

'That's all right, Miss Tuppence. Splendid! I guess that hundred thousand pounds will look just as good in the morning to the lady as it did over night. There's nothing to worry over. She won't speak without the cash anyway, you bet!'

There was certainly a good deal of common sense in this, and Tuppence felt a little comforted.

'What you say is true,' said Sir James meditatively. 'I must confess, however, that I cannot help wishing we had not interrupted at the minute we did. Still, it cannot be helped, it is only a matter of waiting until the morning.'

He looked across at the inert figure on the bed. Mrs Vandemeyer lay perfectly passive with closed eyes. He shook his head.

'Well,' said Tuppence, with an attempt at cheerfulness, 'we must wait until the morning, that's all. But I don't think we ought to leave the flat.'

'What about leaving that bright boy of yours on guard?'

'Albert? And suppose she came round again and hooked it. Albert couldn't stop her.'

'I guess she won't want to make tracks away from the dollars.'

'She might. She seemed very frightened of "Mr Brown."'

'What? Real plumb scared of him?'

'Yes. She looked round and said even walls had ears.'

'Maybe she meant a dictaphone,' said Julius with interest.

'Miss Tuppence is right,' said Sir James quietly. 'We must not leave the flat—if only for Mrs Vandemeyer's sake.'

Julius stared at him.

'You think he'd get after her? Between now and tomorrow morning. How could he know, even?'

'You forget your own suggestion of a dictaphone,' said Sir James dryly. 'We have a very formidable adversary. I believe, if we exercise all due care, that there is a very good chance of his being delivered into our hands. But we must neglect no precaution. We have an important witness, but she must be safeguarded. I would suggest that Miss Tuppence should go to bed, and that you and I, Mr Hersheimmer, should share the vigil.'

Tuppence was about to protest, but happening to glance at the bed she saw Mrs Vandemeyer, her eyes half-open, with such an expression of mingled fear and malevolence on her face that it quite froze the words on her lips.

For a moment she wondered whether the faint and the heart attack had been a gigantic sham, but remembering the deadly pallor she could hardly credit the supposition. As she looked the expression disappeared as by magic, and Mrs Vandemeyer lay inert and motionless as before. For a moment the girl fancied she must have dreamt it. But she determined nevertheless to be on the alert.

'Well,' said Julius, 'I guess we'd better make a move out of here anyway.'

The others fell in with his suggestion. Sir James again felt Mrs Vandemeyer's pulse.

'Perfectly satisfactory,' he said in a low voice to Tuppence. 'She'll be absolutely all right after a night's rest.'

The girl hesitated a moment by the bed. The intensity of the expression she had surprised had impressed her powerfully. Mrs Vandemeyer lifted her eyelids. She seemed to be struggling to speak. Tuppence bent over her.

'Don't—leave—' she seemed unable to proceed, murmuring something that sounded like 'sleepy'. Then she tried again.

Tuppence bent lower still. It was only a breath.

'Mr—Brown—' The voice stopped.

But the half-closed eyes seemed still to send an agonized message.

Moved by a sudden impulse, the girl said quickly:

'I shan't leave the flat. I shall sit up all night.'

A flash of relief showed before the lids descended once more. Apparently Mrs Vandemeyer slept. But her words had awakened a new uneasiness in Tuppence. What had she meant by that low murmur. 'Mr Brown?' Tuppence caught herself nervously looking over her shoulder. The big wardrobe loomed up in a sinister fashion before her eyes. Plenty of room for a man to hide in that... Half-ashamed of herself Tuppence pulled it open and looked inside. No one—of course! She stooped down and looked under the bed. There was no other possible hiding-place.

Tuppence gave her familiar shake of the shoulders. It was absurd, this giving way to nerves! Slowly she went out of the room. Julius and Sir James were talking in a low voice. Sir James turned to her.

'Lock the door on the outside, please, Miss Tuppence, and take out the key. There must be no chance of anyone entering that room.'

The gravity of his manner impressed them, and Tuppence felt less ashamed of her attack of 'nerves.'

'Say,' remarked Julius suddenly, 'there's Tuppence's bright boy. I guess I'd better go down and ease his young mind. That's some lad, Tuppence.'

'How did you get in, by the way?' asked Tuppence suddenly. 'I forgot to ask.'

'Well, Albert got me on the phone all right. I ran round for Sir James here, and we came right on. The boy was on the look out for us, and was just a mite worried about what might have happened to you. He'd been listening outside the door of the flat, but couldn't hear anything.

Anyhow he suggested sending us up in the coal lift instead of ringing the bell. And sure enough we landed in the scullery and came right along to find you. Albert's still below, and must be hopping mad by this time.' With which Julius departed abruptly.

'Now then, Miss Tuppence,' said Sir James, 'you know this place better than I do. Where do you suggest we should take up our quarters?'

Tuppence considered for a moment or two.

'I think Mrs Vandemeyer's boudoir would be the most comfortable,' she said at last, and led the way there.

Sir James looked round approvingly.

'This will do very well, and now, my dear young lady, do go to bed and get some sleep.'

Tuppence shook her head resolutely.

'I couldn't, thank you, Sir James. I should dream of Mr Brown all night!'

'But you'll be so tired, child.'

'No, I shan't. I'd rather stay up—really.'

The lawyer gave in.

Julius reappeared some minutes later, having reassured Albert and rewarded him lavishly for his services. Having in his turn failed to persuade Tuppence to go to bed, he said decisively:

'At any rate, you've got to have something to eat right away. Where's the larder?'

Tuppence directed him, and he returned in a few minutes with a cold pie and three plates.

After a hearty meal, the girl felt inclined to pooh-pooh

her fancies of half an hour before. The power of the money bribe could not fail.

'And now, Miss Tuppence,' said Sir James, 'we want to hear your adventures.'

'That's so,' agreed Julius.

Tuppence narrated her adventures with some complacence. Julius occasionally interjected an admiring 'Bully.' Sir James said nothing until she had finished, when his quiet 'Well done, Miss Tuppence,' made her flush with pleasure.

'There's one thing I don't get clearly,' said Julius. 'What put her up to clearing out?'

'I don't know,' confessed Tuppence.

Sir James stroked his chin thoughtfully.

'The room was in great disorder. That looks as though her flight was unpremeditated. Almost as though she got a sudden warning to go from someone.'

'Mr Brown, I suppose,' said Julius scoffingly.

The lawyer looked at him deliberately for a minute or two.

'Why not?' he said. 'Remember, you yourself have once been worsted by him.'

Julius flushed with vexation.

'I feel just mad when I think of how I handed out Jane's photograph to him like a lamb. Gee, if I ever lay hands on it again, I'll freeze on to it—like hell!'

'That contingency is likely to be a remote one,' said the other dryly.

'I guess you're right,' said Julius frankly. 'And, in any case, it's the original I'm out after. Where do you think she can be, Sir James?'

The lawyer shook his head.

'Impossible to say. But I've a very good idea where she *has* been.'

'You have? Where?'

Sir James smiled.

'At the scene of your nocturnal adventures, the Bournemouth nursing home.'

'There? Impossible. I asked.'

'No, my dear sir, you asked if anyone of the name of Jane Finn had been there. Now, if the girl had been placed there it would almost certainly be under an assumed name.'

'Bully for you,' cried Julius. 'I never thought of that!'

'It was fairly obvious,' said the other.

'Perhaps the doctor's in it too,' suggested Tuppence.

Julius shook his head.

'I don't think so. I took to him at once. No, I'm pretty sure Dr Hall's all right.'

'Hall, did you say?' asked Sir James. 'That is curious— really very curious.'

'Why?' demanded Tuppence.

'Because I happened to meet him this morning. I've known him slightly on and off for some years, and this morning I ran across him in the street. Staying at the Metropole, he told me.' He turned to Julius. 'Didn't he tell you he was coming up to town?'

Julius shook his head.

'Curious,' mused Sir James. 'You did not mention his name this afternoon, or I would have suggested your going to him for further information with my card as introduction.'

'I guess I'm a mutt,' said Julius with unusual humility. 'I ought to have thought of the false name stunt.'

'How could you think of anything after falling out of that tree?' cried Tuppence. 'I'm sure anyone else would have been killed right off.'

'Well, I guess it doesn't matter now, anyway,' said Julius. 'We've got Mrs Vandemeyer on a string, and that's all we need.'

'Yes,' said Tuppence, but there was a lack of assurance in her voice.

A silence settled down over the party. Little by little the magic of the night began to gain hold on them. There were sudden creaks in the furniture, imperceptible rustlings in the curtains. Suddenly Tuppence sprang up with a cry.

'I can't help it. I know Mr Brown's somewhere in the flat! I can *feel* him.'

'Sure, Tuppence, how could he be? This door's open into the hall. No one could have come in by the front door without our seeing and hearing him.'

'I can't help it. I *feel* he's here!'

She looked appealingly at Sir James, who replied gravely:

'With due deference to your feelings, Miss Tuppence (and mine as well for that matter), I do not see how it is humanly possible for anyone to be in the flat without our knowledge.'

The girl was a little comforted by his words.

'Sitting up at night is always rather jumpy,' she confessed.

'Yes,' said Sir James. 'We are in the condition of people holding a séance. Perhaps if a medium were present we might get some marvellous results.'

'Do you believe in spiritualism?' asked Tuppence, opening her eyes wide.

The lawyer shrugged his shoulders.

'There is some truth in it, without a doubt. But most of the testimony would not pass muster in the witness-box.'

The hours drew on. With the first faint glimmerings of dawn, Sir James drew aside the curtains. They beheld, what few Londoners see, the slow rising of the sun over the sleeping city. Somehow, with the coming of the light, the dreads and fancies of the past night seemed absurd. Tuppence's spirits revived to the normal.

'Hooray!' she said. 'It's going to be a gorgeous day. And we shall find Tommy. And Jane Finn. And everything will be lovely. I shall ask Mr Carter if I can't be made a Dame!'

At seven o'clock Tuppence volunteered to go and make some tea. She returned with a tray, containing the teapot and four cups.

'Who's the other cup for?' inquired Julius.

'The prisoner, of course. I suppose we might call her that?'

'Taking her tea seems a kind of anti-climax to last night,' said Julius thoughtfully.

'Yes, it does,' admitted Tuppence. 'But, anyway, here goes. Perhaps you'd both come, too, in case she springs on me, or anything. You see, we don't know what mood she'll wake up in.'

Sir James and Julius accompanied her to the door.

'Where's the key? Oh, of course, I've got it myself.'

She put it in the lock, and turned it, then paused.

'Supposing, after all, she's escaped?' she murmured in a whisper.

'Plumb impossible,' replied Julius reassuringly.

But Sir James said nothing.

Tuppence drew a long breath and entered. She heaved a sigh of relief as she saw that Mrs Vandemeyer was lying on the bed.

'Good morning,' she remarked cheerfully. 'I've brought you some tea.'

Mrs Vandemeyer did not reply. Tuppence put down the cup on the table by the bed and went across to draw up the blinds. When she turned, Mrs Vandemeyer still lay without a movement. With a sudden fear clutching at her heart, Tuppence ran to the bed. The hand she lifted was cold as ice... Mrs Vandemeyer would never speak now...

Her cry brought the others. A very few minutes sufficed. Mrs Vandemeyer was dead—must have been dead some hours. She had evidently died in her sleep.

'If that isn't the cruellest luck,' cried Julius in despair.

The lawyer was calmer, but there was a curious gleam in his eyes.

'If it is luck,' he replied.

'You don't think—but, say, that's plumb impossible—no one could have got in.'

'No,' admitted the lawyer. 'I don't see how they could. And yet—she is on the point of betraying Mr Brown, and—she dies. Is it only chance?'

'But how—'

'Yes, *how*! That is what we must find out.' He stood there silently, gently stroking his chin. 'We must find out,' he said quietly, and Tuppence felt that if she was Mr Brown she would not like the tone of those simple words.

Julius's glance went to the window.

'The window's open,' he remarked. 'Do you think—'

Tuppence shook her head.

'The balcony only goes along as far as the boudoir. We were there.'

'He might have slipped out—' suggested Julius.

But Sir James interrupted him.

'Mr Brown's methods are not so crude. In the meantime we must send for a doctor, but before we do so is there anything in this room that might be of value to us?'

Hastily, the three searched. A charred mass in the grate indicated that Mrs Vandemeyer had been burning papers on the eve of her flight. Nothing of importance remained, though they searched the other rooms as well.

'There's that,' said Tuppence suddenly, pointing to a small, old-fashioned safe let into the wall. 'It's for jewellery, I believe, but there might be something else in it.'

The key was in the lock, and Julius swung open the door, and searched inside. He was some time over the task.

'Well,' said Tuppence impatiently.

There was a pause before Julius answered, then he withdrew his head and shut the door.

'Nothing,' he said.

In five minutes a brisk young doctor arrived, hastily summoned. He was deferential to Sir James, whom he recognized.

'Heart failure, or possibly an overdose of some sleeping-draught.' He sniffed. 'Rather an odour of chloral in the air.'

Tuppence remembered the glass she had upset. A new thought drove her to the wash-stand. She found the little bottle from which Mrs Vandemeyer had poured a few drops. It had been three parts full. Now—*it was empty*.

CHAPTER 14

A Consultation

Nothing was more surprising and bewildering to Tuppence than the ease and simplicity with which everything was arranged, owing to Sir James's skilful handling. The doctor accepted quite readily the theory that Mrs Vandemeyer had accidentally taken an overdose of chloral. He doubted whether an inquest would be necessary. If so, he would let Sir James know. He understood that Mrs Vandemeyer was on the eve of departure for abroad, and that the servants had already left? Sir James and his young friends had been paying a call upon her, when she was suddenly stricken down and they had spent the night in the flat, not liking to leave her alone. Did they know of any relatives? They did not, but Sir James referred him to Mrs Vandemeyer's solicitor.

Shortly afterwards a nurse arrived to take charge, and the others left the ill-omened building.

'And what now?' asked Julius, with a gesture of despair. 'I guess we're down and out for good.'

Sir James stroked his chin thoughtfully.

'No,' he said quietly. 'There is still the chance that Dr Hall may be able to tell us something.'

'Gee! I'd forgotten him.'

'The chance is slight, but it must not be neglected. I think I told you that he is staying at the Metropole. I should suggest that we call upon him there as soon as possible. Shall we say after a bath and breakfast?'

It was arranged that Tuppence and Julius should return to the Ritz, and call for Sir James in the car. The programme was faithfully carried out, and a little after eleven they drew up before the Metropole. They asked for Dr Hall, and a page-boy went in search of him. In a few minutes the little doctor came hurrying towards them.

'Can you spare us a few minutes, Dr Hall?' said Sir James pleasantly. 'Let me introduce you to Miss Cowley. Mr Hersheimmer, I think, you already know.'

A quizzical gleam came into the doctor's eye as he shook hands with Julius.

'Ah, yes, my young friend of the tree episode! Ankle all right, eh?'

'I guess it's cured owing to your skilful treatment, doc.'

'And the heart trouble? Ha! ha!'

'Still searching,' said Julius briefly.

'To come to the point, can we have a word with you in private?' asked Sir James.

'Certainly. I think there is a room here where we shall be quite undisturbed.'

He led the way, and the others followed him. They sat down, and the doctor looked inquiringly at Sir James.

'Dr Hall, I am very anxious to find a certain young lady for the purpose of obtaining a statement from her. I have reason to believe that she has been at one time or another in your establishment at Bournemouth. I hope I am transgressing no professional etiquette in questioning you on the subject?'

'I suppose it is a matter of testimony?'

Sir James hesitated a moment, then he replied:

'Yes.'

'I shall be pleased to give you any information in my power. What is the young lady's name? Mr Hersheimmer asked me, I remember—' He half turned to Julius.

'The name,' said Sir James bluntly, 'is really immaterial. She would be almost certainly sent to you under an assumed one. But I should like to know if you are acquainted with a Mrs Vandemeyer?'

'Mrs Vandemeyer, of 20 South Audley Mansions? I know her slightly.'

'You are not aware of what has happened?'

'What do you mean?'

'You do not know that Mrs Vandemeyer is dead?'

'Dear, dear, I had no idea of it! When did it happen?'

'She took an overdose of chloral last night.'

'Purposely?'

'Accidentally, it is believed. I should not like to say myself. Anyway, she was found dead this morning.'

'Very sad. A singularly handsome woman. I presume she was a friend of yours, since you are acquainted with all these details.'

'I am acquainted with the details because—well, it was I who found her dead.'

'Indeed,' said the doctor, starting.

'Yes,' said Sir James, and stroked his chin reflectively.

'This is very sad news, but you will excuse me if I say that I do not see how it bears on the subject of your inquiry?'

'It bears on it in this way, is it not a fact that Mrs Vandemeyer committed a young relative of hers to your charge?'

Julius leaned forward eagerly.

'That is the case,' said the doctor quietly.

'Under the name of—?'

'Janet Vandemeyer. I understood her to be a niece of Mrs Vandemeyer's.'

'And she came to you?'

'As far as I can remember in June or July of 1915.'

'Was she a mental case?'

'She is perfectly sane, if that is what you mean. I understood from Mrs Vandemeyer that the girl had been with her on the *Lusitania* when that ill-fated ship was sunk, and had suffered a severe shock in consequence.'

'We're on the right track, I think?' Sir James looked round.

'As I said before, I'm a mutt!' returned Julius.

The doctor looked at them all curiously.

'You spoke of wanting a statement from her,' he said. 'Supposing she is not able to give one?'

'What? You have just said that she is perfectly sane.'

'So she is. Nevertheless, if you want a statement from her concerning any events prior to May 7, 1915, she will not be able to give it to you.'

They looked at the little man, stupefied. He nodded cheerfully.

'It's a pity,' he said. 'A great pity, especially as I gather, Sir James, that the matter is important. But there it is, she can tell you nothing.'

'But why, man? Darn it all, why?'

The little man shifted his benevolent glance to the excited young American.

'Because Janet Vandemeyer is suffering from a complete loss of memory!'

'*What?*'

'Quite so. An interesting case, a *very* interesting case. Not so uncommon, really, as you would think. There are several very well known parallels. It's the first case of the kind that I've had under my own personal observation, and I must admit that I've found it of absorbing interest.' There was something rather ghoulish in the little man's satisfaction.

'And she remembers nothing,' said Sir James slowly.

'Nothing prior to May 7, 1915. After that date her memory is as good as yours or mine.'

'Then the first thing she remembers?'

'Is landing with the survivors. Everything before that is a blank. She did not know her own name, or where she had come from, or where she was. She couldn't even speak her own tongue.'

'But surely all this is most unusual?' put in Julius.

'No, my dear sir. Quite normal under the circumstances. Severe shock to the nervous system. Loss of memory proceeds nearly always on the same lines. I suggested a specialist, of course. There's a very good man in Paris—makes a study of these cases—but Mrs Vandemeyer opposed the idea of publicity that might result from such a course.'

'I can imagine she would,' said Sir James grimly.

'I fell in with her views. There *is* a certain notoriety given to these cases. And the girl was very young—nineteen, I believe. It seemed a pity that her infirmity should be talked about—might damage her prospects. Besides, there is no special treatment to pursue in such cases. It is really a matter of waiting.'

'Waiting?'

'Yes, sooner or later, the memory will return—as suddenly as it went. But in all probability the girl will have entirely forgotten the intervening period, and will take up life where she left off—at the sinking of the *Lusitania*.'

'And when do you expect this to happen?'

The doctor shrugged his shoulders.

'Ah, that I cannot say. Sometimes it is a matter of months, sometimes it has been known to be as long as twenty years! Sometimes another shock does the trick. One restores what the other took away.'

'Another shock, eh?' said Julius thoughtfully.

'Exactly. There was a case in Colorado—' The little man's voice trailed on, voluble, mildly enthusiastic.

Julius did not seem to be listening. He had relapsed into his own thoughts and was frowning. Suddenly he came out of his brown study, and hit the table such a resounding bang with his fist that everyone jumped, the doctor most of all.

159

Agatha Christie

'I've got it! I guess, doc, I'd like your medical opinion on the plan I'm about to outline. Say Jane was to cross the herring pond again, and the same thing was to happen. The submarine, the sinking ship, everyone to take to the boats—and so on. Wouldn't that do the trick? Wouldn't it give a mighty big bump to her subconscious self, or whatever the jargon is, and start it functioning again right away?'

'A very interesting speculation, Mr Hersheimmer. In my own opinion, it would be successful. It is unfortunate that there is no chance of the conditions repeating themselves as you suggest.'

'Not by nature, perhaps, doc. But I'm talking about art.'

'Art?'

'Why, yes. What's the difficulty? Hire a liner—'

'A liner!' murmured Dr Hall faintly.

'Hire some passengers, hire a submarine—that's the only difficulty, I guess. Governments are apt to be a bit hidebound over their engines of war. They won't sell to the first-comer. Still, I guess that can be got over. Ever heard of the word "graft," sir? Well, graft gets there every time! I reckon that we shan't really need to fire a torpedo. If everyone hustles round and screams loud enough that the ship is sinking, it ought to be enough for an innocent young girl like Jane. By the time she's got a life-belt on her, and is being hustled into a boat, with a well-drilled lot of artistes doing the hysterical stunt on deck, why—she ought to be right back again where she was in May, 1915. How's that for the bare outline?'

Dr Hall looked at Julius. Everything that he was for the moment incapable of saying was eloquent in that look.

'No,' said Julius, in answer to it, 'I'm not crazy. The thing's perfectly possible. It's done every day in the States for the movies. Haven't you seen trains in collision on the screen? What's the difference between buying up a train and buying up a liner? Get the properties and you can go right ahead!'

Dr Hall found his voice.

'But the expense, my dear sir.' His voice rose. 'The expense! It will be *colossal*!'

'Money doesn't worry me any,' explained Julius simply.

Dr Hall turned an appealing face to Sir James, who smiled slightly.

'Mr Hersheimmer is very well off—very well off indeed.'

The doctor's glance came back to Julius with a new and subtle quality in it. This was no longer an eccentric young fellow with a habit of falling off trees. The doctor's eyes held the deference accorded to a really rich man.

'Very remarkable plan. Very remarkable,' he murmured. 'The movies—of course! Your American word for the cinema. Very interesting. I fear we are perhaps a little behind the times over here in our methods. And you really mean to carry out this remarkable plan of yours.'

'You bet your bottom dollar I do.'

The doctor believed him—which was a tribute to his nationality. If an Englishman had suggested such a thing, he would have had grave doubts as to his sanity.

'I cannot guarantee a cure,' he pointed out. 'Perhaps I ought to make that quite clear.'

'Sure, that's all right,' said Julius. 'You just trot out Jane, and leave the rest to me.'

'Jane?'

'Miss Janet Vandemeyer, then. Can we get on the long distance to your place right away, and ask them to send her up; or shall I run down and fetch her in my car?'

The doctor stared.

'I beg your pardon, Mr Hersheimmer. I thought you understood.'

'Understood what?'

'That Miss Vandemeyer is no longer under my care.'

CHAPTER 15

Tuppence Receives a Proposal

Julius sprang up.

'What?'

'I thought you were aware of that.'

'When did she leave?'

'Let me see. Today is Monday, is it not? It must have been last Wednesday—why, surely—yes, it was the same evening that you—er—fell out of my tree.'

'That evening? Before, or after?'

'Let me see—oh yes, afterwards. A very urgent message arrived from Mrs Vandemeyer. The young lady and the nurse who was in charge of her left by the night train.'

Julius sank back again into his chair.

'Nurse Edith—left with a patient—I remember,' he muttered. 'My God, to have been so near!'

Dr Hall looked bewildered.

'I don't understand. Is the young lady not with her aunt, after all?'

Tuppence shook her head. She was about to speak when

a warning glance from Sir James made her hold her tongue. The lawyer rose.

'I'm much obliged to you, Hall. We're very grateful for all you've told us. I'm afraid we're now in the position of having to track Miss Vandemeyer anew. What about the nurse who accompanied her; I suppose you don't know where she is?'

The doctor shook his head.

'We've not heard from her, as it happens. I understood she was to remain with Miss Vandemeyer for a while. But what can have happened? Surely the girl has not been kidnapped.'

'That remains to be seen,' said Sir James gravely.

The other hesitated.

'You do not think I ought to go to the police?'

'No, no. In all probability the young lady is with other relations.'

The doctor was not completely satisfied, but he saw that Sir James was determined to say no more, and realized that to try to extract more information from the famous K.C. would be mere waste of labour. Accordingly, he wished them goodbye, and they left the hotel. For a few minutes they stood by the car talking.

'How maddening,' cried Tuppence. 'To think that Julius must have been actually under the same roof with her for a few hours.'

'I was a darned idiot,' muttered Julius gloomily.

'You couldn't know,' Tuppence consoled him. 'Could he?' She appealed to Sir James.

'I should advise you not to worry,' said the latter kindly. 'No use crying over spilt milk, you know.'

'The great thing is what to do next,' added Tuppence the practical.

Sir James shrugged his shoulders.

'You might advertise for the nurse who accompanied the girl. That is the only course I can suggest, and I must confess I do not hope for much result. Otherwise there is nothing to be done.'

'Nothing?' said Tuppence blankly. 'And—Tommy?'

'We must hope for the best,' said Sir James. 'Oh yes, we must go on hoping.'

But over her downcast head his eyes met Julius's, and almost imperceptibly he shook his head. Julius understood. The lawyer considered the case hopeless. The young American's face grew grave. Sir James took Tuppence's hand.

'You must let me know if anything further comes to light. Letters will always be forwarded.'

Tuppence stared at him blankly.

'You are going away?'

'I told you. Don't you remember? To Scotland.'

'Yes, but I thought—' The girl hesitated.

Sir James shrugged his shoulders.

'My dear young lady, I can do nothing more, I fear. Our clues have all ended in thin air. You can take my word for it that there is nothing more to be done. If anything should arise, I shall be glad to advise you in any way I can.'

His words gave Tuppence an extraordinary desolate feeling.

'I suppose you're right,' she said. 'Anyway, thank you very much for trying to help us. Goodbye.'

Julius was bending over the car. A momentary pity came into Sir James's keen eyes, as he gazed into the girl's downcast face.

'Don't be too disconsolate, Miss Tuppence,' he said in a low voice. 'Remember, holiday-time isn't always all playtime. One sometimes manages to put in some work as well.'

Something in his tone made Tuppence glance up sharply. He shook his head with a smile.

'No, I shan't say any more. Great mistake to say too much. Remember that. Never tell all you know—not even to the person you know best. Understand? Goodbye.'

He strode away. Tuppence stared after him. She was beginning to understand Sir James's methods. Once before he had thrown her a hint in the same careless fashion. Was this a hint? What exactly lay behind those last brief words? Did he mean that, after all, he had not abandoned the case: that secretly, he would be working on it still while—

Her meditations were interrupted by Julius, who adjured her to 'get right in'.

'You're looking kind of thoughtful,' he remarked as they started off. 'Did the old guy say anything more?'

Tuppence opened her mouth impulsively, and then shut it again. Sir James's words sounded in her ears: 'Never tell all you know—not even to the person you know best.' And like a flash there came into her mind another memory. Julius before the safe in the flat, her own question and the pause

166

before his reply, 'Nothing.' Was there really nothing? Or had he found something he wished to keep to himself ? If he could make a reservation, so could she.

'Nothing particular,' she replied.

She felt rather than saw Julius throw a sideways glance at her.

'Say, shall we go for a spin in the park?'

'If you like.'

For a while they ran on under the trees in silence. It was a beautiful day. The keen rush through the air brought a new exhilaration to Tuppence.

'Say, Miss Tuppence, do you think I'm ever going to find Jane?'

Julius spoke in a discouraged voice. The mood was so alien to him that Tuppence turned and stared at him in surprise. He nodded.

'That's so. I'm getting down and out over the business. Sir James today hadn't got any hope at all, I could see that, I don't like him—we don't gee together somehow—but he's pretty cute, and I guess he wouldn't quit if there was any chance of success—now, would he?'

Tuppence felt rather uncomfortable, but clinging to her belief that Julius also had withheld something from her, she remained firm.

'He suggested advertising for the nurse,' she reminded him.

'Yes, with a "forlorn hope" flavour to his voice! No—I'm about fed up. I've half a mind to go back to the States right away.'

'Oh no!' cried Tuppence. 'We've got to find Tommy.'

'I sure forgot Beresford,' said Julius contritely. 'That's so. We must find him. But after—well, I've been day-dreaming ever since I started on this trip—and these dreams are rotten poor business. I'm quit of them. Say, Miss Tuppence, there's something I'd like to ask you.'

'Yes.'

'You and Beresford. What about it?'

'I don't understand you,' replied Tuppence with dignity, adding rather inconsequently: 'And, anyway, you're wrong!'

'Not got a sort of kindly feeling for one another?'

'Certainly not,' said Tuppence with warmth. 'Tommy and I are friends—nothing more.'

'I guess every pair of lovers has said that some time or another,' observed Julius.

'Nonsense!' snapped Tuppence. 'Do I look the sort of girl that's always falling in love with every man she meets?'

'You do not. You look the sort of girl that's mighty often getting fallen in love with!'

'Oh!' said Tuppence, rather taken aback. 'That's a compliment, I suppose?'

'Sure. Now let's get down to this. Supposing we never find Beresford and—and—'

'All right—say it! I can face facts. Supposing he's—dead! Well?'

'And all this business fiddles out. What are you going to do?'

'I don't know,' said Tuppence forlornly.

'You'll be darned lonesome, you poor kid.'

'I shall be all right,' snapped Tuppence with her usual resentment of any kind of pity.

168

'What about marriage?' inquired Julius. 'Got any views on the subject?'

'I intend to marry, of course,' replied Tuppence. 'That is, if'—she paused, knew a momentary longing to draw back, and then stuck to her guns bravely—'I can find some one rich enough to make it worth my while. That's frank, isn't it? I dare say you despise me for it.'

'I never despise business instinct,' said Julius. 'What particular figure have you in mind?'

'Figure?' asked Tuppence, puzzled. 'Do you mean tall or short?'

'No. Sum—income.'

'Oh, I—haven't quite worked that out.'

'What about me?'

'*You?*'

'Sure thing.'

'Oh, I couldn't!'

'Why not?'

'I tell you I couldn't.'

'Again, why not?'

'It would seem so unfair.'

'I don't see anything unfair about it. I call your bluff, that's all. I admire you immensely, Miss Tuppence, more than any girl I've ever met. You're so darned plucky. I'd just love to give you a real, rattling good time. Say the word, and we'll run round right away to some high-class jeweller, and fix up the ring business.'

'I can't,' gasped Tuppence.

'Because of Beresford?'

'No, no, *no*!'

'Well then?'

Tuppence merely continued to shake her head violently.

'You can't reasonably expect more dollars than I've got.'

'Oh, it isn't that,' gasped Tuppence with an almost hysterical laugh. 'But thanking you very much, and all that, I think I'd better say no.'

'I'd be obliged if you'd do me the favour to think it over until tomorrow.'

'It's no use.'

'Still, I guess we'll leave it like that.'

'Very well,' said Tuppence meekly.

Neither of them spoke again until they reached the Ritz.

Tuppence went upstairs to her room. She felt morally battered to the ground after her conflict with Julius's vigorous personality. Sitting down in front of the glass, she stared at her own reflection for some minutes.

'Fool,' murmured Tuppence at length, making a grimace. 'Little fool. Everything you want—everything you've ever hoped for, and you go and bleat out "no" like an idiotic little sheep. It's your one chance. Why don't you take it? Grab it? Snatch at it? What more do you want?'

As if in answer to her own question, her eyes fell on a small snapshot of Tommy that stood on her dressing-table in a shabby frame. For a moment she struggled for self-control, and then abandoning all pretence, she held it to her lips and burst into a fit of sobbing.

'Oh, Tommy, Tommy,' she cried, 'I do love you so—and I may never see you again...'

At the end of five minutes Tuppence sat up, blew her nose, and pushed back her hair.

'That's that,' she observed sternly. 'Let's look facts in the face. I seem to have fallen in love—with an idiot of a boy who probably doesn't care two straws about me.' Here she paused. 'Anyway,' she resumed, as though arguing with an unseen opponent, 'I don't *know* that he does. He'd never have dared to say so. I've always jumped on sentiment—and here I am being more sentimental than anybody. What idiots girls are! I've always thought so. I suppose I shall sleep with his photograph under my pillow, and dream about him all night. It's dreadful to feel you've been false to your principles.'

Tuppence shook her head sadly, as she reviewed her back-sliding.

'I don't know what to say to Julius, I'm sure. Oh, what a fool I feel! I'll have to say *something*—he's so American and thorough, he'll insist upon having a reason. I wonder if he did find anything in that safe—'

Tuppence's meditations went off on another track. She reviewed the events of last night carefully and persistently. Somehow, they seemed bound up with Sir James's enigmatical words...

Suddenly she gave a great start—the colour faded out of her face. Her eyes, fascinated, gazed in front of her, the pupils dilated.

'Impossible,' she murmured. 'Impossible! I must be going mad even to think of such a thing...'

Monstrous—yet it explained everything...

After a moment's reflection she sat down and wrote a note, weighing each word as she did so. Finally she nodded her head as though satisfied, and slipped it into an envelope which she addressed to Julius. She went down the passage to his sitting-room and knocked at the door. As she had expected, the room was empty. She left the note on the table.

A small page-boy was waiting outside her own door when she returned to it.

'Telegram for you, miss.'

Tuppence took it from the salver, and tore it open carelessly. Then she gave a cry. The telegram was from Tommy!

CHAPTER 16

Further Adventures of Tommy

From a darkness punctuated with throbbing stabs of fire, Tommy dragged his senses slowly back to life. When he at last opened his eyes, he was conscious of nothing but an excruciating pain through his temples. He was vaguely aware of unfamiliar surroundings. Where was he? What had happened? He blinked feebly. This was not his bedroom at the Ritz. And what the devil was the matter with his head?

'Damn!' said Tommy, and tried to sit up. He had remembered. He was in that sinister house in Soho. He uttered a groan and fell back. Through his almost-closed eyelids he reconnoitred carefully.

'He is coming to,' remarked a voice very near Tommy's ear. He recognized it at once for that of the bearded and efficient German, and lay artistically inert. He felt that it would be a pity to come round too soon; and until the pain in his head became a little less acute, he felt quite incapable of collecting his wits. Painfully he tried to puzzle out what had happened. Obviously somebody must have crept up behind him as he listened and struck him down with a blow on the head. They knew him now for a spy, and would in all probability give him short shrift. Undoubtedly he was in a tight place. Nobody knew where he was, therefore he need expect no outside assistance, and must depend solely on his own wits.

'Well, here goes,' murmured Tommy to himself, and repeated his former remark.

'Damn!' he observed, and this time succeeded in sitting up.

In a minute the German stepped forward and placed a glass to his lips, with the brief command 'Drink.' Tommy obeyed. The potency of the draught made him choke, but it cleared his brain in a marvellous manner.

He was lying on a couch in the room in which the meeting had been held. On one side of him was the German, on the other the villainous-faced doorkeeper who had let him in. The others were grouped together at a little distance away. But Tommy missed one face. The man known as Number One was no longer of the company.

'Feel better?' asked the German, as he removed the empty glass.

'Yes, thanks,' returned Tommy cheerfully.

'Ah, my young friend, it is lucky for you your skull is so thick. The good Conrad struck hard.' He indicated the evil-faced doorkeeper by a nod.

The man grinned.

Tommy twisted his head round with an effort.

'Oh,' he said, 'so you're Conrad, are you? It strikes me the thickness of my skull was lucky for you too. When I look at you I feel it's almost a pity I've enabled you to cheat the hangman.'

The man snarled, and the bearded man said quietly:

'He would have run no risk of that.'

'Just as you like,' replied Tommy. 'I know it's the fashion to run down the police. I rather believe in them myself.'

His manner was nonchalant to the last degree. Tommy Beresford was one of those young Englishmen not distinguished by any special intellectual ability, but who are emphatically at their best in what is known as a 'tight place'. Their natural diffidence and caution falls from them then like a glove. Tommy realized perfectly that in his own wits lay the only chance of escape, and behind his casual manner he was racking his brains furiously.

The cold accents of the German took up the conversation:

'Have you anything to say before you are put to death as a spy?'

'Simply lots of things,' replied Tommy with the same urbanity as before.

'Do you deny that you were listening at that door?'

'I do not. I must really apologize—but your conversation was so interesting that it overcame my scruples.'

'How did you get in?'

'Dear old Conrad here.' Tommy smiled deprecatingly at him. 'I hesitate to suggest pensioning off a faithful servant, but you really ought to have a better watchdog.'

Conrad snarled impotently, and said sullenly, as the man with the beard swung round upon him:

'He gave the word. How was I to know?'

'Yes,' Tommy chimed in. 'How was he to know? Don't blame the poor fellow. His hasty action has given me the pleasure of seeing you all face to face.'

He fancied that his words caused some discomposure among the group, but the watchful German stilled it with a wave of his hand.

'Dead men tell no tales,' he said evenly.

'Ah,' said Tommy, 'but I'm not dead yet!'

'You soon will be, my young friend,' said the German.

An assenting murmur came from the others.

Tommy's heart beat faster, but his casual pleasantness did not waver.

'I think not,' he said firmly. 'I should have a great objection to dying.'

He had got them puzzled, he saw that by the look on his captor's face.

'Can you give us any reason why we should not put you to death?' asked the German.

'Several,' replied Tommy. 'Look here, you've been asking me a lot of questions. Let me ask you one for a change. Why didn't you kill me off at once before I regained consciousness?'

The German hesitated, and Tommy seized his advantage.

'Because you didn't know how much I knew—and where I obtained that knowledge. If you kill me now, you never will know.'

But here the emotions of Boris became too much for him. He stepped forward waving his arms.

'You hell-hound of a spy,' he screamed. 'We will give you short shrift. Kill him! Kill him!'

There was a roar of applause.

'You hear?' said the German, his eyes on Tommy. 'What have you got to say to that?'

'Say?' Tommy shrugged his shoulders. 'Pack of fools. Let them ask themselves a few questions. How did I get into this place? Remember what dear old Conrad said—*with your own password*, wasn't it? How did I get hold of that? You don't suppose I came up those steps haphazard and said the first thing that came into my head?'

Tommy was pleased with the concluding words of this speech. His only regret was that Tuppence was not present to appreciate its full flavour.

'That is true,' said the working man suddenly. 'Comrades, we have been betrayed!'

An ugly murmur arose. Tommy smiled at them encouragingly.

'That's better. How can you hope to make a success of any job if you don't use your brains?'

'You will tell us who has betrayed us,' said the German. 'But that shall not save you—oh, no! You shall tell us all that you know. Boris, here, knows pretty ways of making people speak!'

'Bah!' said Tommy scornfully, fighting down a singularly unpleasant feeling in the pit of his stomach. 'You will neither torture me nor kill me.'

'And why not?' asked Boris.

'Because you'd kill the goose that lays the golden eggs,' replied Tommy quietly.

There was a momentary pause. It seemed as though Tommy's persistent assurance was at last conquering. They

177

were no longer completely sure of themselves. The man in the shabby clothes stared at Tommy searchingly.

'He's bluffing you, Boris,' he said quietly.

Tommy hated him. Had the man seen through him?

The German, with an effort, turned roughly to Tommy.

'What do you mean?'

'What do you think I mean?' parried Tommy, searching desperately in his own mind.

Suddenly Boris stepped forward, and shook his fist in Tommy's face.

'Speak, you swine of an Englishman—speak!'

'Don't get so excited, my good fellow,' said Tommy calmly. 'That's the worst of you foreigners. You can't keep calm. Now, I ask you, do I look as though I thought there were the least chance of your killing me?'

He looked confidently round, and was glad they could not hear the persistent beating of his heart which gave the lie to his words.

'No,' admitted Boris at last sullenly, 'you do not.'

'Thank God, he's not a mind reader,' thought Tommy. Aloud he pursued his advantage:

'And why am I so confident? Because I know something that puts me in a position to propose a bargain.'

'A bargain?' The bearded man took him up sharply.

'Yes—a bargain. My life and liberty against—' He paused.

'Against what?'

The group pressed forward. You could have heard a pin drop.

Slowly Tommy spoke.

'The papers that Danvers brought over from America in the *Lusitania*.'

The effect of his words was electrical. Everyone was on his feet. The German waved them back. He leaned over Tommy, his face purple with excitement.

'*Himmel*! You have got them, then?'

With magnificent calm Tommy shook his head.

'You know where they are?' persisted the German.

Again Tommy shook his head. 'Not in the least.'

'Then—then—' angry and baffled, the words failed him.

Tommy looked round. He saw anger and bewilderment on every face, but his calm assurance had done its work—no one doubted but that something lay behind his words.

'I don't know where the papers are—but I believe that I can find them. I have a theory—'

'Pah!'

Tommy raised his hand, and silenced the clamours of disgust. 'I call it a theory—but I'm pretty sure of my facts—facts that are known to no one but myself. In any case what do you lose? If I can produce the papers—you give me my life and liberty in exchange. Is it a bargain?'

'And if we refuse?' said the German quietly.

Tommy lay back on the couch.

'The 29th,' he said thoughtfully, 'is less than a fortnight ahead—'

For a moment the German hesitated. Then he made a sign to Conrad.

'Take him into the other room.'

For five minutes Tommy sat on the bed in the dingy room next door. His heart was beating violently. He had risked all on this throw. How would they decide? And all the while that this agonized questioning went on within him, he talked flippantly to Conrad, enraging the cross-grained doorkeeper to the point of homicidal mania.

At last the door opened, and the German called imperiously to Conrad to return.

'Let's hope the judge hasn't put his black cap on,' remarked Tommy frivolously. 'That's right, Conrad, march me in. The prisoner is at the bar, gentlemen.'

The German was seated once more behind the table. He motioned to Tommy to sit down opposite to him.

'We accept,' he said harshly, 'on terms. The papers must be delivered to us before you go free.'

'Idiot!' said Tommy amiably. 'How do you think I can look for them if you keep me tied by the leg here?'

'What do you expect, then?'

'I must have liberty to go about the business in my own way.'

The German laughed.

'Do you think we are little children to let you walk out of here leaving us a pretty story full of promises?'

'No,' said Tommy thoughtfully. 'Though infinitely simpler for me, I did not really think you would agree to that plan. Very well, we must arrange a compromise. How would it be if you attached little Conrad here to my person. He's a faithful fellow, and very ready with the fist.'

'We prefer,' said the German coldly, 'that you should remain here. One of our number will carry out your instructions

180

minutely. If the operations are complicated, he will return to you with a report and you can instruct him further.'

'You're trying my hands,' complained Tommy. 'It's a very delicate affair, and the other fellow will muff it up as likely as not, and then where shall I be? I don't believe one of you has got an ounce of tact.'

The German rapped the table.

'Those are our terms. Otherwise, death!'

Tommy leaned back wearily.

'I like your style. Curt, but attractive. So be it, then. But one thing is essential, I must see the girl.'

'What girl?'

'Jane Finn, of course.'

The other looked at him curiously for some minutes, then he said slowly, and as though choosing his words with care:

'Do you not know that she can tell you nothing?'

Tommy's heart beat a little faster. Would he succeed in coming face to face with the girl he was seeking?

'I shall not ask her to tell me anything,' he said quietly. 'Not in so many words, that is.'

'Then why see her?'

Tommy paused.

'To watch her face when I ask her one question,' he replied at last.

Again there was a look in the German's eyes that Tommy did not quite understand.

'She will not be able to answer your question.'

'That does not matter. I shall have seen her face when I ask it.'

'And you think that will tell you anything?' He gave a short disagreeable laugh. More than ever, Tommy felt that there was a factor somewhere that he did not understand. The German looked at him searchingly. 'I wonder whether, after all, you know as much as we think?' he said softly.

Tommy felt his ascendancy less sure than a moment before. His hold had slipped a little. But he was puzzled. What had he said wrong? He spoke out on the impulse of the moment.

'There may be things that you know which I do not. I have not pretended to be aware of all the details of your show. But equally I've got something up my sleeve that *you* don't know about. And that's where I mean to score. Danvers was a damned clever fellow—' He broke off as if he had said too much.

But the German's face had lightened a little.

'Danvers,' he murmured. I see—' He paused a minute, then waved to Conrad. 'Take him away. Upstairs—you know.'

'Wait a minute,' said Tommy. 'What about the girl?'

'That may perhaps be arranged.'

'It must be.'

'We will see about it. Only one person can decide that.'

'Who?' asked Tommy. But he knew the answer.

'Mr Brown—'

'Shall I see him?'

'Perhaps.'

'Come,' said Conrad harshly.

Tommy rose obediently. Outside the door his gaoler motioned to him to mount the stairs. He himself followed close behind. On the floor above Conrad opened a door and Tommy passed into a small room. Conrad lit a hissing gas burner and went out. Tommy heard the sound of the key being turned in the lock.

He set to work to examine his prison. It was a smaller room than the one downstairs, and there was something peculiarly airless about the atmosphere of it. Then he realized that there was no window. He walked round it. The walls were filthily dirty, as everywhere else. Four pictures hung crookedly on the wall representing scenes from 'Faust,' Marguerite with her box of jewels, the church scene, Siebel and his flowers, and Faust and Mephistopheles. The latter brought Tommy's mind back to Mr Brown again. In this sealed and closed chamber, with its close-fitting heavy door, he felt cut off from the world, and the sinister power of the arch-criminal seemed more real. Shout as he would, no one could ever hear him. The place was a living tomb...

With an effort Tommy pulled himself together. He sank on to the bed and gave himself up to reflection. His head ached badly; also, he was hungry. The silence of the place was dispiriting.

'Anyway,' said Tommy, trying to cheer himself, 'I shall see the chief—the mysterious Mr Brown, and with a bit of luck in bluffing I shall see the mysterious Jane Finn also. After that—'

After that Tommy was forced to admit the prospect looked dreary.

CHAPTER 17

Annette

The troubles of the future, however, soon faded before the troubles of the present. And of these, the most immediate and pressing was that of hunger. Tommy had a healthy and vigorous appetite. The steak and chips partaken of for lunch seemed now to belong to another decade. He regretfully recognized the fact that he would not make a success of a hunger strike.

He prowled aimlessly about his prison. Once or twice he discarded dignity, and pounded on the door. But nobody answered the summons.

'Hang it all!' said Tommy indignantly. 'They can't mean to starve me to death.' A new-born fear passed through his mind that this might, perhaps, be one of those 'pretty ways' of making a prisoner speak, which had been attributed to Boris. But on reflection he dismissed the idea.

'It's that sour-faced brute Conrad,' he decided. 'That's a fellow I shall enjoy getting even with one of these days. This is just a bit of spite on his part. I'm certain of it.'

Further meditations induced in him the feeling that it would be extremely pleasant to bring something down with a whack on Conrad's egg-shaped head. Tommy stroked his own head tenderly, and gave himself up to the pleasures of imagination. Finally a bright idea flashed across his brain. Why not convert imagination into reality! Conrad was undoubtedly the tenant of the house. The others, with the possible exception of the bearded German, merely used it as a rendezvous. Therefore, why not wait in ambush for Conrad behind the door, and when he entered bring down a chair, or one of the decrepit pictures, smartly on to his head. One would, of course, be careful not to hit too hard. And then—and then, simply walk out! If he met anyone on the way down, well—Tommy brightened at the thought of an encounter with his fists. Such an affair was infinitely more in his line than the verbal encounter of this afternoon. Intoxicated by his plan, Tommy gently unhooked the picture of the Devil and Faust, and settled himself in position. His hopes were high. The plan seemed to him simple but excellent.

Time went on, but Conrad did not appear. Night and day were the same in this prison room, but Tommy's wrist-watch, which enjoyed a certain degree of accuracy, informed him that it was nine o'clock in the evening. Tommy reflected gloomily that if supper did not arrive soon it would be a question of waiting for breakfast. At ten o'clock hope deserted him, and he flung himself on the bed to seek consolation in sleep. In five minutes his woes were forgotten.

The sound of the key turning in the lock awoke him from his slumbers. Not belonging to the type of hero who is famous for awaking in full possession of his faculties, Tommy merely blinked at the ceiling and wondered vaguely where he was. Then he remembered, and looked at his watch. It was eight o'clock.

'It's either early morning tea or breakfast,' deduced the young man, 'and pray God it's the latter!'

The door swung open. Too late, Tommy remembered his scheme of obliterating the unprepossessing Conrad. A moment later he was glad that he had, for it was not Conrad who entered, but a girl. She carried a tray which she set down on the table.

In the feeble light of the gas burner Tommy blinked at her. He decided at once that she was one of the most beautiful girls he had ever seen. Her hair was a full rich brown, with sudden glints of gold in it as though there were imprisoned sunbeams struggling in its depths. There was a wild-rose quality about her face. Her eyes, set wide apart, were hazel, a golden hazel that again recalled a memory of sunbeams.

A delirious thought shot through Tommy's mind.

'Are you Jane Finn?' he asked breathlessly.

The girl shook her head wonderingly.

'My name is Annette, monsieur.'

She spoke in a soft, broken English.

'Oh!' said Tommy, rather taken aback. '*Française?*' he hazarded.

'Oui, monsieur. Monsieur parle français?'

'Not for any length of time,' said Tommy. 'What's that? Breakfast?'

186

The girl nodded. Tommy dropped off the bed and came and inspected the contents of the tray. It consisted of a loaf, some margarine, and a jug of coffee.

'The living is not equal to the Ritz,' he observed with a sigh. 'But for what we are at last about to receive the Lord has made me truly thankful. Amen.'

He drew up a chair, and the girl turned away to the door.

'Wait a sec,' cried Tommy. 'There are lots of things I want to ask you, Annette. What are you doing in this house? Don't tell me you're Conrad's niece, or daughter, or anything, because I can't believe it.'

'I do the *service*, monsieur. I am not related to anybody.'

'I see,' said Tommy. 'You know what I asked you just now. Have you ever heard that name?'

'I have heard people speak of Jane Finn, I think.'

'You don't know where she is?'

Annette shook her head.

'She's not in this house, for instance?'

'Oh no, monsieur. I must go now—they will be waiting for me.'

She hurried out. The key turned in the lock.

'I wonder who "they" are,' mused Tommy, as he continued to make inroads on the loaf. 'With a bit of luck, that girl might help me to get out of here. She doesn't look like one of the gang.'

At one o'clock Annette reappeared with another tray, but this time Conrad accompanied her.

'Good morning,' said Tommy amiably. 'You have *not* used Pear's soap, I see.'

Conrad growled threateningly.

'No light repartee, have you, old bean? There, there, we can't always have brains as well as beauty. What have we for lunch? Stew? How did I know? Elementary, my dear Watson—the smell of onions is unmistakable.'

'Talk away,' grunted the man. 'It's little enough time you'll have to talk in, maybe.'

The remark was unpleasant in its suggestion, but Tommy ignored it. He sat down at the table.

'Retire, varlet,' he said, with a wave of his hand. 'Prate not to thy betters.'

That evening Tommy sat on the bed, and cogitated deeply. Would Conrad again accompany the girl? If he did not, should he risk trying to make an ally of her? He decided that he must leave no stone unturned. His position was desperate.

At eight o'clock the familiar sound of the key turning made him spring to his feet. The girl was alone.

'Shut the door,' he commanded. 'I want to speak to you.' She obeyed.

'Look here, Annette, I want you to help me get out of this.' She shook her head.

'Impossible. There are three of them on the floor below.'

'Oh!' Tommy was secretly grateful for the information. 'But you would help me if you could?'

'No, monsieur.'

'Why not?'

The girl hesitated.

'I think—they are my own people. You have spied upon them. They are quite right to keep you here.'

188

'They're a bad lot, Annette. If you'll help me, I'll take you away from the lot of them. And you'd probably get a good whack of money.'

But the girl merely shook her head.

'I dare not, monsieur. I am afraid of them.'

She turned away.

'Wouldn't you do anything to help another girl?' cried Tommy. 'She's about your age too. Won't you save her from their clutches?'

'You mean Jane Finn?'

'Yes.'

'It is her you came here to look for? Yes?'

'That's it.'

The girl looked at him, then passed her hand across her forehead.

'Jane Finn. Always I hear that name. It is familiar.'

Tommy came forward eagerly.

'You must know *something* about her?'

But the girl turned away abruptly.

'I know nothing—only the name.' She walked towards the door. Suddenly she uttered a cry. Tommy stared. She had caught sight of the picture he had laid against the wall the night before. For a moment he caught a look of terror in her eyes. As inexplicably it changed to relief. Then abruptly, she went out of the room. Tommy could make nothing of it. Did she fancy that he had meant to attack her with it? Surely not. He rehung the picture on the wall thoughtfully.

Three more days went by in dreary inaction. Tommy felt the strain telling on his nerves. He saw no one but Conrad and Annette, and the girl had become dumb. She spoke only in monosyllables. A kind of dark suspicion smouldered in her eyes. Tommy felt that if this solitary confinement went on much longer he would go mad. He gathered from Conrad that they were waiting for orders from 'Mr Brown'. Perhaps, thought Tommy, he was abroad or away, and they were obliged to wait for his return.

But the evening of the third day brought a rude awakening.

It was barely seven o'clock when he heard the tramp of footsteps outside in the passage. In another minute the door was flung open. Conrad entered. With him was the evil-looking Number Fourteen. Tommy's heart sank at the sight of them.

'Evenin', gov'nor,' said the man with a leer. 'Got those ropes, mate?'

The silent Conrad produced a length of fine cord. The next minute Number Fourteen's hands, horribly dexterous, were winding the cord round his limbs, while Conrad held him down.

'What the devil—?' began Tommy.

But the slow, speechless grin of the silent Conrad froze the words on his lips.

Number Fourteen proceeded deftly with his task. In another minute Tommy was a mere helpless bundle. Then at last Conrad spoke:

'Thought you'd bluffed us, did you? With what you knew, and what you didn't know. Bargained with us! And all the time it was bluff ! Bluff ! You know less than a kitten. But your number's up all right, you b—— swine.'

Tommy lay silent. There was nothing to say. He had failed. Somehow or other the omnipotent Mr Brown had seen through his pretensions. Suddenly a thought occurred to him.

'A very good speech, Conrad,' he said approvingly. 'But wherefore the bonds and fetters? Why not let this kind gentleman here cut my throat without delay?'

'Garn,' said Number Fourteen unexpectedly. 'Think we're as green as to do you in here, and have the police nosing round? Not 'alf ! We've ordered the carriage for your lordship tomorrow mornin', but in the meantime we're not taking any chances, see!'

'Nothing,' said Tommy, 'could be plainer than your words—unless it was your face.'

'Stow it,' said Number Fourteen.

'With pleasure,' replied Tommy. 'You're making a sad mistake—but yours will be the loss.'

'You don't kid us that way again,' said Number Fourteen. 'Talking as though you were still at the blooming Ritz, aren't you?'

Tommy made no reply. He was engaged in wondering how Mr Brown had discovered his identity. He decided that Tuppence, in the throes of anxiety, had gone to the police, and that his disappearance having been made public the gang had not been slow to put two and two together.

The two men departed and the door slammed. Tommy was left to his meditations. They were not pleasant ones. Already his limbs felt cramped and stiff. He was utterly helpless, and he could see no hope anywhere.

About an hour had passed when he heard the key softly turned, and the door opened. It was Annette. Tommy's heart beat a little faster. He had forgotten the girl. Was it possible that she had come to his help?

Suddenly he heard Conrad's voice:

'Come out of it, Annette. He doesn't want any supper tonight.'

'*Oui, oui, je sais bien.* But I must take the other tray. We need the things on it.'

'Well, hurry up,' growled Conrad.

Without looking at Tommy the girl went over to the table, and picked up the tray. She raised a hand and turned out the light.

'Curse you,'—Conrad had come to the door—'why did you do that?'

'I always turn it out. You should have told me. Shall I relight it, Monsieur Conrad?'

'No, come on out of it.'

'*Le beau petit monsieur,*' cried Annette, pausing by the bed in the darkness. 'You have tied him up well, *hein*? He is like a trussed chicken!' The frank amusement in her tone jarred on the boy but at that moment to his amazement, he felt her hand running lightly over his bonds, and something small and cold was pressed into the palm of his hand.

'Come on, Annette.'

'*Mais me voilà.*'

The door shut. Tommy heard Conrad say:

'Lock it and give me the key.'

The footsteps died away. Tommy lay petrified with amazement. The object Annette had thrust into his hand was a small penknife, the blade open. From the way she had studiously avoided looking at him, and her action with the light, he came to the conclusion that the room was overlooked. There must be a peep-hole somewhere in the walls. Remembering how guarded she had always been in her manner, he saw that he had probably been under observation all the time. Had he said anything to give himself away? Hardly. He had revealed a wish to escape and a desire to find Jane Finn, but nothing that could have given a clue to his own identity. True, his question to Annette had proved that he was personally unacquainted with Jane Finn, but he had never pretended otherwise. The question now was, did Annette really know more? Were her denials intended primarily for the listeners? On that point he could come to no conclusion.

But there was a more vital question that drove out all others. Could he, bound as he was, manage to cut his bonds? He essayed cautiously to rub the open blade up and down on the cord that bound his two wrists together. It was an awkward business and drew a smothered 'Ow' of pain from him as the knife cut into his wrist. But slowly and doggedly he went on sawing to and fro. He cut the flesh badly, but at last he felt the cord slacken. With his hands free, the rest was easy. Five minutes later he stood upright with some difficulty owing to the cramp in his limbs. His first care was to bind up his bleeding wrist. Then he sat on the edge of the bed to think. Conrad had taken the key of the door, so he could expect little more assistance from Annette. The only outlet from the room was the door, consequently he would perforce have to wait until the two men returned to fetch him. But when they did… Tommy smiled! Moving with infinite caution in the dark room, he found and unhooked the famous picture. He felt an economical pleasure that his first plan would not be wasted. There was now nothing to do but to wait. He waited.

The night passed slowly. Tommy lived through an eternity of hours, but at last he heard footsteps. He stood upright, drew a deep breath, and clutched the picture firmly.

The door opened. A faint light streamed in from outside. Conrad went straight towards the gas to light it. Tommy deeply regretted that it was he who had entered first. It would have been pleasant to get even with Conrad. Number Fourteen followed. As he stepped across the threshold, Tommy brought the picture down with terrific force on his head. Number Fourteen went down amidst a stupendous crash of broken glass. In a minute Tommy had slipped out and pulled to the door. The key was in the lock. He turned it and withdrew it just as Conrad hurled himself against the door from the inside with a volley of curses.

For a moment Tommy hesitated. There was the sound of someone stirring on the floor below. Then the German's voice came up the stairs.

'*Gott im Himmel*! Conrad, what is it?'

Tommy felt a small hand thrust into his. Beside him stood Annette. She pointed up a rickety ladder that apparently led to some attics.

'Quick—up here!' She dragged him after her up the ladder. In another moment they were standing in a dusty garret littered with lumber. Tommy looked round.

'This won't do. It's a regular trap. There's no way out.'

'Hush! Wait.' The girl put her finger to her lips. She crept to the top of the ladder and listened.

The banging and beating on the door was terrific. The German and another were trying to force the door in. Annette explained in a whisper:

'They will think you are still inside. They cannot hear what Conrad says. The door is too thick.'

'I thought you could hear what went on in the room?'

'There is a peep-hole into the next room. It was clever of you to guess. But they will not think of that—they are only anxious to get in.'

'Yes—but look here—'

'Leave it to me.' She bent down. To his amazement, Tommy saw that she was fastening the end of a long piece of string to the handle of a big cracked jug. She arranged it carefully, then turned to Tommy.

'Have you the key of the door?'

'Yes.'

'Give it to me.'

He handed it to her.

'I am going down. Do you think you can go half-way, and then swing yourself down *behind* the ladder, so that they will not see you?'

Tommy nodded.

'There's a big cupboard in the shadow of the landing.

195

Agatha Christie

Stand behind it. Take the end of this string in your hand. When I've let the others out—*pull* !'

Before he had time to ask her anything more, she had flitted lightly down the ladder and was in the midst of the group with a loud cry:

'*Mon Dieu! Mon Dieu! Qu'est-ce qu'il y a?*'

The German turned on her with an oath.

'Get out of this. Go to your room!'

Very cautiously Tommy swung himself down the back of the ladder. So long as they did not turn round, all was well. He crouched behind the cupboard. They were still between him and the stairs.

'Ah!' Annette appeared to stumble over something. She stooped. '*Mon Dieu, voilà la clef* !'

The German snatched it from her. He unlocked the door. Conrad stumbled out, swearing.

'Where is he? Have you got him?'

'We have seen no one,' said the German sharply. His face paled. 'Who do you mean?'

Conrad gave vent to another oath.

'He's got away.'

'Impossible. He would have passed us.'

At that moment, with an ecstatic smile Tommy pulled the string. A crash of crockery came from the attic above. In a trice the men were pushing each other up the rickety ladder and had disappeared into the darkness above.

Quick as a flash Tommy leapt from his hiding-place and dashed down the stairs, pulling the girl with him. There was no one in the hall. He fumbled over the bolts and chain. At

196

last they yielded, the door swung open. He turned. Annette had disappeared.

Tommy stood spell-bound. Had she run upstairs again? What madness possessed her! He fumed with impatience, but he stood his ground. He would not go without her.

And suddenly there was an outcry overhead, an exclamation from the German, and then Annette's voice, clear and high:

'*Ma foi*, he has escaped! And quickly! Who would have thought it?'

Tommy still stood rooted to the ground. Was that a command to him to go? He fancied it was.

And then, louder still, the words floated down to him:

'This is a terrible house. I want to go back to Marguerite. To Marguerite. *To Marguerite*!'

Tommy had run back to the stairs. She wanted him to go and leave her? But why? At all costs he must try to get her away with him. Then his heart sank. Conrad was leaping down the stairs uttering a savage cry at the sight of him. After him came the others.

Tommy stopped Conrad's rush with a straight blow with his fist. It caught the other on the point of the jaw and he fell like a log. The second man tripped over his body and fell. From higher up the staircase there was a flash, and a bullet grazed Tommy's ear. He realized that it would be good for his health to get out of this house as soon as possible. As regards Annette he could do nothing. He had got even with Conrad, which was one satisfaction. The blow had been a good one.

He leapt for the door, slamming it behind him. The square was deserted. In front of the house was a baker's van. Evidently he was to have been taken out of London in that, and his body found many miles from the house in Soho. The driver jumped to the pavement and tried to bar Tommy's way. Again Tommy's fist shot out, and the driver sprawled on the pavement.

Tommy took to his heels and ran—none too soon. The front door opened and a hail of bullets followed him. Fortunately none of them hit him. He turned the corner of the square.

'There's one thing,' he thought to himself, 'they can't go on shooting. They'll have the police after them if they do. I wonder they dared to there.'

He heard the footsteps of his pursuers behind him, and redoubled his own pace. Once he got out of these by-ways he would be safe. There would be a policeman about somewhere—not that he really wanted to invoke the aid of the police if he could possibly do without it. It meant explanation, and general awkwardness. In another moment he had reason to bless his luck. He stumbled over a prostrate figure, which started up with a yell of alarm and dashed off down the street. Tommy drew back into a doorway. In a minute he had the pleasure of seeing his two pursuers, of whom the German was one, industriously tracking down the red herring!

Tommy sat down quietly on the doorstep and allowed a few moments to elapse while he recovered his breath. Then he strolled gently in the opposite direction. He glanced at his watch. It was a little after half-past five. It was rapidly growing light. At the next corner he passed a policeman. The policeman cast a suspicious eye on him. Tommy felt slightly offended. Then, passing his hand over his face, he laughed. He had not shaved or washed for three days! What a guy he must look.

He betook himself without more ado to a Turkish Bath establishment which he knew to be open all night. He emerged into the busy daylight feeling himself once more, and able to make plans.

First of all, he must have a square meal. He had eaten nothing since midday yesterday. He turned into an A.B.C. shop and ordered eggs and bacon and coffee. Whilst he ate, he read a morning paper propped up in front of him. Suddenly he stiffened. There was a long article on Kramenin, who was described as the 'man behind Bolshevism' in Russia, and who had just arrived in London—some thought as an unofficial envoy. His career was sketched lightly, and it was firmly asserted that he, and not the figurehead leaders, had been the author of the Russian Revolution.

In the centre of the page was his portrait.

'So that's who Number One is,' said Tommy with his mouth full of eggs and bacon. 'Not a doubt about it. I must push on.'

He paid for his breakfast, and betook himself to Whitehall. There he sent up his name, and the message that it was urgent. A few minutes later he was in the presence of the man who did not here go by the name of 'Mr Carter'. There was a frown on his face.

'Look here, you've no business to come asking for me in this way. I thought that was distinctly understood?'

'It was, sir. But I judged it important to lose no time.'

And as briefly and succinctly as possible he detailed the experiences of the last few days.

Half-way through, Mr Carter interrupted him to give a few cryptic orders through the telephone. All traces of displeasure had now left his face. He nodded energetically when Tommy had finished.

'Quite right. Every moment's of value. Fear we shall be too late anyway. They wouldn't wait. Would clear out at once. Still, they may have left something behind them that will be a clue. You say you've recognized Number One to be Kramenin? That's important. We want something against him badly to prevent the Cabinet falling on his neck too freely. What about the others? You say two faces were familiar to you? One's a Labour man, you think? Just look through these photos, and see if you can spot him.'

A minute later, Tommy held one up. Mr Carter exhibited some surprise.

'Ah, Westway! Shouldn't have thought it. Poses as being moderate. As for the other fellow, I think I can give a good guess.' He handed another photograph to Tommy, and smiled at the other's exclamation. 'I'm right, then. Who is he? Irishman. Prominent Unionist M.P. All a blind, of course. We've suspected it—but couldn't get any proof. Yes, you've done very well, young man. The 29th, you say, is the date. That gives us very little time—very little time indeed.'

'But—' Tommy hesitated.

Mr Carter read his thoughts.

'We can deal with the General Strike menace, I think. It's a toss-up—but we've got a sporting chance! But if that draft treaty turns up—we're done. England will be plunged in anarchy. Ah, what's that? The car? Come on, Beresford, we'll go and have a look at this house of yours.'

Two constables were on duty in front of the house in Soho. An inspector reported to Mr Carter in a low voice. The latter turned to Tommy.

'The birds have flown—as we thought. We might as well go over it.'

Going over the deserted house seemed to Tommy to partake of the character of a dream. Everything was just as it had been. The prison room with the crooked pictures, the broken jug in the attic, the meeting room with its long table. But nowhere was there a trace of papers. Everything of that kind had either been destroyed or taken away. And there was no sign of Annette.

'What you tell me about the girl puzzled me,' said Mr Carter. 'You believe that she deliberately went back?'

'It would seem so, sir. She ran upstairs while I was getting the door open.'

'H'm, she must belong to the gang, then; but, being a woman, didn't feel like standing by to see a personable young man killed. But evidently she's in with them, or she wouldn't have gone back.'

'I can't believe she's really one of them, sir. She—seemed so different—'

'Good-looking, I suppose?' said Mr Carter with a smile that made Tommy flush to the roots of his hair.

He admitted Annette's beauty rather shame-facedly.

'By the way,' observed Mr Carter, 'have you shown yourself to Miss Tuppence yet? She's been bombarding me with letters about you.'

'Tuppence? I was afraid she might get a bit rattled. Did she go to the police?'

Mr Carter shook his head.

'Then I wonder how they twigged me.'

Mr Carter looked inquiringly at him, and Tommy explained. The other nodded thoughtfully.

'True, that's rather a curious point. Unless the mention of the Ritz was an accidental remark?'

'It might have been, sir. But they must have found out about me suddenly in some way.'

'Well,' said Mr Carter, looking round him, 'there's nothing more to be done here. What about some lunch with me?'

'Thanks awfully, sir. But I think I'd better get back and rout out Tuppence.'

'Of course. Give her my kind regards and tell her not to believe you're killed too readily next time.'

Tommy grinned.

'I take a lot of killing, sir.'

'So I perceive,' said Mr Carter dryly. 'Well, goodbye. Remember you're a marked man now, and take reasonable care of yourself.'

'Thank you, sir.'

Hailing a taxi briskly Tommy stepped in, and was swiftly borne to the Ritz, dwelling the while on the pleasurable anticipation of startling Tuppence.

'Wonder what she's been up to. Dogging "Rita" most likely. By the way, I suppose that's who Annette meant by Marguerite. I didn't get it at the time.' The thought saddened him a little, for it seemed to prove that Mrs Vandemeyer and the girl were on intimate terms.

The taxi drew up at the Ritz. Tommy burst into its sacred portals eagerly, but his enthusiasm received a check. He was informed that Miss Cowley had gone out a quarter of an hour ago.

CHAPTER 18

The Telegram

Baffled for the moment, Tommy strolled into the restaurant, and ordered a meal of surpassing excellence. His four days' imprisonment had taught him anew to value good food.

He was in the middle of conveying a particularly choice morsel of *sole à la Jeannette* to his mouth, when he caught sight of Julius entering the room. Tommy waved a menu cheerfully, and succeeded in attracting the other's attention. At the sight of Tommy, Julius's eyes seemed as though they would pop out of his head. He strode across, and pump-handled Tommy's hand with what seemed to the latter quite unnecessary vigour.

'Holy snakes!' he ejaculated. 'Is it really you?'

'Of course it is. Why shouldn't it be?'

'Why shouldn't it be? Say, man, don't you know you've been given up for dead? I guess we'd have had a solemn requiem for you in another few days.'

'Who thought I was dead?' demanded Tommy.

'Tuppence.'

'She remembered the proverb about the good dying young, I suppose. There must be a certain amount of original sin in me to have survived. Where is Tuppence, by the way?'

'Isn't she here?'

'No, the fellows at the office said she'd just gone out.'

'Gone shopping, I guess. I dropped her here in the car about an hour ago. But, say, can't you shed that British calm of yours, and get down to it? What on God's earth have you been doing all this time?'

'If you're feeding here,' replied Tommy, 'order now. It's going to be a long story.'

Julius drew up a chair to the opposite side of the table, summoned a hovering waiter, and dictated his wishes. Then he turned to Tommy.

'Fire ahead. I guess you've had some few adventures.'

'One or two,' replied Tommy modestly, and plunged into his recital.

Julius listened spell-bound. Half the dishes that were placed before him he forgot to eat. At the end he heaved a long sigh.

'Bully for you. Reads like a dime novel!'

'And now for the home front,' said Tommy, stretching out his hand for a peach.

'W—ell,' drawled Julius, 'I don't mind admitting we've had some adventures too.'

He, in his turn, assumed the rôle of narrator. Beginning with his unsuccessful reconnoitring at Bournemouth, he passed on to his return to London, the buying of the car, the growing anxieties of Tuppence, the call upon Sir James, and the sensational occurrences of the previous night.

'But who killed her?' asked Tommy. 'I don't quite understand.'

'The doctor kidded himself she took it herself,' replied Julius dryly.

'And Sir James? What did he think?'

'Being a legal luminary, he is likewise a human oyster,' replied Julius. 'I should say he "reserved judgment."' He went on to detail the events of the morning.

'Lost her memory, eh?' said Tommy with interest. 'By Jove, that explains why they looked at me so queerly when I spoke of questioning her. Bit of a slip on my part, that! But it wasn't the sort of thing a fellow would be likely to guess.'

'They didn't give you any sort of hint as to where Jane was?'

Tommy shook his head regretfully.

'Not a word. I'm a bit of an ass, as you know. I ought to have got more out of them somehow.'

'I guess you're lucky to be here at all. That bluff of yours was the goods all right. How you ever came to think of it all so pat beats me to a frazzle!'

'I was in such a funk I had to think of something,' said Tommy simply.

There was a moment's pause, and then Tommy reverted to Mrs Vandemeyer's death.

'There's no doubt it was chloral?'

'I believe not. At least they call it heart failure induced by an overdose, or some such claptrap. It's all right. We don't want to be worried with an inquest. But I guess Tuppence and I and even the highbrow Sir James have all got the same idea.'

'Mr Brown?' hazarded Tommy.

'Sure thing.'

Tommy nodded.

'All the same,' he said thoughtfully, 'Mr Brown hasn't got wings. I don't see how he got in and out.'

'How about some high-class thought transference stunt? Some magnetic influence that irresistibly impelled Mrs Vandemeyer to commit suicide?'

Tommy looked at him with respect.

'Good, Julius. Distinctly good. Especially the phraseology. But it leaves me cold. I yearn for a real Mr Brown of flesh and blood. I think the gifted young detectives must get to work, study the entrances and exits, and tap the bumps on their foreheads until the solution of the mystery dawns on them. Let's go round to the scene of the crime. I wish we could get hold of Tuppence. The Ritz would enjoy the spectacle of the glad reunion.'

Inquiry at the office revealed the fact that Tuppence had not yet returned.

'All the same, I guess I'll have a look round upstairs,' said Julius. 'She might be in my sitting-room.' He disappeared.

Suddenly a diminutive boy spoke at Tommy's elbow:

'The young lady—she's gone away by train, I think, sir,' he murmured shyly.

'What?' Tommy wheeled round upon him.

The small boy became pinker than before.

'The taxi, sir. I heard her tell the driver Charing Cross and to look sharp.'

Tommy stared at him, his eyes opening wide in surprise. Emboldened, the small boy proceeded. 'So I thought, having asked for an A.B.C. and a Bradshaw.'

Tommy interrupted him:

'When did she ask for an A.B.C. and a Bradshaw?'

'When I took her the telegram, sir.'

'A telegram?'

'Yes, sir.'

'When was that?'

'About half-past twelve, sir.'

'Tell me exactly what happened.'

The small boy drew a long breath.

'I took up a telegram to No. 891—the lady was there. She opened it and gave a gasp, and then she said, very jolly like: "Bring me up a Bradshaw, and an A.B.C., and look sharp, Henry." My name isn't Henry, but—'

'Never mind your name,' said Tommy impatiently. 'Go on.'

'Yes, sir. I brought them, and she told me to wait, and looked up something. And then she looks up at the clock, and "Hurry up," she says. "Tell them to get me a taxi," and she begins a-shoving on of her hat in front of the glass, and she was down in two ticks, almost as quick as I was, and I seed her going down the steps and into the taxi, and I heard her call out what I told you.'

The small boy stopped and replenished his lungs. Tommy continued to stare at him. At that moment Julius rejoined him. He held an open letter in his hand.

'I say, Hersheimmer,'—Tommy turned to him—'Tuppence has gone off sleuthing on her own.'

'Shucks!'

'Yes, she has. She went off in a taxi to Charing Cross in the deuce of a hurry after getting a telegram.' His eye fell on the letter in Julius's hand. 'Oh; she left a note for you. That's all right. Where's she off to?'

Almost unconsciously, he held out his hand for the letter, but Julius folded it up and placed it in his pocket. He seemed a trifle embarrassed.

'I guess this is nothing to do with it. It's about something else—something I asked her that she was to let me know about.'

'Oh!' Tommy looked puzzled, and seemed waiting for more.

'See here,' said Julius suddenly, 'I'd better put you wise. I asked Miss Tuppence to marry me this morning.'

'Oh!' said Tommy mechanically. He felt dazed. Julius's words were totally unexpected. For the moment they benumbed his brain.

'I'd like to tell you,' continued Julius, 'that before I suggested anything of the kind to Miss Tuppence, I made it clear that I didn't want to butt in in any way between her and you—'

Tommy roused himself.

'That's all right,' he said quickly. 'Tuppence and I have been pals for years. Nothing more.' He lit a cigarette with a hand that shook ever so little. 'That's quite all right. Tuppence always said that she was looking out for—'

He stopped abruptly, his face crimsoning, but Julius was in no way discomposed.

'Oh, I guess it'll be the dollars that'll do the trick. Miss Tuppence put me wise to that right away. There's no humbug about her. We ought to gee along together very well.'

Tommy looked at him curiously for a minute, as though he were about to speak, then changed his mind and said nothing. Tuppence and Julius! Well, why not? Had she not lamented the fact that she knew no rich men? Had she not openly avowed her intention of marrying for money if she ever had the chance? Her meeting with the young American millionaire had given her the chance—and it was unlikely she would be slow to avail herself of it. She was out for money. She had always said so. Why blame her because she had been true to her creed?

Nevertheless, Tommy did blame her. He was filled with a passionate and utterly illogical resentment. It was all very well to *say* things like that—but a *real* girl would never marry for money. Tuppence was utterly cold-blooded and selfish, and he would be delighted if he never saw her again! And it was a rotten world!

Julius's voice broke in on these meditations.

'Yes, we ought to gee along together very well. I've heard that a girl always refuses you once—a sort of convention.'

Tommy caught his arm.

'Refuses? Did you say *refuses*?'

'Sure thing. Didn't I tell you that? She just rapped out a "no" without any kind of reason to it. The eternal feminine, the Huns call it, I've heard. But she'll come round right enough. Likely enough, I hustled her some—'

But Tommy interrupted regardless of decorum.

'What did she say in that note?' he demanded fiercely.

The obliging Julius handed it to him.

'There's no earthly clue in it as to where she's gone,' he assured Tommy. 'But you might as well see for yourself if you don't believe me.'

The note, in Tuppence's well-known schoolboy writing, ran as follows:

Dear Julius,

It's always better to have things in black and white. I don't feel I can be bothered to think of marriage until Tommy is found. Let's leave it till then.

Yours affectionately,

Tuppence.

Tommy handed it back, his eyes shining. His feelings had undergone a sharp reaction. He now felt that Tuppence was all that was noble and disinterested. Had she not refused Julius without hesitation? True, the note betokened signs of weakening, but he could excuse that. It read almost like a bribe to Julius to spur him on in his efforts to find Tommy, but he supposed she had not really meant it that way. Darling Tuppence, there was not a girl in the world to touch her! When he saw her—His thoughts were brought up with a sudden jerk.

'As you say,' he remarked, pulling himself together, 'there's not a hint here as to what she's up to. Hi—Henry!'

The small boy came obediently. Tommy produced five shillings.

'One thing more. Do you remember what the young lady did with the telegram?'

Henry gasped and spoke.

'She crumpled it up into a ball and threw it into the grate, and made a sort of noise like "Whoop!" sir.'

'Very graphic, Henry,' said Tommy. 'Here's your five shillings. Come on, Julius. We must find that telegram.'

They hurried upstairs. Tuppence had left the key in her door. The room was as she had left it. In the fire-place was a crumpled ball of orange and white. Tommy disentangled it and smoothed out the telegram.

Come at once, Moat House, Ebury, Yorkshire, great developments—Tommy.

They looked at each other in stupefaction. Julius spoke first:

'*You* didn't send it?'

'Of course not. What does it mean?'

'I guess it means the worst,' said Julius quietly. 'They've got her.'

'*What*?'

'Sure thing! They signed your name, and she fell into the trap like a lamb.'

'My God! What shall we do?'

'Get busy, and go after her! Right now! There's no time to waste. It's almighty luck that she didn't take the wire with her. If she had we'd probably never have traced her. But we've got to hustle. Where's that Bradshaw?'

The energy of Julius was infectious. Left to himself, Tommy would probably have sat down to think things out for a good half-hour before he decided on a plan of action. But with Julius Hersheimmer about, hustling was inevitable.

After a few muttered imprecations he handed the Bradshaw to Tommy as being more conversant with its mysteries. Tommy abandoned it in favour of an A.B.C.

'Here we are. Ebury, Yorks. From King's Cross. Or St Pancras. (Boy must have made a mistake. It was King's Cross, not *Charing* Cross) 12.50, that's the train she went by; 2.10, that's gone; 3.20 is the next—and a damned slow train, too.'

'What about the car?'

Tommy shook his head.

'Send it up if you like, but we'd better stick to the train. The great thing is to keep calm.'

Julius groaned.

'That's so. But it gets my goat to think of that innocent young girl in danger!'

Tommy nodded abstractedly. He was thinking. In a moment or two, he said:

'I say, Julius, what do they want her for, anyway?'

'Eh? I don't get you?'

'What I mean is that I don't think it's their game to do her any harm,' explained Tommy, puckering his brow with the strain of his mental processes. 'She's a hostage, that's what she is. She's in no immediate danger, because if we tumble on to anything, she'd be damned useful to them. As long as they've got her, they've got the whip hand of us. See?'

'Sure thing,' said Julius thoughtfully. 'That's so.'

'Besides,' added Tommy, as an afterthought, 'I've great faith in Tuppence.'

The journey was wearisome, with many stops, and crowded carriages. They had to change twice, once at Doncaster, once at a small junction. Ebury was a deserted station with a solitary porter, to whom Tommy addressed himself:

'Can you tell me the way to the Moat House?'

'The Moat House? It's a tidy step from here. The big house near the sea, you mean?'

Tommy assented brazenly. After listening to the porter's meticulous but perplexing directions, they prepared to leave the station. It was beginning to rain, and they turned up the collars of their coats as they trudged through the slush of the road. Suddenly Tommy halted.

'Wait a moment.' He ran back to the station and tackled the porter anew.

'Look here, do you remember a young lady who arrived by an earlier train, the 12.10 from London? She'd probably ask you the way to the Moat House.'

He described Tuppence as well as he could, but the porter shook his head. Several people had arrived by the train in question. He could not call to mind one young lady in particular. But he was quite certain that no one had asked him the way to the Moat House.

Tommy rejoined Julius, and explained. Depression was settling down on him like a leaden weight. He felt convinced that their quest was going to be unsuccessful. The enemy had over three hours' start. Three hours was more than enough for Mr Brown. He would not ignore the possibility of the telegram having been found.

The way seemed endless. Once they took the wrong turning and went nearly half a mile out of their direction. It was past seven o'clock when a small boy told them that 't' Moat House' was just past the next corner.

A rusty iron gate swinging dismally on its hinges! An overgrown drive thick with leaves. There was something about the place that struck a chill to both their hearts. They went up the deserted drive. The leaves deadened their footsteps. The daylight was almost gone. It was like walking in a world of ghosts. Overhead the branches flapped and creaked with a mournful note. Occasionally a sodden leaf drifted silently down, startling them with its cold touch on their cheeks.

A turn of the drive brought them in sight of the house. That, too, seemed empty and deserted. The shutters were closed, the steps up to the door overgrown with moss. Was it indeed to this desolate spot that Tuppence had been decoyed? It seemed hard to believe that a human footstep had passed this way for months.

Julius jerked the rusty bell handle. A jangling peal rang discordantly, echoing through the emptiness within. No one came. They rang again and again—but there was no sign of life. Then they walked completely round the house. Everywhere silence, and shuttered windows. If they could believe the evidence of their eyes the place was empty.

'Nothing doing,' said Julius.

They retraced their steps slowly to the gate.

'There must be a village handy,' continued the young American. 'We'd better make inquiries there. They'll know something about the place, and whether there's been anyone there lately.'

'Yes, that's not a bad idea.'

Proceeding up the road they soon came to a little hamlet. On the outskirts of it, they met a workman swinging his bag of tools, and Tommy stopped him with a question.

'The Moat House? It's empty. Been empty for years. Mrs Sweeney's got the key if you want to go over it—next to the post office.'

Tommy thanked him. They soon found the post office, which was also a sweet and general fancy shop, and knocked at the door of the cottage next to it. A clean, wholesome-looking woman opened it. She readily produced the key of the Moat House.

'Though I doubt if it's the kind of place to suit you, sir. In a terrible state of repair. Ceilings leaking and all. 'Twould need a lot of money spent on it.'

'Thanks,' said Tommy cheerily. 'I dare say it'll be a wash-out, but houses are scarce nowadays.'

'That they are,' declared the woman heartily. 'My daughter and son-in-law have been looking for a decent cottage for I don't know how long. It's all the war. Upset things terribly, it has. But excuse me, sir, it'll be too dark for you to see much of the house. Hadn't you better wait until tomorrow?'

'That's all right. We'll have a look round this evening, anyway. We'd have been here before only we lost our way. What's the best place to stay at for the night round here?'

Mrs Sweeney looked doubtful.

'There's the Yorkshire Arms, but it's not much of a place for gentlemen like you.'

'Oh, it will do very well. Thanks. By the way, you've not had a young lady here asking for this key today?'

The woman shook her head.

'No one's been over the place for a long time.'

'Thanks very much.'

They retraced their steps to the Moat House. As the front door swung back on its hinges, protesting loudly, Julius struck a match and examined the floor carefully. Then he shook his head.

'I'd swear no one's passed this way. Look at the dust. Thick. Not a sign of a footmark.'

They wandered round the deserted house. Everywhere the same tale. Thick layers of dust apparently undisturbed.

'This gets me,' said Julius. 'I don't believe Tuppence was ever in this house.'

'She must have been.'

Julius shook his head without replying.

'We'll go over it again tomorrow,' said Tommy. 'Perhaps we'll see more in the daylight.'

On the morrow they took up the search once more, and were reluctantly forced to the conclusion that the house had not been invaded for some considerable time. They might have left the village altogether but for a fortunate discovery of Tommy's. As they were retracing their steps to the gate, he gave a sudden cry, and stooping, picked something up from among the leaves, and held it out to Julius. It was a small gold brooch.

'That's Tuppence's!'

'Are you sure?'

'Absolutely. I've often seen her wear it.'

Julius drew a deep breath.

'I guess that settles it. She came as far as here, anyway. We'll make that pub our headquarters, and raise hell round here until we find her. Somebody *must* have seen her.'

Forthwith the campaign began. Tommy and Julius worked separately and together, but the result was the same. Nobody answering to Tuppence's description had been seen in the vicinity. They were baffled—but not discouraged. Finally they altered their tactics. Tuppence had certainly not remained long in the neighbourhood of the Moat House. That pointed to her having been overcome and carried away in a car. They renewed inquiries. Had anyone seen a car standing somewhere near the Moat House that day? Again they met with no success.

Julius wired to town for his own car, and they scoured the neighbourhood daily with unflagging zeal. A grey limousine on which they had set high hopes was traced to Harrogate, and turned out to be the property of a highly respectable maiden lady!

Each day saw them set out on a new quest. Julius was like a hound on the leash. He followed up the slenderest clue. Every car that had passed through the village on the fateful day was tracked down. He forced his way into country properties and submitted the owners of the cars to searching cross-examination. His apologies were as thorough as his methods, and seldom failed in disarming the indignation of his victims; but, as day succeeded day, they were no nearer to discovering Tuppence's whereabouts. So well had the abduction been planned that the girl seemed literally to have vanished into thin air.

And another preoccupation was weighing on Tommy's mind.

'Do you know how long we've been here?' he asked one morning as they sat facing each other at breakfast. 'A week! We're no nearer to finding Tuppence, *and next Sunday is the 29th*!'

'Shucks!' said Julius thoughtfully. 'I'd almost forgotten about the 29th. I've been thinking of nothing but Tuppence.'

'So have I. At least, I hadn't forgotten about the 29th, but it didn't seem to matter a damn in comparison to finding Tuppence. But today's the 23rd, and time's getting short. If we're ever going to get hold of her at all, we must do it before the 29th—her life won't be worth an hour's purchase afterwards. The hostage game will be played out by then. I'm beginning to feel that we've made a big mistake in the way we've set about this. We've wasted time and we're no forrader.'

'I'm with you there. We've been a couple of mutts, who've bitten off a bigger bit than they can chew. I'm going to quit fooling right away!'

'What do you mean?'

'I'll tell you. I'm going to do what we ought to have done a week ago. I'm going right back to London to put the case in the hands of your British police. We fancied ourselves as sleuths. Sleuths! It was a piece of damn-fool foolishness! I'm through! I've had enough of it. Scotland Yard for me!'

'You're right,' said Tommy slowly. 'I wish to God we'd gone there right away.'

'Better late than never. We've been like a couple of babes playing "Here we go round the Mulberry Bush." Now I'm going right along to Scotland Yard to ask them to take me by the hand and show me the way I should go. I guess the professional always scores over the amateur in the end. Are you coming along with me?'

Tommy shook his head.

'What's the good? One of us is enough. I might as well stay here and nose round a bit longer. Something *might* turn up. One never knows.'

'Sure thing. Well, so long. I'll be back in a couple of shakes with a few inspectors along. I shall tell them to pick out their brightest and best.'

But the course of events was not to follow the plan Julius had laid down. Later in the day Tommy received a wire:

Join me Manchester Midland Hotel. Important news
—JULIUS.

At 7.30 that night Tommy alighted from a slow cross-country train. Julius was on the platform.

'Thought you'd come by this train if you weren't out when my wire arrived.'

Tommy grasped him by the arm.

'What is it? Is Tuppence found?'

Julius shook his head.

'No. But I found this waiting in London. Just arrived.'

He handed the telegraph form to the other. Tommy's eyes opened as he read:

Jane Finn found. Come Manchester Midland Hotel immediately—PEEL EDGERTON.

Julius took the form back and folded it up.

'Queer,' he said thoughtfully. 'I thought that lawyer chap had quit!'

221

CHAPTER 19

Jane Finn

'My train got in half an hour ago,' explained Julius, as he led the way out of the station. 'I reckoned you'd come by this before I left London, and wired accordingly to Sir James. He's booked rooms for us, and will be round to dine at eight.'

'What made you think he'd ceased to take any interest in the case?' asked Tommy curiously.

'What he said,' replied Julius dryly. 'The old bird's as close as an oyster! Like all the darned lot of them, he wasn't going to commit himself till he was sure he could deliver the goods.'

'I wonder,' said Tommy thoughtfully.

Julius turned on him.

'You wonder what?'

'Whether that was his real reason.'

'Sure. You bet your life it was.'

Tommy shook his head unconvinced.

Sir James arrived punctually at eight o'clock, and Julius introduced Tommy. Sir James shook hands with him warmly.

'I am delighted to make your acquaintance, Mr Beresford. I have heard so much about you from Miss Tuppence'—he smiled involuntarily—'that it really seems as though I already know you quite well.'

'Thank you, sir,' said Tommy with his cheerful grin. He scanned the great lawyer eagerly. Like Tuppence, he felt the magnetism of the other's personality. He was reminded of Mr Carter. The two men, totally unlike so far as physical resemblance went, produced a similar effect. Beneath the weary manner of the one and the professional reserve of the other, lay the same quality of mind, keen-edged like a rapier.

In the meantime he was conscious of Sir James's close scrutiny. When the lawyer dropped his eyes the young man had the feeling that the other had read him through and through like an open book. He could not but wonder what the final judgment was, but there was little chance of learning that. Sir James took in everything, but gave out only what he chose. A proof of that occurred almost at once.

Immediately the first greetings were over Julius broke out into a flood of eager questions. How had Sir James managed to track the girl? Why had he not let them know that he was still working on the case? And so on.

Sir James stroked his chin and smiled. At last he said:

'Just so, just so. Well, she's found. And that's the great thing, isn't it? Eh! Come now, that's the great thing?'

'Sure it is. But just how did you strike her trail? Miss Tuppence and I thought you'd quit for good and all.'

'Ah!' The lawyer shot a lightning glance at him, then resumed operations on his chin. 'You thought that, did you? Did you really? H'm, dear me.'

'But I guess I can take it we were wrong,' pursued Julius.

'Well, I don't know that I should go so far as to say that. But it's certainly fortunate for all parties that we've managed to find the young lady.'

'But where is she?' demanded Julius, his thoughts flying off on another tack. 'I thought you'd be sure to bring her along?'

'That would hardly be possible,' said Sir James gravely.

'Why?'

'Because the young lady was knocked down in a street accident, and has sustained slight injuries to the head. She was taken to the infirmary, and on recovering consciousness gave her name as Jane Finn. When—ah!—I heard that, I arranged for her to be removed to the house of a doctor— a friend of mine, and wired at once for you. She relapsed into unconsciousness and has not spoken since.'

'She's not seriously hurt?'

'Oh, a bruise and a cut or two; really, from a medical point of view, absurdly slight injuries to have produced such a condition. Her state is probably to be attributed to the mental shock consequent on recovering her memory.'

'It's come back?' cried Julius excitedly.

Sir James tapped the table rather impatiently.

'Undoubtedly, Mr Hersheimmer, since she was able to give her real name. I thought you had appreciated that point.'

'And you just happened to be on the spot,' said Tommy. 'Seems quite like a fairy tale?'

224

But Sir James was far too wary to be drawn.

'Coincidences are curious things,' he said dryly.

Nevertheless, Tommy was now certain of what he had before only suspected. Sir James's presence in Manchester was not accidental. Far from abandoning the case, as Julius supposed, he had by some means of his own successfully run the missing girl to earth. The only thing that puzzled Tommy was the reason for all this secrecy? He concluded that it was a foible of the legal mind.

Julius was speaking.

'After dinner,' he announced, 'I shall go right away and see Jane.'

'That will be impossible, I fear,' said Sir James. 'It is very unlikely they would allow her to see visitors at this time of night. I should suggest tomorrow morning about ten o'clock.'

Julius flushed. There was something in Sir James which always stirred him to antagonism. It was a conflict of two masterful personalities.

'All the same, I reckon I'll go round there tonight and see if I can't ginger them up to break through their silly rules.'

'It will be quite useless, Mr Hersheimmer.'

The words came out like the crack of a pistol, and Tommy looked up with a start. Julius was nervous and excited. The hand with which he raised his glass to his lips shook slightly, but his eyes held Sir James's defiantly. For a moment the hostility between the two seemed likely to burst into flame, but in the end Julius lowered his eyes, defeated.

'For the moment, I reckon you're the boss.'

'Thank you,' said the other. 'We will say ten o'clock then?' With consummate ease of manner he turned to Tommy. 'I must confess, Mr Beresford, that it was something of a surprise to me to see you here this evening. The last I heard of you was that your friends were in grave anxiety on your behalf. Nothing had been heard of you for some days, and Miss Tuppence was inclined to think you had got into difficulties.'

'I had, sir!' Tommy grinned reminiscently. 'I was never in a tighter place in my life.'

Helped out by questions from Sir James, he gave an abbreviated account of his adventures. The lawyer looked at him with renewed interest as he brought the tale to a close.

'You got yourself out of a tight place very well,' he said gravely. 'I congratulate you. You displayed a great deal of ingenuity and carried your part through well.'

Tommy blushed, his face assuming a prawn-like hue at the praise.

'I couldn't have got away but for the girl, sir.'

'No.' Sir James smiled a little. 'It was lucky for you she happened to—er—take a fancy to you.' Tommy appeared about to protest, but Sir James went on. 'There's no doubt about her being one of the gang, I suppose?'

'I'm afraid not, sir. I thought perhaps they were keeping her there by force, but the way she acted didn't fit in with that. You see, she went back to them when she could have got away.'

Sir James nodded thoughtfully.

'What did she say? Something about wanting to be taken to Marguerite?'

226

'Yes, sir. I suppose she meant Mrs Vandemeyer.'

'She always signed herself Rita Vandemeyer. All her friends spoke of her as Rita. Still, I suppose the girl must have been in the habit of calling her by her full name. And, at the moment she was crying out to her, Mrs Vandemeyer was either dead or dying! Curious! There are one or two points that strike me as being obscure—their sudden change of attitude towards yourself, for instance. By the way, the house was raided, of course?'

'Yes, sir, but they'd cleared out.'

'Naturally,' said Sir James dryly.

'And not a clue left behind.'

'I wonder—' The lawyer tapped the table thoughtfully. Something in his voice made Tommy look up. Would this man's eyes have seen something where theirs had been blind? He spoke impulsively:

'I wish you'd been there, sir, to go over the house!'

'I wish I had,' said Sir James quietly. He sat for a moment in silence. Then he looked up. 'And since then? What have you been doing?'

For a moment, Tommy stared at him. Then it dawned on him that of course the lawyer did not know.

'I forgot that you didn't know about Tuppence,' he said slowly. The sickening anxiety, forgotten for a while in the excitement of knowing Jane Finn found at last, swept over him again.

The lawyer laid down his knife and fork sharply.

'Has anything happened to Miss Tuppence?' His voice was keen-edged.

'She's disappeared,' said Julius.

'When?'

'A week ago.'

'How?'

Sir James's questions fairly shot out. Between them Tommy and Julius gave the history of the last week and their futile search.

Sir James went at once to the root of the matter.

'A wire signed with your name? They knew enough of you both for that. They weren't sure of how much you had learnt in that house. Their kidnapping of Miss Tuppence is the counter-move to your escape. If necessary they could seal your lips with what might happen to her.'

Tommy nodded.

'That's just what I thought, sir.'

Sir James looked at him keenly. '*You* had worked that out, had you? Not bad—not at all bad. The curious thing is that they certainly did not know anything about you when they first held you prisoner. You are sure that you did not in any way disclose your identity?'

Tommy shook his head.

'That's so,' said Julius with a nod. 'Therefore I reckon someone put them wise—and not earlier than Sunday afternoon.'

'Yes, but who?'

'That almighty omniscient Mr Brown, of course!'

There was a faint note of derision in the American's voice which made Sir James look up sharply.

'You don't believe in Mr Brown, Mr Hersheimmer?'

'No, sir, I do not,' returned the young American with emphasis. 'Not as such, that is to say. I reckon it out that he's a figurehead—just a bogy name to frighten the children with. The real head of this business is that Russian chap Kramenin. I guess he's quite capable of running revolutions in three countries at once if he chose! The man Whittington is probably the head of the English branch.'

'I disagree with you,' said Sir James shortly. 'Mr Brown exists.' He turned to Tommy. 'Did you happen to notice where that wire was handed in?'

'No, sir, I'm afraid I didn't.'

'H'm. Got it with you?'

'It's upstairs, sir, in my kit.'

'I'd like to have a look at it sometime. No hurry. You've wasted a week'—Tommy hung his head—'a day or so more is immaterial. We'll deal with Miss Jane Finn first. Afterwards, we'll set to work to rescue Miss Tuppence from bondage. I don't think she's in any immediate danger. That is, so long as they don't know that we've got Jane Finn, and that her memory has returned. We must keep that dark at all costs. You understand?'

The other two assented, and, after making arrangements for meeting on the morrow, the great lawyer took his leave.

At ten o'clock, the two young men were at the appointed spot. Sir James had joined them on the doorstep. He alone appeared unexcited. He introduced them to the doctor.

'Mr Hersheimmer—Mr Beresford—Dr Roylance. How's the patient?'

'Going on well. Evidently no idea of the flight of time. Asked this morning how many had been saved from the *Lusitania*. Was it in the papers yet? That, of course, was only what was to be expected. She seems to have something on her mind, though.'

'I think we can relieve her anxiety. May we go up?'

'Certainly.'

Tommy's heart beat sensibly faster as they followed the doctor upstairs. Jane Finn at last! The long-sought, the mysterious, the elusive Jane Finn! How wildly improbable success had seemed! And here in this house, her memory almost miraculously restored, lay the girl who held the future of England in her hands. A half groan broke from Tommy's lips. If only Tuppence could have been at his side to share in the triumphant conclusion of their joint venture! Then he put the thought of Tuppence resolutely aside. His confidence in Sir James was growing. There was a man who would unerringly ferret out Tuppence's whereabouts. In the meantime, Jane Finn! And suddenly a dread clutched at his heart. It seemed too easy... Suppose they should find her dead... stricken down by the hand of Mr Brown?

In another minute he was laughing at these melodramatic fancies. The doctor held open the door of a room and they passed in. On the white bed, bandages round her head, lay the girl. Somehow the whole scene seemed unreal. It was so exactly what one expected that it gave the effect of being beautifully staged.

The girl looked from one to the other of them with large wondering eyes. Sir James spoke first.

'Miss Finn,' he said, 'this is your cousin, Mr Julius P. Hersheimmer.'

A faint flush flitted over the girl's face, as Julius stepped forward and took her hand.

'How do, Cousin Jane?' he said lightly.

But Tommy caught the tremor in his voice.

'Are you really Uncle Hiram's son?' she asked wonderingly.

Her voice, with the slight warmth of the Western accent, had an almost thrilling quality. It seemed vaguely familiar to Tommy, but he thrust the impression aside as impossible.

'Sure thing.'

'We used to read about Uncle Hiram in the newspapers,' continued the girl, in her soft tones. 'But I never thought I'd meet you one day. Mother figured it out that Uncle Hiram would never get over being mad with her.'

'The old man was like that,' admitted Julius. 'But I guess the new generation's sort of different. Got no use for the family feud business. First thing I thought about, soon as the war was over, was to come along and hunt you up.'

A shadow passed over the girl's face.

'They've been telling me things—dreadful things—that my memory went, and that there are years I shall never know about—years lost out of my life.'

'You didn't realize that yourself ?'

The girl's eyes opened wide.

'Why, no. It seems to me as though it were no time since we were being hustled into those boats. I can see it all now!' She closed her eyes with a shudder.

Julius looked across at Sir James, who nodded.

'Don't worry any. It isn't worth it. Now, see here, Jane, there's something we want to know about. There was a man aboard that boat with some mighty important papers on him, and the big guns in this country have got a notion that he passed on the goods to you. Is that so?'

The girl hesitated, her glance shifting to the other two. Julius understood.

'Mr Beresford is commissioned by the British Government to get those papers back. Sir James Peel Edgerton is an English Member of Parliament, and might be a big gun in the Cabinet if he liked. It's owing to him that we've ferreted you out at last. So you can go right ahead and tell us the whole story. Did Danvers give you the papers?'

'Yes. He said they'd have a better chance with me, because they would have the women and children first.'

'Just as we thought,' said Sir James.

'He said they were very important—that they might make all the difference to the Allies. But, if it's all so long ago, and the war's over, what does it matter now?'

'I guess history repeats itself, Jane. First there was a great hue and cry over those papers, then it all died down, and now the whole caboodle's started all over again—for rather different reasons. Then you can hand them over to us right away?'

'But I can't.'

'What?'

'I haven't got them.'

'You—haven't—got them?' Julius punctuated the words with little pauses

'No—I hid them.'

'You *hid* them?'

'Yes. I got uneasy. People seemed to be watching me. It scared me—badly.' She put her hand to her head. 'It's almost the last thing I remember before waking up in the hospital...'

'Go on,' said Sir James, in his quiet penetrating tones. 'What do you remember?'

She turned to him obediently.

'It was at Holyhead. I came that way—I don't remember why...'

'That doesn't matter. Go on.'

'In the confusion on the quay I slipped away. Nobody saw me. I took a car. Told the man to drive me out of the town. I watched when we got on the open road. No other car was following us. I saw a path at the side of the road. I told the man to wait.'

She paused, then went on. 'The path led to the cliff, and down to the sea between big yellow gorse bushes—they were like golden flames. I looked round. There wasn't a soul in sight. But just level with my head there was a hole in the rock. It was quite small—I could only just get my hand in, but it went a long way back. I took the oilskin packet from round my neck and shoved it right in as far as I could. Then I tore off a bit of gorse—My! but it did prick—and plugged the hole with it so that you'd never guess there was a crevice of any kind there. Then I marked the place carefully in my own mind, so that I'd find it again. There was a queer boulder in the path just there—for all the world like a dog sitting up begging. Then I went back to the road. The car was waiting, and I drove back. I just caught the train. I was a bit ashamed of myself for fancying things maybe, but, by and by, I saw the man opposite me wink at a woman who was sitting next to me, and I felt scared again, and was glad the papers were safe. I went out in the corridor to get a little air. I thought I'd slip into another carriage. But the woman called me back, said I'd dropped something, and when I stooped to look, something seemed to hit me—here.' She placed her hand to the back of her head. 'I don't remember anything more until I woke up in the hospital.'

There was a pause.

'Thank you, Miss Finn.' It was Sir James who spoke. 'I hope we have not tired you?'

'Oh, that's all right. My head aches a little, but otherwise I feel fine.'

Julius stepped forward and took her hand again.

'So long, Cousin Jane. I'm going to get busy after those papers, but I'll be back in two shakes of a dog's tail, and I'll tote you up to London and give you the time of your young life before we go back to the States! I mean it—so hurry up and get well.'

CHAPTER 20

Too Late

In the street they held an informal council of war. Sir James had drawn a watch from his pocket.

'The boat train to Holyhead stops at Chester at 12.14. If you start at once I think you can catch the connexion.'

Tommy looked up, puzzled.

'Is there any need to hurry, sir? Today is only the 24th.'

'I guess it's always well to get up early in the morning,' said Julius, before the lawyer had time to reply. 'We'll make tracks for the depot right away.'

A little frown had settled on Sir James's brow.

'I wish I could come with you. I am due to speak at a meeting at two o'clock. It is unfortunate.'

The reluctance in his tone was very evident. It was clear, on the other hand, that Julius was easily disposed to put up with the loss of the other's company.

'I guess there's nothing complicated about this deal,' he remarked. 'Just a game of hide-and-seek, that's all.'

'I hope so,' said Sir James.

235

'Sure thing. What else could it be?'

'You are still young, Mr Hersheimmer. At my age you will probably have learnt one lesson: "Never underestimate your adversary."'

The gravity of his tone impressed Tommy, but had little effect upon Julius.

'You think Mr Brown might come along and take a hand! If he does, I'm ready for him.' He slapped his pocket. 'I carry a gun. Little Willie here travels round with me everywhere.' He produced a murderous-looking revolver, and tapped it affectionately before returning it to its home. 'But he won't be needed on this trip. There's nobody to put Mr Brown wise.'

The lawyer shrugged his shoulders.

'There was nobody to put Mr Brown wise to the fact that Mrs Vandemeyer meant to betray him. Nevertheless, *Mrs Vandemeyer died without speaking.*'

Julius was silenced for once, and Sir James added on a lighter note:

'I only want to put you on your guard. Goodbye, and good luck. Take no unnecessary risks once the papers are in your hands. If there is any reason to believe that you have been shadowed, destroy them at once. Good luck to you. The game is in your hands now.' He shook hands with them both.

Ten minutes later the two men were seated in a first-class carriage *en route* for Chester.

For a long time neither of them spoke. When at length Julius broke the silence, it was with a totally unexpected remark.

'Say,' he observed thoughtfully, 'did you ever make a darn fool of yourself over a girl's face?'

Tommy, after a moment's astonishment, searched his mind.

'Can't say I have,' he replied at last. 'Not that I can recollect, anyhow. Why?'

'Because for the last two months I've been making a sentimental idiot of myself over Jane! First moment I clapped eyes on her photograph my heart did all the usual stunts you read about in novels. I guess I'm ashamed to admit it, but I came over here determined to find her and fix it all up, and take her back as Mrs Julius P. Hersheimmer!'

'Oh!' said Tommy, amazed.

Julius uncrossed his legs brusquely and continued:

'Just shows what an almighty fool a man can make of himself! One look at the girl in the flesh, and I was cured!'

Feeling more tongue-tied than ever, Tommy ejaculated 'Oh!' again.

'No disparagement to Jane, mind you,' continued the other. 'She's a real nice girl, and some fellow will fall in love with her right away.'

'I thought her a very good-looking girl,' said Tommy, finding his tongue.

'Sure she is. But she's not like her photo one bit. At least I suppose she is in a way—must be—because I recognized her right off. If I'd seen her in a crowd I'd have said "There's a girl whose face I know" right away without hesitation. But there was something about that photo'—Julius shook his head, and heaved a sigh—'I guess romance is a mighty queer thing!'

'It must be,' said Tommy coldly, 'if you can come over here in love with one girl, and propose to another within a fortnight.'

Julius had the grace to look discomposed.

'Well, you see, I'd got sort of tired feeling that I'd never find Jane—and that it was all plumb foolishness anyway. And then—oh well, the French, for instance, are much more sensible in the way they look at things. They keep romance and marriage apart—'

Tommy flushed.

'Well, I'm damned! If that's—'

Julius hastened to interrupt.

'Say now, don't be hasty. I don't mean what you mean. I take it Americans have a higher opinion of morality than you have even. What I meant was that the French set about marriage in a business-like way—find two people who are suited to one another, look after the money affairs, and see the whole thing practically, and in a business-like spirit.'

'If you ask me,' said Tommy, 'we're all too damned business-like nowadays. We're always saying, "Will it pay?" The men are bad enough, and the girls are worse!'

'Cool down, son. Don't get so heated.'

'I feel heated,' said Tommy.

Julius looked at him and judged it wise to say no more.

However, Tommy had plenty of time to cool down before they reached Holyhead, and the cheerful grin had returned to his countenance as they alighted at their destination.

After consultation and with the aid of a road map, they were fairly well agreed as to direction, so were able to hire a taxi without more ado and drive out on the road leading to Treaddur Bay. They instructed the man to go slowly, and watched narrowly so as not to miss the path. They came to it not long after leaving the town, and Tommy stopped the car promptly, asked in a casual tone whether the path led down to the sea, and hearing it did paid off the man in handsome style.

A moment later the taxi was slowly chugging back to Holyhead. Tommy and Julius watched it out of sight, and then turned to the narrow path.

'It's the right one, I suppose?' asked Tommy doubtfully. 'There must be simply heaps along here.'

'Sure it is. Look at the gorse. Remember what Jane said?'

Tommy looked at the swelling hedges of golden blossom which bordered the path on either side, and was convinced.

They went down in single file, Julius leading. Twice Tommy turned his head uneasily. Julius looked back.

'What is it?'

'I don't know. I've got the wind up somehow. Keep fancying there's someone following us.'

'Can't be,' said Julius positively. 'We'd see him.'

Tommy had to admit that this was true. Nevertheless, his sense of uneasiness deepened. In spite of himself he believed in the omniscience of the enemy.

'I rather wish that fellow would come along,' said Julius. He patted his pocket. 'Little William here is just aching for exercise!'

'Do you always carry it—him—with you?' inquired Tommy with burning curiosity.

'Most always. I guess you never know what might turn up.'

Tommy kept a respectful silence. He was impressed by Little William. It seemed to remove the menace of Mr Brown farther away.

The path was now running along the side of the cliff, parallel to the sea. Suddenly Julius came to such an abrupt halt that Tommy cannoned into him.

'What's up?' he inquired.

'Look there. If that doesn't beat the band!'

Tommy looked. Standing out and half obstructing the path was a huge boulder which certainly bore a fanciful resemblance to a 'begging' terrier.

'Well,' said Tommy, refusing to share Julius's emotion, 'it's what we expected to see, isn't it?'

Julius looked at him sadly and shook his head.

'British phlegm! Sure we expected it—but it kind of rattles me, all the same, to see it sitting there just where we expected to find it!'

Tommy, whose calm was, perhaps, more assumed than natural, moved his feet impatiently.

'Push on. What about the hole?'

They scanned the cliff-side narrowly. Tommy heard himself saying idiotically:

'The gorse won't be there after all these years.'

And Julius replied solemnly:

'I guess you're right.'

Tommy suddenly pointed with a shaking hand.

'What about that crevice there?'

Julius replied in an awestricken voice:

'That's it—for sure.'

They looked at each other.

'When I was in France,' said Tommy reminiscently, 'whenever my batman failed to call me, he always said that he had come over queer. I never believed it. But whether he felt it or not, there *is* such a sensation. I've got it now! Badly!'

He looked at the rock with a kind of agonized passion.

'Damn it!' he cried. 'It's impossible! Five years! Think of it! Birds'-nesting boys, picnic parties, thousands of people passing! It can't be there! It's a hundred to one against its being there! It's against all reason!'

Indeed, he felt it to be impossible—more, perhaps, because he could not believe in his own success where so many others had failed. The thing was too easy, therefore it could not be. The hole would be empty.

Julius looked at him with a widening smile.

'I guess you're rattled now all right,' he drawled with some enjoyment. 'Well, here goes!' He thrust his hand into the crevice, and made a slight grimace. 'It's a tight fit. Jane's hand must be a few sizes smaller than mine. I don't feel anything—no—say, what's this? Gee whiz!' And with a flourish he waved aloft a small discoloured packet. 'It's the goods all right. Sewn up in oilskin. Hold it while I get my penknife.'

The unbelievable had happened. Tommy held the precious packet tenderly between his hands. They had succeeded!

'It's queer,' he murmured idly, 'you'd think the stitches would have rotted. They look just as good as new.'

241

They cut them carefully and ripped away the oilskin. Inside was a small folded sheet of paper. With trembling fingers they unfolded it. The sheet was blank! They stared at each other, puzzled.

'A dummy!' hazarded Julius. 'Was Danvers just a decoy?'

Tommy shook his head. That solution did not satisfy him. Suddenly his face cleared.

'I've got it! *Sympathetic ink!*'

'You think so?'

'Worth trying anyhow. Heat usually does the trick. Get some sticks. We'll make a fire.'

In a few minutes the little fire of twigs and leaves was blazing merrily. Tommy held the sheet of paper near the glow. The paper curled a little with the heat. Nothing more.

Suddenly Julius grasped his arm, and pointed to where characters were appearing in a faint brown colour.

'Gee whiz! You've got it! Say, that idea of yours was great. It never occurred to me.'

Tommy held the paper in position some minutes longer until he judged the heat had done its work. Then he withdrew it. A moment later he uttered a cry.

Across the sheet in neat brown printing ran the words:

WITH THE COMPLIMENTS OF MR BROWN.

CHAPTER 21

Tommy Makes a Discovery

For a moment or two they stood staring at each other stupidly, dazed with the shock. Somehow, inexplicably, Mr Brown had forestalled them. Tommy accepted defeat quietly. Not so Julius.

'How in tarnation did he get ahead of us? That's what beats me!' he ended up.

Tommy shook his head, and said dully:

'It accounts for the stitches being new. We might have guessed...'

'Never mind the darned stitches. How did he get ahead of us? We hustled all we knew. It's downright impossible for anyone to get here quicker than we did. And, anyway, how did he know? Do you reckon there was a dictaphone in Jane's room? I guess there must have been.'

But Tommy's common sense pointed out objections.

'No one could have known beforehand that she was going to be in that house—much less that particular room.'

'That's so,' admitted Julius. 'Then one of the nurses was a crook and listened at the door. How's that?'

'I don't see that it matters anyway,' said Tommy wearily. 'He may have found out some months ago, and removed the papers, then—No, by Jove, that won't wash! They'd have been published at once.'

'Sure thing they would! No, someone's got ahead of us today by an hour or so. But how they did it gets my goat.'

'I wish that chap Peel Edgerton had been with us,' said Tommy thoughtfully.

'Why?' Julius stared. 'The mischief was done when we came.'

'Yes—' Tommy hesitated. He could not explain his own feeling—the illogical idea that the K.C.'s presence would somehow have averted the catastrophe. He reverted to his former point of view. 'It's no good arguing about how it was done. The game's up. We've failed. There's only one thing for me to do.'

'What's that?'

'Get back to London as soon as possible. Mr Carter must be warned. It's only a matter of hours now before the blow falls. But, at any rate, he ought to know the worst.'

The duty was an unpleasant one, but Tommy had no intention of shirking it. He must report his failure to Mr Carter. After that his work was done. He took the midnight mail to London. Julius elected to stay the night at Holyhead.

Half an hour after arrival, haggard and pale, Tommy stood before his chief.

'I've come to report, sir. I've failed—failed badly.'

Mr Carter eyed him sharply.

'You mean that the treaty—'

'Is in the hands of Mr Brown, sir.'

'Ah!' said Mr Carter quietly. The expression on his face did not change, but Tommy caught the flicker of despair in his eyes. It convinced him as nothing else had done that the outlook was hopeless.

'Well,' said Mr Carter after a minute or two, 'we mustn't sag at the knees, I suppose. I'm glad to know definitely. We must do what we can.'

Through Tommy's mind flashed the assurance: 'It's hopeless, and he knows it's hopeless!'

The other looked up at him.

'Don't take it to heart, lad,' he said kindly. 'You did your best. You were up against one of the biggest brains of the century. And you came very near success. Remember that.'

'Thank you, sir. It's awfully decent of you.'

'I blame myself. I have been blaming myself ever since I heard this other news.'

Something in his tone attracted Tommy's attention. A new fear gripped at his heart.

'Is there—something more, sir?'

'I'm afraid so,' said Mr Carter gravely. He stretched out his hand to a sheet on the table.

'Tuppence—?' faltered Tommy.

'Read for yourself.'

The typewritten words danced before his eyes. The description of a green toque, a coat with a handkerchief in the pocket marked P.L.C. He looked an agonized question at Mr Carter. The latter replied to it:

'Washed up on the Yorkshire coast—near Ebury. I'm afraid—it looks very much like foul play.'

'My God!' gasped Tommy. '*Tuppence!* Those devils—I'll never rest till I've got even with them! I'll hunt them down! I'll—'

The pity on Mr Carter's face stopped him.

'I know what you feel like, my poor boy. But it's no good. You'll waste your strength uselessly. It may sound harsh, but my advice to you is: Cut your losses. Time's merciful. You'll forget.'

'Forget Tuppence? Never!'

Mr Carter shook his head.

'So you think now. Well, it won't bear thinking of—that brave little girl! I'm sorry about the whole business—confoundedly sorry.'

Tommy came to himself with a start.

'I'm taking up your time, sir,' he said with an effort. 'There's no need for you to blame yourself. I dare say we were a couple of young fools to take on such a job. You warned us all right. But I wish to God *I'd* been the one to get it in the neck. Goodbye, sir.'

Back at the Ritz, Tommy packed up his few belongings mechanically, his thoughts far away. He was still bewildered by the introduction of tragedy into his cheerful commonplace existence. What fun they had had together, he and Tuppence! And now—oh, he couldn't believe it—it couldn't be true! *Tuppence—dead!* Little Tuppence, brimming over with life! It was a dream, a horrible dream. Nothing more.

They brought him a note, a few kind words of sympathy from Peel Edgerton, who had read the news in the paper. (There had been a large headline: EX-V.A.D. FEARED DROWNED.) The letter ended with the offer of a post on a ranch in the Argentine, where Sir James had considerable interests.

'Kind old beggar,' muttered Tommy, as he flung it aside.

The door opened, and Julius burst in with his usual violence. He held an open newspaper in his hand.

'Say, what's all this? They seem to have got some fool idea about Tuppence.'

'It's true,' said Tommy quietly.

'You mean they've done her in?'

Tommy nodded.

'I suppose when they got the treaty she—wasn't any good to them any longer, and they were afraid to let her go.'

'Well, I'm darned!' said Julius. 'Little Tuppence. She sure was the pluckiest little girl—'

But suddenly something seemed to crack in Tommy's brain. He rose to his feet.

'Oh, get out! You don't really care, damn you! You asked her to marry you in your rotten cold-blooded way, but I *loved* her. I'd have given the soul out of my body to save her from harm. I'd have stood by without a word and let her marry you, because you could have given her the sort of time she ought to have had, and I was only a poor devil without a penny to bless himself with. But it wouldn't have been because I didn't care!'

'See here,' began Julius temperately.

'Oh, go to the devil! I can't stand your coming here and talking about "little Tuppence". Go and look after your cousin. Tuppence is my girl! I've always loved her, from the time we played together as kids. We grew up and it was just the same. I shall never forget when I was in hospital, and she came in in that ridiculous cap and apron! It was like a miracle to see the girl I loved turn up in a nurse's kit—'

But Julius interrupted him.

'A nurse's kit! Gee whiz! I must be going to Coney Hatch! I could swear I've seen Jane in a nurse's cap too. And that's plumb impossible! No, by gum, I've got it! It was her I saw talking to Whittington at that nursing home in Bournemouth. She wasn't a patient there! She was a nurse!'

'I dare say,' said Tommy angrily, 'she's probably been in with them from the start. I shouldn't wonder if she stole those papers from Danvers to begin with.'

'I'm darned if she did!' shouted Julius. 'She's my cousin, and as patriotic a girl as ever stepped.'

'I don't care a damn who she is, but get out of here!' retorted Tommy also at the top of his voice.

The young men were on the point of coming to blows. But suddenly, with an almost magical abruptness, Julius's anger abated.

'All right, son,' he said quietly, 'I'm going. I don't blame you any for what you've been saying. It's mighty lucky you did say it. I've been the most almighty blithering darned idiot that it's possible to imagine. Calm down,'—Tommy had made an impatient gesture—'I'm going right away now—going to the London and North Western Railway depot, if you want to know.'

'I don't care a damn where you're going,' growled Tommy.

As the door closed behind Julius, he returned to his suitcase.

'That's the lot,' he murmured, and rang the bell.

'Take my luggage down.'

'Yes, sir. Going away, sir?'

'I'm going to the devil,' said Tommy, regardless of the menial's feelings.

That functionary, however, merely replied respectfully:

'Yes, sir. Shall I call a taxi?'

Tommy nodded.

Where was he going? He hadn't the faintest idea. Beyond a fixed determination to get even with Mr Brown he had no plans. He had re-read Sir James's letter, and shook his head. Tuppence must be avenged. Still, it was kind of the old fellow.

'Better answer it, I suppose.' He went across to the writing-table. With the usual perversity of bedroom stationery, there were innumerable envelopes and no paper. He rang. No one came. Tommy fumed at the delay. Then he remembered that there was a good supply in Julius's sitting-room. The American had announced his immediate departure. There would be no fear of running up against him. Besides, he wouldn't mind if he did. He was beginning to be rather ashamed of the things he had said. Old Julius had taken them jolly well. He'd apologize if he found him there.

Agatha Christie

But the room was deserted. Tommy walked across to the writing-table, and opened the middle drawer. A photograph, carelessly thrust in face upwards, caught his eye. For a moment he stood rooted to the ground. Then he took it out, shut the drawer, walked slowly over to an arm-chair, and sat down still staring at the photograph in his hand.

What on earth was a photograph of the French girl Annette doing in Julius Hersheimmer's writing-table?

CHAPTER 22

In Downing Street

The Prime Minister tapped the desk in front of him with nervous fingers. His face was worn and harassed. He took up his conversation with Mr Carter at the point it had broken off.

'I don't understand,' he said. 'Do you really mean that things are not so desperate after all?'

'So this lad seems to think.'

'Let's have a look at his letter again.'

Mr Carter handed it over. It was written in a sprawling boyish hand.

Dear Mr Carter,

Something's turned up that has given me a jar. Of course I may be simply making an awful ass of myself, but I don't think so. If my conclusions are right, that girl at Manchester was just a plant. The whole thing was prearranged, sham packet and all, with the object of making us think the game was up—therefore I fancy that we must have been pretty hot on the scent.

251

I think I know who the real Jane Finn is, and I've even got an idea where the papers are. That last's only a guess, of course, but I've a sort of feeling it'll turn out right. Anyhow, I enclose it in a sealed envelope for what it's worth. I'm going to ask you not to open it until the very last moment, midnight on the 28th, in fact. You'll understand why in a minute. You see, I've figured it out that those things of Tuppence's are a plant too, and she's no more drowned than I am. The way I reason is this: as a last chance they'll let Jane Finn escape in the hope that she's been shamming this memory stunt, and that once she thinks she's free she'll go right away to the cache. Of course it's an awful risk for them to take, because she knows all about them—but they're pretty desperate to get hold of that treaty. But if they know that the papers have been recovered by us, *neither of those two girls' lives will be worth an hour's purchase. I must try and get hold of Tuppence before Jane escapes.*

I want a repeat of that telegram that was sent to Tuppence at the Ritz. Sir James Peel Edgerton said you would be able to manage that for me. He's frightfully clever.

One last thing—please have that house in Soho watched day and night.

Yours, etc.,

Thomas Beresford.

The Prime Minister looked up.

'The enclosure?'

Mr Carter smiled dryly.

'In the vaults of the Bank. I am taking no chances.'

'You don't think'—the Prime Minister hesitated a minute—'that it would be better to open it now? Surely we ought to secure the document, that is, provided the young man's guess turns out to be correct, at once. We can keep the fact of having done so quite secret.'

'Can we? I'm not so sure. There are spies all round us. Once it's known I wouldn't give that'—he snapped his fingers—'for the life of those two girls. No, the boy trusted me, and I shan't let him down.'

'Well, well, we must leave it at that, then. What's he like, this lad?'

'Outwardly, he's an ordinary clean-limbed, rather block-headed young Englishman. Slow in his mental processes. On the other hand, it's quite impossible to lead him astray through his imagination. He hasn't got any—so he's difficult to deceive. He worries things out slowly, and once he's got hold of anything he doesn't let go. The little lady's quite different. More intuition and less common sense. They make a pretty pair working together. Pace and stamina.'

'He seems confident,' mused the Prime Minister.

'Yes, and that's what gives me hope. He's the kind of diffident youth who would have to be *very* sure before he ventured an opinion at all.'

A half smile came to the other's lips.

'And it is this—boy who will defeat the master criminal of our time?'

'This—boy, as you say! But I sometimes fancy I see a shadow behind.'

'You mean?'

'Peel Edgerton.'

'Peel Edgerton?' said the Prime Minister in astonishment.

'Yes. I see his hand in *this*.' He struck the open letter. 'He's there—working in the dark, silently, unobtrusively. I've always felt that if anyone was to run Mr Brown to earth, Peel Edgerton would be the man. I tell you he's on the case now, but doesn't want it known. By the way, I got rather an odd request from him the other day.'

'Yes?'

'He sent me a cutting from some American paper. It referred to a man's body found near the docks in New York about three weeks ago. He asked me to collect any information on the subject I could.'

'Well?'

Carter shrugged his shoulders.

'I couldn't get much. Young fellow about thirty-five—poorly dressed—face very badly disfigured. He was never identified.'

'And you fancy that the two matters are connected in some way?'

'Somehow I do. I may be wrong, of course.'

There was a pause, then Mr Carter continued:

'I asked him to come round here. Not that we'll get anything out of him he doesn't want to tell. His legal instincts are too strong. But there's no doubt he can throw light on one or two obscure points in young Beresford's letter. Ah, here he is!'

The two men rose to greet the newcomer. A half whimsical thought flashed across the Premier's mind. 'My successor, perhaps!'

'We've had a letter from young Beresford,' said Mr Carter, coming to the point at once. 'You've seen him, I suppose?'

'You suppose wrong,' said the lawyer.

'Oh!' Mr Carter was a little nonplussed.

Sir James smiled, and stroked his chin.

'He rang me up,' he volunteered.

'Would you have any objection to telling us exactly what passed between you?'

'Not at all. He thanked me for a certain letter which I had written to him—as a matter of fact, I had offered him a job. Then he reminded me of something I had said to him at Manchester respecting that bogus telegram which lured Miss Cowley away. I asked him if anything untoward had occurred. He said it had—that in a drawer in Mr Hersheimmer's room he had discovered a photograph.' The lawyer paused, then continued: 'I asked him if the photograph bore the name and address of a Californian photographer. He replied: "You're on to it, sir. It had." Then he went on to tell me something I *didn't* know. The original of that photograph was the French girl, Annette, who saved his life.'

'What?'

'Exactly. I asked the young man with some curiosity what he had done with the photograph. He replied that he had put it back where he found it.' The lawyer paused again. 'That was good, you know—distinctly good. He can use his brains, that young fellow. I congratulated him. The discovery was a providential one. Of course, from the moment that the girl in Manchester was proved to be a plant everything was altered. Young Beresford saw that for himself without my having to tell it him. But he felt he couldn't trust his judgment on the subject of Miss Cowley. Did I think she was alive? I told him, duly weighing the evidence, that there was a very decided chance in favour of it. That brought us back to the telegram.'

'Yes?'

'I advised him to apply to you for a copy of the original wire. It had occurred to me as probable that, after Miss Cowley flung it on the floor, certain words might have been erased and altered with the express intention of setting searchers on a false trail.'

Carter nodded. He took a sheet from his pocket, and read aloud:

Come at once, Astley Priors, Gatehouse, Kent. Great developments—Tommy.

'Very simple,' said Sir James, 'and very ingenious. Just a few words to alter, and the thing was done. And the one important clue they overlooked.'

'What was that?'

'The page-boy's statement that Miss Cowley drove to Charing Cross. They were so sure of themselves that they took it for granted he had made a mistake.'

'Then young Beresford is now?'

'At Gatehouse, Kent, unless I am much mistaken.'

Mr Carter looked at him curiously.

'I rather wonder you're not there too, Peel Edgerton?'

'Ah, I'm busy on a case.'

'I thought you were on your holiday?'

'Oh, I've not been briefed. Perhaps it would be more correct to say I'm preparing a case. Any more facts about that American chap for me?'

'I'm afraid not. Is it important to find out who he was?'

'Oh, I know who he was,' said Sir James easily. 'I can't prove it yet—but I know.'

The other two asked no questions. They had an instinct that it would be mere waste of breath.

'But what I don't understand,' said the Prime Minister suddenly, 'is how that photograph came to be in Mr Hersheimmer's drawer?'

'Perhaps it never left it,' suggested the lawyer gently.

'But the bogus inspector? Inspector Brown?'

'Ah!' said Sir James thoughtfully. He rose to his feet. 'I mustn't keep you. Go on with the affairs of the nation. I must get back to—my case.'

Two days later Julius Hersheimmer returned from Manchester. A note from Tommy lay on his table:

Dear Hersheimmer,

Sorry I lost my temper. In case I don't see you again, goodbye. I've been offered a job in the Argentine, and might as well take it.

Yours,

Tommy Beresford.

A peculiar smile lingered for a moment on Julius's face. He threw the letter into the waste-paper basket.

'The darned fool!' he murmured.

CHAPTER 23

A Race Against Time

After ringing up Sir James, Tommy's next procedure was to make a call at South Audley Mansions. He found Albert discharging his professional duties, and introduced himself without more ado as a friend of Tuppence's. Albert unbent immediately.

'Things has been very quiet here lately,' he said wistfully. 'Hope the young lady's keeping well, sir?'

'That's just the point, Albert. She's disappeared.'

'You don't mean as the crooks have got her?'

'They have.'

'In the Underworld?'

'No, dash it all, in this world!'

'It's a h'expression, sir,' explained Albert. 'At the pictures the crooks always have a restoorant in the Underworld. But do you think as they've done her in, sir?'

'I hope not. By the way, have you by any chance an aunt, a cousin, grandmother, or any other suitable female relation who might be represented as being likely to kick the bucket?'

A delighted grin spread slowly over Albert's countenance.

'I'm on, sir. My poor aunt what lives in the country has been mortal bad for a long time, and she's asking for me with her dying breath.'

Tommy nodded approval.

'Can you report this in the proper quarter and meet me at Charing Cross in an hour's time?'

'I'll be there, sir. You can count on me.'

As Tommy had judged, the faithful Albert proved an invaluable ally. The two took up their quarters at the inn in Gatehouse. To Albert fell the task of collecting information. There was no difficulty about it.

Astley Priors was the property of a Dr Adams. The doctor no longer practised, had retired, the landlord believed, but he took a few private patients—here the good fellow tapped his forehead knowingly—'Balmy ones! You understand!' The doctor was a popular figure in the village, subscribed freely to all the local sports—'a very pleasant affable gentleman.' Been there long? Oh, a matter of ten years or so—might be longer. Scientific gentleman, he was. Professors and people often came down from town to see him. Anyway, it was a gay house, always visitors.

In the face of all this volubility, Tommy felt doubts. Was it possible that this genial, well-known figure could be in reality a dangerous criminal? His life seemed so open and above-board. No hint of sinister doings. Suppose it was all a gigantic mistake? Tommy felt a cold chill at the thought.

Then he remembered the private patients—'balmy ones.' He inquired carefully if there was a young lady amongst them, describing Tuppence. But nothing much seemed to be known about the patients—they were seldom seen outside the grounds. A guarded description of Annette also failed to provoke recognition.

Astley Priors was a pleasant red-brick edifice, surrounded by well-wooded grounds which effectually shielded the house from observation from the road.

On the first evening Tommy, accompanied by Albert, explored the grounds. Owing to Albert's insistence they dragged themselves along painfully on their stomachs, thereby producing a great deal more noise than if they had stood upright. In any case, these precautions were totally unnecessary. The grounds, like those of any other private house after nightfall, seemed untenanted. Tommy had imagined a possible fierce watchdog. Albert's fancy ran to a puma, or a tame cobra. But they reached a shrubbery near the house quite unmolested.

The blinds of the dining-room window were up. There was a large company assembled round the table. The port was passing from hand to hand. It seemed a normal, pleasant company. Through the open window scraps of conversation floated out disjointedly on the night air. It was a heated discussion on county cricket!

Again Tommy felt that cold chill of uncertainty. It seemed impossible to believe that these people were other than they seemed. Had he been fooled once more? The fair-bearded, spectacled gentleman who sat at the head of the table looked singularly honest and normal.

Tommy slept badly that night. The following morning the indefatigable Albert, having cemented an alliance with the greengrocer's boy, took the latter's place and ingratiated himself with the cook at Malthouse. He returned with the information that she was undoubtedly 'one of the crooks,' but Tommy mistrusted the vividness of his imagination. Questioned, he could adduce nothing in support of his statement except his own opinion that she wasn't the usual kind. You could see that at a glance.

The substitution being repeated (much to the pecuniary advantage of the real greengrocer's boy) on the following day, Albert brought back the first piece of hopeful news. There *was* a French young lady staying in the house. Tommy put his doubts aside. Here was confirmation of his theory. But time pressed. Today was the 27th. The 29th was the much-talked-of 'Labour Day,' about which all sorts of rumours were running riot. Newspapers were getting agitated. Sensational hints of a Labour *coup d'état* were freely reported. The Government said nothing. It knew and was prepared. There were rumours of dissension among the Labour leaders. They were not of one mind. The more far-seeing among them realized that what they proposed might well be a death-blow to the England that at heart they loved. They shrank from the starvation and misery a general strike would entail, and were willing to meet the Government half-way. But behind them were subtle, insistent forces at work, urging the memories of old wrongs, deprecating the weakness of half-and-half measures, fomenting misunderstandings.

Tommy felt that, thanks to Mr Carter, he understood the position fairly accurately. With the fatal document in the hands of Mr Brown, public opinion would swing to the side of the Labour extremists and revolutionists. Failing that, the battle was an even chance. The Government with a loyal army and police force behind them might win—but at a cost of great suffering. But Tommy nourished another and a preposterous dream. With Mr Brown unmasked and captured he believed, rightly or wrongly, that the whole organization would crumble ignominiously and instantaneously. The strange permeating influence of the unseen chief held it together. Without him, Tommy believed an instant panic would set in; and, the honest men left to themselves, an eleventh-hour reconciliation would be possible.

'This is a one-man show,' said Tommy to himself. 'The thing to do is to get hold of the man.'

It was partly in furtherance of this ambitious design that he had requested Mr Carter not to open the sealed envelope. The draft treaty was Tommy's bait. Every now and then he was aghast at his own presumption. How dared he think that he had discovered what so many wiser and cleverer men had overlooked? Nevertheless, he stuck tenaciously to his idea.

That evening he and Albert once more penetrated the grounds of Astley Priors. Tommy's ambition was somehow or other to gain admission to the house itself. As they approached cautiously, Tommy gave a sudden gasp.

On the second-floor window someone standing between the window and the light in the room threw a silhouette on the blind. It was one Tommy would have recognized anywhere! Tuppence was in that house!

He clutched Albert by the shoulder.

'Stay here! When I begin to sing, watch that window.'

He retreated hastily to a position on the main drive, and began in a deep roar, coupled with an unsteady gait, the following ditty:

'I am a soldier
A jolly British soldier;
You can see that I'm a soldier by my feet...'

It had been a favourite on the gramophone in Tuppence's hospital days. He did not doubt but that she would recognize it and draw her own conclusions. Tommy had not a note of music in his voice, but his lungs were excellent. The noise he produced was terrific.

Presently an unimpeachable butler, accompanied by an equally unimpeachable footman, issued from the front door. The butler remonstrated with him. Tommy continued to sing, addressing the butler affectionately as 'dear old whiskers'. The footman took him by one arm, the butler by the other. They ran him down the drive, and neatly out of the gate. The butler threatened him with the police if he intruded again. It was beautifully done—soberly and with perfect decorum. Anyone would have sworn that the butler was a real butler, the footman a real footman—only, as it happened, the butler was Whittington!

Tommy retired to the inn and waited for Albert's return. At last that worthy made his appearance.

'Well?' cried Tommy eagerly.

'It's all right. While they was a-running of you out the window opened, and something was chucked out.' He handed a scrap of paper to Tommy. 'It was wrapped round a letter-weight.'

On the paper were scrawled three words: 'Tomorrow—same time.'

'Good egg!' cried Tommy. 'We're getting going.'

'I wrote a message on a piece of paper, wrapped it round a stone, and chucked it through the window,' continued Albert breathlessly.

Tommy groaned.

'Your zeal will be the undoing of us, Albert. What did you say?'

'Said we was a-staying at the inn. If she could get away, to come there and croak like a frog.'

'She'll know that's you,' said Tommy with a sigh of relief. 'Your imagination runs away with you, you know, Albert. Why, you wouldn't recognize a frog croaking if you heard it.'

Albert looked rather crestfallen.

'Cheer up,' said Tommy. 'No harm done. That butler's an old friend of mine—I bet he knew who I was, though he didn't let on. It's not their game to show suspicion. That's why we've found it fairly plain sailing. They don't want to discourage me altogether. On the other hand, they don't want to make it too easy. I'm a pawn in their game, Albert, that's what I am. You see, if the spider lets the fly walk out too easily, the fly might suspect it was a put-up job. Hence the usefulness of that promising youth, Mr T. Beresford, who's blundered in just at the right moment for them. But later, Mr T. Beresford had better look out!'

Tommy retired for the night in a state of some elation. He had elaborated a careful plan for the following evening.

He felt sure that the inhabitants of Astley Priors would not interfere with him up to a certain point. It was after that that Tommy proposed to give them a surprise.

About twelve o'clock, however, his calm was rudely shaken. He was told that someone was demanding him in the bar. The applicant proved to be a rude-looking carter well coated with mud.

'Well, my good fellow, what is it?' asked Tommy.

'Might this be for you, sir?' The carter held out a very dirty folded note, on the outside of which was written: 'Take this to the gentleman at the inn near Astley Priors. He will give you ten shillings.'

The handwriting was Tuppence's. Tommy appreciated her quick-wittedness in realizing that he might be staying at the inn under an assumed name. He snatched at it.

'That's all right.'

The man withheld it.

'What about my ten shillings?'

Tommy hastily produced a ten-shilling note, and the man relinquished his find. Tommy unfastened it.

Dear Tommy,

I knew it was you last night. Don't go this evening. They'll be lying in wait for you. They're taking us away this morning. I heard something about Wales—Holyhead, I think. I'll drop this on the road if I get a chance. Annette told me how you'd escaped. Buck up.

Yours,

Twopence.

Tommy raised a shout for Albert before he had even finished perusing this characteristic epistle.

'Pack my bag! We're off !'

'Yes, sir.' The boots of Albert could be heard racing upstairs.

Holyhead? Did that mean that, after all—Tommy was puzzled. He read on slowly.

The boots of Albert continued to be active on the floor above.

Suddenly a second shout came from below.

'Albert! I'm a damned fool! Unpack that bag!'

'Yes, sir.'

Tommy smoothed out the note thoughtfully.

'Yes, a damned fool,' he said softly. 'But so's someone else! And at last I know who it is!'

CHAPTER 24

Julius Takes a Hand

In his suite at Claridge's, Kramenin reclined on a couch and dictated to his secretary in sibilant Russian.

Presently the telephone at the secretary's elbow purred, and he took up the receiver, spoke for a minute or two, then turned to his employer.

'Someone below is asking for you.'

'Who is it?'

'He gives the name of Mr Julius P. Hersheimmer.'

'Hersheimmer,' repeated Kramenin thoughtfully. 'I have heard that name before.'

'His father was one of the steel kings of America,' explained the secretary, whose business it was to know everything. 'This young man must be a millionaire several times over.'

The other's eyes narrowed appreciatively.

'You had better go down and see him, Ivan. Find out what he wants.'

The secretary obeyed, closing the door noiselessly behind him. In a few minutes he returned.

267

'He declines to state his business—says it is entirely private and personal, and that he must see you.'

'A millionaire several times over,' murmured Kramenin. 'Bring him up, my dear Ivan.'

The secretary left the room once more, and returned escorting Julius.

'Monsieur Kramenin?' said the latter abruptly.

The Russian, studying him attentively with his pale venomous eyes, bowed.

'Pleased to meet you,' said the American. 'I've got some very important business I'd like to talk over with you, if I can see you alone.' He looked pointedly at the other.

'My secretary, Monsieur Grieber, from whom I have no secrets.'

'That may be so—but I have,' said Julius dryly. 'So I'd be obliged if you'd tell him to scoot.'

'Ivan,' said the Russian softly, 'perhaps you would not mind retiring into the next room—'

'The next room won't do,' interrupted Julius. 'I know these ducal suites—and I want this one plumb empty except for you and me. Send him round to a store to buy a penn'orth of peanuts.'

Though not particularly enjoying the American's free and easy manner of speech, Kramenin was devoured by curiosity.

'Will your business take long to state?'

'Might be an all night job if you caught on.'

'Very good. Ivan, I shall not require you again this evening. Go to the theatre—take a night off.'

'Thank you, your excellency.'

268

The secretary bowed and departed.

Julius stood at the door watching his retreat. Finally, with a satisfied sigh, he closed it, and came back to his position in the centre of the room.

'Now, Mr Hersheimmer, perhaps you will be so kind as to come to the point?'

'I guess that won't take a minute,' drawled Julius. Then, with an abrupt change of manner: 'Hands up—or I shoot!'

For a moment Kramenin stared blindly into the big revolver, then, with almost comical haste, he flung up his hands above his head. In that instant Julius had taken his measure. The man he had to deal with was an abject physical coward—the rest would be easy.

'This is an outrage,' cried the Russian in a high hysterical voice. 'An outrage! Do you mean to kill me?'

'Not if you keep your voice down. Don't go edging sideways towards that bell. That's better.'

'What do you want? Do nothing rashly. Remember my life is of the utmost value to my country. I may have been maligned—'

'I reckon,' said Julius, 'that the man who let daylight into you would be doing humanity a good turn. But you needn't worry any. I'm not proposing to kill you this trip—that is, if you're reasonable.'

The Russian quailed before the stern menace in the other's eyes. He passed his tongue over his dry lips.

'What do you want? Money?'

'No. I want Jane Finn.'

'Jane Finn? I—never heard of her!'

269

'You're a darned liar! You know perfectly who I mean.'

'I tell you I've never heard of the girl.'

'And I tell you,' retorted Julius, 'that Little Willie here is just hopping mad to go off!'

The Russian wilted visibly.

'You wouldn't dare—'

'Oh, yes I would, son!'

Kramenin must have recognized something in the voice that carried conviction, for he said sullenly:

'Well? Granted I do know who you mean—what of it?'

'You will tell me now—right here—where she is to be found.'

Kramenin shook his head.

'I daren't.'

'Why not?'

'I daren't. You ask an impossibility.'

'Afraid, eh? Of whom? Mr Brown? Ah, that tickles you up! There is such a person, then? I doubted it. And the mere mention of him scares you stiff !'

'I have seen him,' said the Russian slowly. 'Spoken to him face to face. I did not know it until afterwards. He was one of the crowd. I should not know him again. Who is he really? I do not know. But I know this—he is a man to fear.'

'He'll never know,' said Julius.

'He knows everything—and his vengeance is swift. Even I—Kramenin!—would not be exempt!'

'Then you won't do as I ask you?'

'You ask an impossibility.'

'Sure that's a pity for you,' said Julius cheerfully. 'But the world in general will benefit.' He raised the revolver.

'Stop,' shrieked the Russian. 'You cannot mean to shoot me?'

'Of course I do. I've always heard you Revolutionists held life cheap, but it seems there's a difference when it's your own life in question. I gave you just one chance of saving your dirty skin, and that you wouldn't take!'

'They would kill me!'

'Well,' said Julius pleasantly, 'it's up to you. But I'll just say this. Little Willie here is a dead cert, and if I was you I'd take a sporting chance with Mr Brown!'

'You will hang if you shoot me,' muttered the Russian irresolutely.

'No, stranger, that's where you're wrong. You forget the dollars. A big crowd of solicitors will get busy, and they'll get some high-brow doctors on the job, and the end of it all will be that they'll say my brain was unhinged. I shall spend a few months in a quiet sanatorium, my mental health will improve, the doctors will declare me sane again, and all will end happily for little Julius. I guess I can bear a few months' retirement in order to rid the world of you, but don't you kid yourself I'll hang for it!'

The Russian believed him. Corrupt himself, he believed implicitly in the power of money. He had read of American murder trials running much on the lines indicated by Julius. He had bought and sold justice himself. This virile young American with the significant drawling voice, had the whip hand of him.

'I'm going to count five,' continued Julius, 'and I guess, if you let me get past four, you needn't worry any about

271

Mr Brown. Maybe he'll send some flowers to the funeral, but *you* won't smell them! Are you ready? I'll begin. One—two—three—four—'

The Russian interrupted with a shriek:

'Do not shoot. I will do all you wish.'

Julius lowered the revolver.

'I thought you'd hear sense. Where is the girl?'

'At Gatehouse, in Kent. Astley Priors, the place is called.'

'Is she a prisoner there?'

'She's not allowed to leave the house—though it's safe enough really. The little fool has lost her memory, curse her!'

'That's been annoying for you and your friends, I reckon. What about the other girl, the one you decoyed away over a week ago?'

'She's there too,' said the Russian sullenly.

'That's good,' said Julius. 'Isn't it all panning out beautifully? And a lovely night for the run!'

'What run?' demanded Kramenin, with a stare.

'Down to Gatehouse, sure. I hope you're fond of motoring?'

'What do you mean? I refuse to go.'

'Now don't get mad. You must see I'm not such a kid as to leave you here. You'd ring up your friends on that telephone first thing! Ah!' He observed the fall on the other's face. 'You see, you'd got it all fixed. No, sir, you're coming along with me. This your bedroom next door here? Walk right in. Little Willie and I will come behind. Put on a thick coat, that's right. Fur lined? And you a Socialist! Now we're ready. We walk downstairs and out through the hall to where my car's waiting. And don't you forget I've got you covered every inch of the way. I can shoot just as well through my coat pocket. One word or a glance even, at one of those liveried menials, and there'll sure be a strange face in the Sulphur and Brimstone Works!'

Together they descended the stairs, and passed out to the waiting car. The Russian was shaking with rage. The hotel servants surrounded them. A cry hovered on his lips, but at the last minute his nerve failed him. The American was a man of his word.

When they reached the car, Julius breathed a sigh of relief, the danger-zone was passed. Fear had successfully hypnotized the man by his side.

'Get in,' he ordered. Then as he caught the other's side-long glance, 'No, the chauffeur won't help you any. Naval man. Was on a submarine in Russia when the Revolution broke out. A brother of his was murdered by your people. George!'

'Yes, sir?' The chauffeur turned his head.

'This gentleman is a Russian Bolshevik. We don't want to shoot him, but it may be necessary. You understand?'

'Perfectly, sir.'

'I want to go to Gatehouse in Kent. Know the road at all?'

'Yes, sir, it will be about an hour and a half's run.'

'Make it an hour. I'm in a hurry.'

'I'll do my best, sir.' The car shot forward through the traffic.

Julius ensconced himself comfortably by the side of his victim. He kept his hand in the pocket of his coat, but his manner was urbane to the last degree.

'There was a man I shot once in Arizona—' he began cheerfully.

273

At the end of the hour's run the unfortunate Kramenin was more dead than alive. In succession to the anecdote of the Arizona man, there had been a tough from 'Frisco, and an episode in the Rockies. Julius's narrative style, if not strictly accurate, was picturesque!

Slowing down, the chauffeur called over his shoulder that they were just coming into Gatehouse. Julius bade the Russian direct them. His plan was to drive straight up to the house. There Kramenin was to ask for the two girls. Julius explained to him that Little Willie would not be tolerant of failure. Kramenin, by this time, was as putty in the other's hand. The terrific pace they had come had still further unmanned him. He had given himself up for dead at every corner.

The car swept up the drive, and stopped before the porch. The chauffeur looked round for orders.

'Turn the car first, George. Then ring the bell, and get back to your place. Keep the engine going, and be ready to scoot like hell when I give the word.'

'Very good, sir.'

The front door was opened by the butler. Kramenin felt the muzzle of the revolver pressed against his ribs.

'Now,' hissed Julius. 'And be careful.'

The Russian beckoned. His lips were white, and his voice was not very steady:

'It is I—Kramenin! Bring down the girl at once! There is no time to lose!'

Whittington had come down the steps. He uttered an exclamation of astonishment at seeing the other.

'You! What's up? Surely you know the plan—'

Kramenin interrupted him, using the words that have created many unnecessary panics:

'We have been betrayed! Plans must be abandoned. We must save our own skins. The girl! And at once! It's our only chance.'

Whittington hesitated, but for hardly a moment.

'You have orders—from *him?*'

'Naturally! Should I be here otherwise? Hurry! There is no time to be lost. The other little fool had better come too.'

Whittington turned and ran back into the house. The agonizing minutes went by. Then—two figures hastily huddled in cloaks appeared on the steps and were hustled into the car. The smaller of the two was inclined to resist and Whittington shoved her in unceremoniously. Julius leaned forward, and in doing so the light from the open door lit up his face. Another man on the steps behind Whittington gave a startled exclamation. Concealment was at an end.

'Get a move on, George,' shouted Julius.

The chauffeur slipped in his clutch, and with a bound the car started.

The man on the steps uttered an oath. His hand went to his pocket. There was a flash and a report. The bullet just missed the taller girl by an inch.

'Get down, Jane,' cried Julius. 'Flat on the bottom of the car.' He thrust her sharply forward, then standing up, he took careful aim and fired.

'Have you hit him?' cried Tuppence eagerly.

'Sure,' replied Julius. 'He isn't killed, though. Skunks like that take a lot of killing. Are you all right, Tuppence?'

'Of course I am. Where's Tommy? And who's this?' She indicated the shivering Kramenin.

'Tommy's making tracks for the Argentine. I guess he thought you'd turned up your toes. Steady through the gate, George! That's right. It'll take 'em at least five minutes to get busy after us. They'll use the telephone, I guess, so look out for snares ahead—and don't take the direct route. Who's this, did you say, Tuppence? Let me present Monsieur Kramenin. I persuaded him to come on the trip for his health.'

The Russian remained mute, still livid with terror.

'But what made them let us go?' demanded Tuppence suspiciously.

'I reckon Monsieur Kramenin here asked them so prettily they just couldn't refuse!'

This was too much for the Russian. He burst out vehemently:

'Curse you—curse you! They know now that I betrayed them. My life won't be safe for an hour in this country.'

'That's so,' assented Julius. 'I'd advise you to make tracks for Russia right away.'

'Let me go, then,' cried the other. 'I have done what you asked. Why do you still keep me with you?'

'Not for the pleasure of your company. I guess you can get right off now if you want to. I thought you'd rather I tooled you back to London.'

'You may never reach London,' snarled the other. 'Let me go here and now.'

'Sure thing. Pull up, George. The gentleman's not making the return trip. If I ever come to Russia, Monsieur Kramenin, I shall expect a rousing welcome and—'

But before Julius had finished his speech, and before the car had finally halted, the Russian had swung himself out and disappeared into the night.

'Just a mite impatient to leave us,' commented Julius, as the car gathered way again. 'And no idea of saying goodbye politely to the ladies. Say, Jane, you can get up on the seat now.'

For the first time the girl spoke.

'How did you "persuade" him?' she asked.

Julius tapped his revolver.

'Little Willie here takes the credit!'

'Splendid!' cried the girl. The colour surged into her face, her eyes looked admiringly at Julius.

'Annette and I didn't know what was going to happen to us,' said Tuppence. 'Old Whittington hurried us off. We thought it was lambs to the slaughter.'

'Annette,' said Julius. 'Is that what you call her?'

His mind seemed to be trying to adjust itself to a new idea.

'It's her name,' said Tuppence, opening her eyes very wide.

'Shucks!' retorted Julius. 'She may think it's her name, because her memory's gone, poor kid. But it's the one real and original Jane Finn we've got here.'

'What—?' cried Tuppence.

But she was interrupted. With an angry spurt, a bullet embedded itself in the upholstery of the car just behind her head.

277

Agatha Christie

'Down with you,' cried Julius. 'It's an ambush. These guys have got busy pretty quickly. Push her a bit, George.'

The car fairly leapt forward. Three more shots rang out, but went happily wide. Julius, upright, leant over the back of the car.

'Nothing to shoot at,' he announced gloomily. 'But I guess there'll be another little picnic soon. Ah!'

He raised his hand to his cheek.

'You are hurt?' said Annette quickly.

'Only a scratch.'

The girl sprang to her feet.

'Let me out! Let me out, I say! Stop the car. It is me they're after. I'm the one they want. You shall not lose your lives because of me. Let me go.' She was fumbling with the fastenings of the door.

Julius took her by both arms, and looked at her. She had spoken with no trace of foreign accent.

'Sit down, kid,' he said gently. 'I guess there's nothing wrong with your memory. Been fooling them all the time, eh?'

The girl looked at him, nodded, and then suddenly burst into tears. Julius patted her on the shoulder.

'There, there—just you sit tight. We're not going to let you quit.'

Through her sobs the girl said indistinctly:

'You're from home. I can tell by your voice. It makes me homesick.'

'Sure I'm from home. I'm your cousin—Julius Hersheimmer. I came over to Europe on purpose to find you—and a pretty dance you've led me.'

278

The car slackened speed. George spoke over his shoulder:

'Crossroads here, sir. I'm not sure of the way.'

The car slowed down till it hardly moved. As it did so a figure climbed suddenly over the back, and plunged head first into the midst of them.

'Sorry,' said Tommy, extricating himself.

A mass of confused exclamations greeted him. He replied to them severally:

'Was in the bushes by the drive. Hung on behind. Couldn't let you know before at the pace you were going. It was all I could do to hang on. Now then, you girls, get out!'

'Get out?'

'Yes. There's a station just up that road. Train due in three minutes. You'll catch it if you hurry.'

'What the devil are you driving at?' demanded Julius. 'Do you think you can fool them by leaving the car?'

'You and I aren't going to leave the car. Only the girls.'

'You're crazed, Beresford. Stark staring mad! You can't let those girls go off alone. It'll be the end of it if you do.'

Tommy turned to Tuppence.

'Get out at once, Tuppence. Take her with you, and do just as I say. No one will do you any harm. You're safe. Take the train to London. Go straight to Sir James Peel Edgerton. Mr Carter lives out of town, but you'll be safe with him.'

'Darn you!' cried Julius. 'You're mad. Jane, you stay where you are.'

With a sudden swift movement, Tommy snatched the revolver from Julius's hand, and levelled it at him.

'Now will you believe I'm in earnest? Get out, both of you, and do as I say—or I'll shoot!'

Tuppence sprang out, dragging the unwilling Jane after her.

'Come on, it's all right. If Tommy's sure—he's sure. Be quick. We'll miss the train.'

They started running.

Julius's pent-up rage burst forth.

'What the hell—'

Tommy interrupted him.

'Dry up! I want a few words with you, Mr Julius Hersheimmer.'

CHAPTER 25

Jane's Story

Her arm through Jane's, dragging her along, Tuppence reached the station. Her quick ears caught the sound of the approaching train.

'Hurry up,' she panted, 'or we'll miss it.'

They arrived on the platform just as the train came to a standstill. Tuppence opened the door of an empty first-class compartment, and the two girls sank down breathless on the padded seats.

A man looked in, then passed on to the next carriage. Jane started nervously. Her eyes dilated with terror. She looked questioningly at Tuppence.

'Is he one of them, do you think?' she breathed.

Tuppence shook her head.

'No, no. It's all right.' She took Jane's hand in hers. 'Tommy wouldn't have told us to do this unless he was sure we'd be all right.'

'But he doesn't know them as I do!' The girl shivered. 'You can't understand. Five years! Five long years!

281

Sometimes I thought I should go mad.'

'Never mind. It's all over.'

'Is it?'

The train was moving now, speeding through the night at a gradually increasing rate. Suddenly Jane Finn started up.

'What was that? I thought I saw a face—looking in through the window.'

'No, there's nothing. See.' Tuppence went to the window, and lifting the strap let the pane down.

'You're sure?'

'Quite sure.'

The other seemed to feel some excuse was necessary:

'I guess I'm acting like a frightened rabbit, but I can't help it. If they caught me now they'd—' Her eyes opened wide and staring.

'*Don't* !' implored Tuppence. 'Lie back, and *don't think*. You can be quite sure that Tommy wouldn't have said it was safe if it wasn't.'

'My cousin didn't think so. He didn't want us to do this.'

'No,' said Tuppence, rather embarrassed.

'What are you thinking of ?' said Jane sharply.

'Why?'

'Your voice was so—queer!'

'I *was* thinking of something,' confessed Tuppence. 'But I don't want to tell you—not now. I may be wrong, but I don't think so. It's just an idea that came into my head a long time ago. Tommy's got it too—I'm almost sure he has. But don't *you* worry—there'll be time enough for that

282

later. And it mayn't be so at all! Do what I tell you—lie back and don't think of anything.'

'I'll try.' The long lashes drooped over the hazel eyes.

Tuppence, for her part, sat bolt upright—much in the attitude of a watchful terrier on guard. In spite of herself she was nervous. Her eyes flashed continually from one window to the other. She noted the exact position of the communication cord. What it was that she feared, she would have been hard put to it to say. But in her own mind she was far from feeling the confidence displayed in her words. Not that she disbelieved in Tommy, but occasionally she was shaken with doubts as to whether anyone so simple and honest as he was could ever be a match for the fiendish subtlety of the arch-criminal.

If they once reached Sir James Peel Edgerton in safety, all would be well. But would they reach him? Would not the silent forces of Mr Brown already be assembling against them? Even that last picture of Tommy, revolver in hand, failed to comfort her. By now he might be overpowered, borne down by sheer force of numbers... Tuppence mapped out her plan of campaign.

As the train at length drew slowly into Charing Cross, Jane Finn sat up with a start.

'Have we arrived? I never thought we should!'

'Oh, I thought we'd get to London all right. If there's going to be any fun, now is when it will begin. Quick, get out. We'll nip into a taxi.'

In another minute they were passing the barrier, had paid the necessary fares, and were stepping into a taxi.

Agatha Christie

'King's Cross,' directed Tuppence. Then she gave a jump. A man looked in at the window, just as they started. She was almost certain it was the same man who had got into the carriage next to them. She had a horrible feeling of being slowly hemmed in on every side.

'You see,' she explained to Jane, 'if they think we're going to Sir James, this will put them off the scent. Now they'll imagine we're going to Mr Carter. His country place is north of London somewhere.'

Crossing Holborn there was a block, and the taxi was held up. This was what Tuppence had been waiting for.

'Quick,' she whispered. 'Open the right-hand door!'

The two girls stepped out into the traffic. Two minutes later they were seated in another taxi and were retracing their steps, this time direct to Carlton House Terrace.

'There,' said Tuppence, with great satisfaction, 'this ought to do them. I can't help thinking that I'm really rather clever! How that other taxi man will swear! But I took his number, and I'll send him a postal order tomorrow, so that he won't lose by it if he happens to be genuine. What's this thing swerving—Oh!'

There was a grinding noise and a bump. Another taxi had collided with them.

In a flash Tuppence was out on the pavement. A policeman was approaching. Before he arrived Tuppence had handed the driver five shillings, and she and Jane had merged themselves in the crowd.

'It's only a step or two now,' said Tuppence breathlessly. The accident had taken place in Trafalgar Square.

'Do you think the collision was an accident, or done deliberately?'

'I don't know. It might have been either.'

Hand-in-hand, the two girls hurried along.

'It may be my fancy,' said Tuppence suddenly, 'but I feel as though there was someone behind us.'

'Hurry!' murmured the other. 'Oh, hurry!'

They were now at the corner of Carlton House Terrace, and their spirits lightened. Suddenly a large and apparently intoxicated man barred their way.

'Good evening, ladies,' he hiccuped. 'Whither away so fast?'

'Let us pass, please,' said Tuppence imperiously.

'Just a word with your pretty friend here.' He stretched out an unsteady hand, and clutched Jane by the shoulder. Tuppence heard other footsteps behind. She did not pause to ascertain whether they were friends or foes. Lowering her head, she repeated a manœuvre of childish days, and butted their aggressor full in the capacious middle. The success of these unsportsmanlike tactics was immediate. The man sat down abruptly on the pavement. Tuppence and Jane took to their heels. The house they sought was some way down. Other footsteps echoed behind them. Their breath was coming in choking gasps as they reached Sir James's door. Tuppence seized the bell and Jane the knocker.

The man who had stopped them reached the foot of the steps. For a moment he hesitated, and as he did so the door opened. They fell into the hall together. Sir James came forward from the library door.

'Hullo! What's this?'

He stepped forward and put his arm round Jane as she swayed uncertainly. He half carried her into the library, and laid her on the leather couch. From a tantalus on the table he poured out a few drops of brandy, and forced her to drink them. With a sigh she sat up, her eyes still wild and frightened.

'It's all right. Don't be afraid, my child. You're quite safe.'

Her breath came more normally, and the colour was returning to her cheeks. Sir James looked at Tuppence quizzically.

'So you're not dead, Miss Tuppence, any more than that Tommy boy of yours was!'

'The Young Adventurers take a lot of killing,' boasted Tuppence.

'So it seems,' said Sir James dryly. 'Am I right in thinking that the joint venture has ended in success, and that this'— he turned to the girl on the couch—'is Miss Jane Finn?'

Jane sat up.

'Yes,' she said quietly, 'I am Jane Finn. I have a lot to tell you.'

'When you are stronger—'

'No—now!' Her voice rose a little. 'I shall feel safer when I have told everything.'

'As you please,' said the lawyer.

He sat down in one of the big arm-chairs facing the couch. In a low voice Jane began her story.

'I came over on the *Lusitania* to take up a post in Paris. I was fearfully keen about the war, and just dying to help somehow or other. I had been studying French, and my teacher said they were wanting help in a hospital in Paris, so I wrote and offered my services, and they were accepted. I hadn't got any folk of my own, so it made it easy to arrange things.

'When the *Lusitania* was torpedoed, a man came up to me. I'd noticed him more than once—and I'd figured it out in my own mind that he was afraid of somebody or something. He asked me if I was a patriotic American, and told me he was carrying papers which were just life or death to the Allies. He asked me to take charge of them. I was to watch for an advertisement in *The Times*. If it didn't appear, I was to take them to the American Ambassador.

'Most of what followed seems like a nightmare still. I see it in my dreams sometimes... I'll hurry over that part. Mr Danvers had told me to watch out. He might have been shadowed from New York, but he didn't think so. At first I had no suspicions, but on the boat to Holyhead I began to get uneasy. There was one woman who had been very keen to look after me, and chum up with me generally— a Mrs Vandemeyer. At first I'd been only grateful to her for being so kind to me; but all the time I felt there was something about her I didn't like, and on the Irish boat I saw her talking to some queer-looking men, and from the way they looked I saw that they were talking about me. I remembered that she'd been quite near me on the *Lusitania* when Mr Danvers gave me the packet, and before that she'd tried to talk to him once or twice. I began to get scared, but I didn't quite see what to do.

'I had a wild idea of stopping at Holyhead, and not going on to London that day, but I soon saw that would be plumb foolishness. The only thing was to act as though I'd noticed nothing, and hope for the best. I couldn't see how they could get me if I was on my guard. One thing I'd done already as a precaution—ripped open the oilskin packet and substituted blank paper, and then sewn it up again. So, if anyone did manage to rob me of it, it wouldn't matter.

'What to do with the real thing worried me no end. Finally I opened it out flat—there were only two sheets—and laid it between two of the advertisement pages of a magazine. I stuck the two pages together round the edge with some gum off an envelope. I carried the magazine carelessly stuffed into the pocket of my ulster.

'At Holyhead I tried to get into a carriage with people that looked all right, but in a queer way there seemed always to be a crowd round me shoving and pushing me just the way I didn't want to go. There was something uncanny and frightening about it. In the end I found myself in a carriage with Mrs Vandemeyer after all. I went out into the corridor, but all the other carriages were full, so I had to go back and sit down. I consoled myself with the thought that there were other people in the carriage—there was quite a nice-looking man and his wife sitting just opposite. So I felt almost happy about it until just outside London. I had leaned back and closed my eyes. I guess they thought I was asleep, but my eyes weren't quite shut, and suddenly I saw the nice-looking man get something out of his bag and hand it to Mrs Vandemeyer, and as he did so he *winked*...

'I can't tell you how that wink sort of froze me through and through. My only thought was to get out in the corridor as quick as ever I could. I got up, trying to look natural and easy. Perhaps they saw something—I don't know—but suddenly Mrs Vandemeyer said "Now," and flung something over my nose and mouth as I tried to scream. At the same moment I felt a terrific blow on the back of my head...'

She shuddered. Sir James murmured something sympathetically. In a minute she resumed:

'I don't know how long it was before I came back to consciousness. I felt very ill and sick. I was lying on a dirty bed. There was a screen round it, but I could hear two people talking in the room. Mrs Vandemeyer was one of them. I tried to listen, but at first I couldn't take much in. When at last I did begin to grasp what was going on—I was just terrified! I wonder I didn't scream right out there and then.

'They hadn't found the papers. They'd got the oil-skin packet with the blanks, and they were just mad! They didn't know whether *I'*d changed the papers, or whether Danvers had been carrying a dummy message, while the real one was sent another way. They spoke of'—she closed her eyes—'torturing me to find out!'

'I'd never known what fear—really sickening fear—was before! Once they came to look at me. I shut my eyes and pretended to be still unconscious, but I was afraid they'd hear the beating of my heart. However, they went away again. I began thinking madly. What could I do? I knew I wouldn't be able to stand up against torture very long.

'Suddenly something put the thought of loss of memory into my head. The subject had always interested me, and I'd read an awful lot about it. I had the whole thing at my finger-tips. If only I could succeed in carrying the bluff through, it might save me. I said a prayer, and drew a long breath. Then I opened my eyes and started babbling in *French*!

'Mrs Vandemeyer came round the screen at once. Her face was so wicked I nearly died, but I smiled up at her doubtfully, and asked her in French where I was.

'It puzzled her, I could see. She called the man she had been talking to. He stood by the screen with his face in shadow. He spoke to me in French. His voice was very ordinary and quiet but somehow, I don't know why, he scared me, but I went on playing my part. I asked again where I was, and then went on that there was something I *must* remember—*must* remember—*only* for the moment it was all gone. I worked myself up to be more and more distressed. He asked me my name. I said I didn't know—that I couldn't remember anything at all.

'Suddenly he caught my wrist, and began twisting it. The pain was awful. I screamed. He went on. I screamed and screamed, but I managed to shriek out things in French. I don't know how long I could have gone on, but luckily I fainted. The last thing I heard was his voice saying: "That's not bluff ! Anyway, a kid of her age wouldn't know enough." I guess he forgot American girls are older for their age than English ones, and take more interest in scientific subjects.

'When I came to, Mrs Vandemeyer was sweet as honey to me. She'd had her orders, I guess. She spoke to me in

French—told me I'd had a shock and been very ill. I should be better soon. I pretended to be rather dazed—murmured something about the "doctor" having hurt my wrist. She looked relieved when I said that.

'By and by she went out of the room altogether. I was suspicious still, and lay quite quiet for some time. In the end, however, I got up and walked round the room, examining it. I thought that even if anyone *was* watching me from somewhere, it would seem natural enough under the circumstances. It was a squalid, dirty place. There were no windows, which seemed queer. I guessed the door would be locked, but I didn't try it. There were some battered old pictures on the walls, representing scenes from *Faust*.'

Jane's two listeners gave a simultaneous 'Ah!' The girl nodded.

'Yes—it was the place in Soho where Mr Beresford was imprisoned. Of course at the time I didn't even know if I was in London. One thing was worrying me dreadfully, but my heart gave a great throb of relief when I saw my ulster lying carelessly over the back of a chair. *And the magazine was still rolled up in the pocket!*

'If only I could be certain that I was not being overlooked! I looked carefully round the walls. There didn't seem to be a peep-hole of any kind—nevertheless I felt kind of sure there must be. All of a sudden I sat down on the edge of the table, and put my face in my hands, sobbing out a "Mon Dieu! Mon Dieu!" I've got very sharp ears. I distinctly heard the rustle of a dress, and slight creak. That was enough for me. I was being watched!

291

'I lay down on the bed again, and by and by Mrs Vandemeyer brought me some supper. She was still sweet as they make them. I guess she'd been told to win my confidence. Presently she produced the oilskin packet, and asked me if I recognized it, watching me like a lynx all the time.

'I took it and turned it over in a puzzled sort of way. Then I shook my head. I said that I felt I *ought* to remember something about it, that it was just as though it was all coming back, and then, before I could get hold of it, it went again. Then she told me that I was her niece, and that I was to call her "Aunt Rita." I did obediently, and she told me not to worry—my memory would soon come back.

'That was an awful night. I'd made my plan whilst I was waiting for her. The papers were safe so far, but I couldn't take the risk of leaving them there any longer. They might throw that magazine away any minute. I lay awake waiting until I judged it must be about two o'clock in the morning. Then I got up as softly as I could, and felt in the dark along the left-hand wall. Very gently, I unhooked one of the pictures from its nail—Marguerite with her casket of jewels. I crept over to my coat and took out the magazine, and an odd envelope or two that I had shoved in. Then I went to the washstand, and damped the brown paper at the back of the picture all round. Presently I was able to pull it away. I had already torn out the two stuck-together pages from the magazine, and now I slipped them with their precious enclosure between the picture and its brown paper backing. A little gum from the envelopes helped me to stick the latter up again. No one would dream the picture had ever been tampered with. I rehung it on the wall, put the magazine back in my coat pocket, and crept back to bed. I was pleased with my hiding-place. They'd never think of pulling to pieces one of their own pictures. I hoped that they'd come to the conclusion that Danvers had been carrying a dummy all along, and that, in the end, they'd let me go.

'As a matter of fact, I guess that's what they did think at first and, in a way, it was dangerous for me. I learnt afterwards that they nearly did away with me then and there—there was never much chance of their "letting me go"—but the first man, who was the boss, preferred to keep me alive on the chance of my having hidden them, and being able to tell where if I recovered my memory. They watched me constantly for weeks. Sometimes they'd ask me questions by the hour—I guess there was nothing they didn't know about the third degree!—but somehow I managed to hold my own. The strain of it was awful, though...

'They took me back to Ireland, and over every step of the journey again, in case I'd hidden it somewhere *en route*. Mrs Vandemeyer and another woman never left me for a moment. They spoke of me as a young relative of Mrs Vandemeyer's whose mind was affected by the shock of the *Lusitania*. There was no one I could appeal to for help without giving myself away to *them*, and if I risked it and failed—and Mrs Vandemeyer looked so rich, and so beautifully dressed, that I felt convinced they'd take her word against mine, and think it was part of my mental trouble to think myself "persecuted"— I felt that the horrors in store for me would be too awful once they knew I'd been only shamming.'

Sir James nodded comprehendingly.

'Mrs Vandemeyer was a woman of great personality. With that and her social position she would have had little difficulty in imposing her point of view in preference to yours. Your sensational accusations against her would not easily have found credence.'

'That's what I thought. It ended in my being sent to a sanatorium at Bournemouth. I couldn't make up my mind at first whether it was a sham affair or genuine. A hospital nurse had charge of me. I was a special patient. She seemed so nice and normal that at last I determined to confide in her. A merciful providence just saved me in time from falling into the trap. My door happened to be ajar, and I heard her talking to someone in the passage. *She was one of them!* They still fancied it might be a bluff on my part, and she was put in charge of me to make sure! After that, my nerve went completely. I dared trust nobody.

'I think I almost hypnotized myself. After a while, I almost forgot that I was really Jane Finn. I was so bent on playing the part of Janet Vandemeyer that my nerves began to play tricks. I became really ill—for months I sank into a sort of stupor. I felt sure I should die soon, and that nothing really mattered. A sane person shut up in a lunatic asylum often ends by becoming insane, they say. I guess I was like that. Playing my part had become second nature to me. I wasn't even unhappy in the end—just apathetic. Nothing seemed to matter. And the years went on.

'And then suddenly things seemed to change. Mrs Vandemeyer came down from London. She and the doctor asked me questions, experimented with various treatments. There was some talk of sending me to a specialist in Paris. In the end, they did not dare risk it. I overheard something that seemed to show that other people—friends—were looking for me. I learnt later that the nurse who had looked after me went to Paris, and consulted a specialist, representing herself to be me. He put her through some searching tests, and exposed her loss of memory to be fraudulent; but she had taken a note of his methods and reproduced them on me. I dare say I couldn't have deceived the specialist for a minute—a man who has made a lifelong study of a thing is unique—but I managed once again to hold my own with them. The fact that I'd not thought of myself as Jane Finn for so long made it easier.

'One night I was whisked off to London at a moment's notice. They took me back to the house in Soho. Once I got away from the sanatorium I felt different—as though something in me that had been buried for a long time was waking up again.

'They sent me in to wait on Mr Beresford. (Of course I didn't know his name then.) I was suspicious—I thought it was another trap. But he looked so honest, I could hardly believe it. However I was careful in all I said, for I knew we could be overheard. There's a small hole, high up in the wall.

'But on the Sunday afternoon a message was brought to the house. They were all very disturbed. Without their knowing, I listened. Word had come that he was to be killed. I needn't tell the next part, because you know it. I thought I'd have time to rush up and get the papers from their hiding-place, but I was caught. So I screamed out that he was escaping, and I said I wanted to go back to Marguerite. I shouted the name three times very loud. I knew the others would think I meant Mrs Vandemeyer, but I hoped it might make Mr Beresford think of the picture. He'd unhooked one the first day—that's what made me hesitate to trust him.'

She paused.

'Then the papers,' said Sir James slowly, 'are still at the back of the picture in that room.'

'Yes.' The girl had sunk back on the sofa exhausted with the strain of the long story.

Sir James rose to his feet. He looked at his watch.

'Come,' he said, 'we must go at once.'

'Tonight? queried Tuppence, surprised.

'Tomorrow may be too late,' said Sir James gravely. 'Besides, by going tonight we have the chance of capturing that great man and super-criminal—Mr Brown!'

There was dead silence, and Sir James continued:

'You have been followed here—not a doubt of it. When we leave the house we shall be followed again, but not molested *for it is Mr Brown's plan that we are to lead him*. But the Soho house is under police supervision night and day. There are several men watching it. When we enter that house, Mr Brown will not draw back—he will risk all, on the chance of obtaining the spark to fire his mine. And he fancies the risk not great—since he will enter in the guise of a friend!'

Tuppence flushed, then opened her mouth impulsively.

'But there's something you don't know—that we haven't told you.' Her eyes dwelt on Jane in perplexity.

'What is that?' asked the other sharply. 'No hesitations, Miss Tuppence. We need to be sure of our going.'

But Tuppence, for once, seemed tongue-tied.

'It's so difficult—you see, if I'm wrong—oh, it would be dreadful.' She made a grimace at the unconscious Jane. 'Never forgive me,' she observed cryptically.

'You want me to help you out, eh?'

'Yes, please. *You* know who Mr Brown is, don't you?'

'Yes,' said Sir James gravely. 'At last I do.'

'At last?' queried Tuppence doubtfully. 'Oh, but I thought—' She paused.

'You thought correctly, Miss Tuppence. I have been morally certain of his identity for some time—ever since the night of Mrs Vandemeyer's mysterious death.'

'Ah!' breathed Tuppence.

'For there we are up against the logic of facts. There are only two solutions. Either the chloral was administered by her own hand, which theory I reject utterly, or else—'

'Yes?'

'Or else it was administered in the brandy you gave her. Only three people touched that brandy—you, Miss Tuppence, I myself, and one other—Mr Julius Hersheimmer!'

Jane Finn stirred and sat up, regarding the speaker with wide astonished eyes.

'At first, the thing seemed utterly impossible. Mr Hersheimmer, as the son of a prominent millionaire, was a well-known figure in America. It seemed utterly impossible that he and Mr Brown could be one and the same. But you cannot escape from the logic of facts. Since the thing was so—it must be accepted. Remember Mrs Vandemeyer's sudden and inexplicable agitation. Another proof, if proof was needed.

'I took an early opportunity of giving you a hint. From some words of Mr Hersheimmer's at Manchester, I gathered that you had understood and acted on that hint. Then I set to work to prove the impossible possible. Mr Beresford rang me up and told me, what I had already suspected, that the photograph of Miss Jane Finn had never really been out of Mr Hersheimmer's possession—'

But the girl interrupted. Springing to her feet, she cried out angrily:

'What do you mean? What are you trying to suggest? That Mr Brown is *Julius*? Julius—my own cousin!'

'No, Miss Finn,' said Sir James unexpectedly. 'Not your cousin. The man who calls himself Julius Hersheimmer is no relation to you whatsoever.'

CHAPTER 26

Mr Brown

Sir James's words came like a bombshell. Both girls looked equally puzzled. The lawyer went across to his desk, and returned with a small newspaper cutting, which he handed to Jane. Tuppence read it over her shoulder. Mr Carter would have recognized it. It referred to the mysterious man found dead in New York.

'As I was saying to Miss Tuppence,' resumed the lawyer, 'I set to work to prove the impossible possible. The great stumbling-block was the undeniable fact that Julius Hersheimmer was not an assumed name. When I came across this paragraph my problem was solved. Julius Hersheimmer set out to discover what had become of his cousin. He went out West, where he obtained news of her and her photograph to aid him in his search. On the eve of his departure from New York he was set upon and murdered. His body was dressed in shabby clothes, and the face disfigured to prevent identification. Mr Brown took his place. He sailed immediately for England. None of the real Hersheimmer's friends or intimates saw him before he sailed—though indeed it would hardly have mattered if they had, the impersonation was so perfect. Since then he has been hand in glove with those sworn to hunt him down. Every secret of theirs had been known to him. Only once did he come near disaster. Mrs Vandemeyer knew his secret. It was no part of his plan that that huge bribe should ever be offered to her. But for Miss Tuppence's fortunate change of plan, she would have been far away from the flat when we arrived there. Exposure stared him in the face. He took a desperate step, trusting in his assumed character to avert suspicion. He nearly succeeded—but not quite.'

'I can't believe it,' murmured Jane. 'He seemed so splendid.'

'The real Julius Hersheimmer *was* a splendid fellow! And Mr Brown is a consummate actor. But ask Miss Tuppence if she also has not had her suspicions.'

Jane turned mutely to Tuppence. The latter nodded.

'I didn't want to say it, Jane—I knew it would hurt you. And, after all, I couldn't be sure. I still don't understand why, if he's Mr Brown, he rescued us.'

'Was it Julius Hersheimmer who helped you to escape?'

Tuppence recounted to Sir James the exciting events of the evening, ending up: 'But I can't see *why*!'

'Can't you? I can. So can young Beresford, by his actions. As a last hope Jane Finn was to be allowed to escape—and the escape must be managed so that she harbours no suspicions of its being a put-up job. They're not averse to young Beresford's being in the neighbourhood, and, if necessary,

300

communicating with you. They'll take care to get him out of the way at the right minute. Then Julius Hersheimmer dashes up and rescues you in true melodramatic style. Bullets fly—but don't hit anybody. What would have happened next? You would have driven straight to the house in Soho and secured the document which Miss Finn would probably have entrusted to her cousin's keeping. Or, if he conducted the search, he would have pretended to find the hiding-place already rifled. He would have had a dozen ways of dealing with the situation, but the result would have been the same. And I rather fancy some accident would have happened to both of you. You see, you know rather an inconvenient amount. That's a rough outline. I admit I was caught napping; but somebody else wasn't.'

'Tommy,' said Tuppence softly.

'Yes. Evidently when the right moment came to get rid of him—he was too sharp for them. All the same, I'm not too easy in my mind about him.'

'Why?'

'Because Julius Hersheimmer is Mr Brown,' said Sir James dryly. 'And it takes more than one man and a revolver to hold up Mr Brown...'

Tuppence paled a little.

'What can we do?'

'Nothing until we've been to the house in Soho. If Beresford has still got the upper hand, there's nothing to fear. If otherwise, our enemy will come to find us, and he will not find us unprepared!' From a drawer in the desk, he took a Service revolver, and placed it in his coat pocket.

'Now we're ready. I know better than even to suggest going without you, Miss Tuppence—'

'I should think so indeed!'

'But I do suggest that Miss Finn should remain here. She will be perfectly safe, and I am afraid she is absolutely worn out with all she has been through.'

But to Tuppence's surprise Jane shook her head.

'No. I guess I'm going too. Those papers were my trust. I must go through with this business to the end. I'm heaps better now anyway.'

Sir James's car was ordered round. During the short drive Tuppence's heart beat tumultuously. In spite of momentary qualms of uneasiness respecting Tommy, she could not but feel exultation. They were going to win!

The car drew up at the corner of the square and they got out. Sir James went up to a plain-clothes man who was on duty with several others, and spoke to him. Then he rejoined the girls.

'No one has gone into the house so far. It is being watched at the back as well, so they are quite sure of that. Anyone who attempts to enter after we have done so will be arrested immediately. Shall we go in?'

A policeman produced a key. They all knew Sir James well. They had also had orders respecting Tuppence. Only the third member of the party was unknown to them. The three entered the house, pulling the door to behind them. Slowly they mounted the rickety stairs. At the top was the ragged curtain hiding the recess where Tommy had hidden that day. Tuppence had heard the story from Jane in her character of 'Annette'. She looked at the tattered velvet with interest. Even now she could almost swear it moved—as though *someone* was behind it. So strong was the illusion that she almost fancied she could make out the outline of a form... Supposing Mr Brown—Julius—was there waiting...

Impossible of course! Yet she almost went back to put the curtain aside and make sure...

Now they were entering the prison room. No place for anyone to hide here, thought Tuppence, with a sigh of relief, then chided herself indignantly. She must not give way to this foolish fancying—this curious insistent feeling that *Mr Brown was in the house*... Hark! what was that? A stealthy footstep on the stairs? There *was* someone in the house! Absurd! She was becoming hysterical.

Jane had gone straight to the picture of Marguerite. She unhooked it with a steady hand. The dust lay thick upon it, and festoons of cobwebs lay between it and the wall. Sir James handed her a pocket-knife, and she stripped away the brown paper from the back... The advertisement page of a magazine fell out. Jane picked it up. Holding apart the frayed inner edges she extracted two thin sheets covered with writing!

No dummy this time! The real thing!

'We've got it,' said Tuppence. 'At last...'

The moment was almost breathless in its emotion. Forgotten the faint creakings, the imagined noises of a minute ago. None of them had eyes for anything but what Jane held in her hand.

Sir James took it, and scrutinized it attentively.

'Yes,' he said quietly, 'this is the ill-fated draft treaty!'

'We've succeeded,' said Tuppence. There was awe and an almost wondering unbelief in her voice.

Sir James echoed her words as he folded the paper carefully and put it away in his pocket-book, then he looked curiously round the dingy room.

'It was here that your young friend was confined for so long, was it not?' he said. 'A truly sinister room. You notice the absence of windows, and the thickness of the close-fitting door. Whatever took place here would never be heard by the outside world.'

Tuppence shivered. His words woke a vague alarm in her. What if there *was* someone concealed in the house? Someone who might bar that door on them, and leave them to die like rats in a trap? Then she realized the absurdity of her thought. The house was surrounded by police who, if they failed to reappear, would not hesitate to break in and make a thorough search. She smiled at her own foolishness—then looked up with a start to find Sir James watching her. He gave her an emphatic little nod.

'Quite right, Miss Tuppence. You scent danger. So do I. So does Miss Finn.'

'Yes,' admitted Jane. 'It's absurd—but I can't help it.'

Sir James nodded again.

'You feel—as we all feel—*the presence of Mr Brown.* Yes'—as Tuppence made a movement—'not a doubt of it—*Mr Brown is here...*'

'In this house?'

'In this room... You don't understand? *I am Mr Brown...*'

Stupefied, unbelieving, they stared at him. The very lines of his face had changed. It was a different man who stood before them. He smiled a slow cruel smile.

'Neither of you will leave this room alive! You said just now we had succeeded. *I* have succeeded! The draft treaty is mine.' His smile grew wider as he looked at Tuppence. 'Shall I tell you how it will be? Sooner or later the police will break in, and they will find three victims of Mr Brown—three, not two, you understand, but fortunately the third will not be dead, only wounded, and will be able to describe the attack with a wealth of detail! The treaty? It is in the hands of Mr Brown. So no one will think of searching the pockets of Sir James Peel Edgerton!'

He turned to Jane.

'You outwitted me. I make my acknowledgments. But you will not do it again.'

There was a faint sound behind him, but intoxicated with success he did not turn his head.

He slipped his hand into his pocket.

'Checkmate to the Young Adventurers,' he said, and slowly raised the big revolver.

But, even as he did so, he felt himself seized from behind in a grip of iron. The revolver was wrenched from his hand, and the voice of Julius Hersheimmer said drawlingly:

'I guess you're caught red-handed with the goods upon you.'

The blood rushed to the K.C.'s face, but his self-control was marvellous, as he looked from one to the other of his two captors. He looked longest at Tommy.

'You,' he said beneath his breath. '*You!* I might have known.'

Seeing that he was disposed to offer no resistance, their grip slackened. Quick as a flash his left hand, the hand which bore the big signet ring, was raised to his lips...

'"*Ave Cæsar! te morituri salutant*,"' he said, still looking at Tommy.

Then his face changed, and with a long convulsive shudder he fell forward in a crumpled heap, whilst an odour of bitter almonds filled the air.

CHAPTER 27

A Supper Party at the Savoy

The supper party given by Mr Julius Hersheimmer to a few friends on the evening of the 30th will long be remembered in catering circles. It took place in a private room, and Mr Hersheimmer's orders were brief and forcible. He gave carte blanche—and when a millionaire gives carte blanche he usually gets it!

Every delicacy out of season was duly provided. Waiters carried bottles of ancient and royal vintage with loving care. The floral decorations defied the seasons, and fruits of the earth as far apart as May and November found themselves miraculously side by side. The list of guests was small and select. The American Ambassador, Mr Carter, who had taken the liberty, he said, of bringing an old friend, Sir William Beresford, with him, Archdeacon Cowley, Dr Hall, those two youthful adventurers, Miss Prudence Cowley and Mr Thomas Beresford, and last, but not least, as guest of honour, Miss Jane Finn.

Julius had spared no pains to make Jane's appearance a success. A mysterious knock had brought Tuppence to the door of the apartment she was sharing with the American girl. It was Julius. In his hand he held a cheque.

'Say, Tuppence,' he began, 'will you do me a good turn? Take this, and get Jane regularly togged up for this evening. You're all coming to supper with me at the Savoy. See? Spare no expense. You get me?'

'Sure thing,' mimicked Tuppence. 'We shall enjoy ourselves! It will be a pleasure dressing Jane. She's the loveliest thing I've ever seen.'

'That's so,' agreed Mr Hersheimmer fervently.

His fervour brought a momentary twinkle to Tuppence's eye.

'By the way, Julius,' she remarked demurely, 'I—haven't given you my answer yet.'

'Answer?' said Julius. His face paled.

'You know—when you asked me to—marry you,' faltered Tuppence, her eyes downcast in the true manner of the early Victorian heroine, 'and wouldn't take no for an answer. I've thought it well over—'

'Yes?' said Julius. The perspiration stood on his forehead.

Tuppence relented suddenly.

'You great idiot!' she said. 'What on earth induced you to do it? I could see at the time you didn't care a twopenny dip for me!'

'Not at all. I had—and still have—the highest sentiments of esteem and respect—and admiration for you—'

'H'm!' said Tuppence. 'Those are the kind of sentiments that very soon go to the wall when the other sentiment comes along! Don't they, old thing?'

'I don't know what you mean,' said Julius stiffly, but a large and burning blush overspread his countenance.

'Shucks!' retorted Tuppence. She laughed and closed the door, reopening it to add with dignity: 'Morally, I shall always consider I have been jilted!'

'What was it?' asked Jane as Tuppence rejoined her.

'Julius.'

'What did he want?'

'Really, I think, he wanted to see you, but I wasn't going to let him. Not until tonight, when you're going to burst upon everyone like King Solomon in his glory! Come on! *We're going to shop!*'

To most people the 29th, the much-heralded 'Labour Day,' had passed much as any other day. Speeches were made in the Park and Trafalgar Square. Straggling processions, singing *The Red Flag*, wandered through the streets in a more or less aimless manner. Newspapers which had hinted at a general strike, and the inauguration of a reign of terror, were forced to hide their diminished heads. The bolder and more astute among them sought to prove that peace had been effected by following their counsels. In the Sunday papers a brief notice of the sudden death of Sir James Peel Edgerton, the famous K.C., had appeared. Monday's paper dealt appreciatively with the dead man's career. The exact manner of his sudden death was never made public.

Tommy had been right in his forecast of the situation. It had been a one-man show. Deprived of their chief, the organization fell to pieces. Kramenin had made a precipitate return to Russia, leaving England early on Sunday

Agatha Christie

morning. The gang had fled from Astley Priors in a panic, leaving behind, in their haste, various damaging documents which compromised them hopelessly. With these proofs of conspiracy in their hands, aided further by a small brown diary, taken from the pocket of the dead man which had contained a full and damning résumé of the whole plot, the Government had called an eleventh-hour conference. The Labour leaders were forced to recognize that they had been used as a cat's paw. Certain concessions were made by the Government, and were eagerly accepted. It was to be Peace, not War!

But the Cabinet knew by how narrow a margin they had escaped utter disaster. And burnt in on Mr Carter's brain was the strange scene which had taken place in the house in Soho the night before.

He had entered the squalid room to find that great man, the friend of a lifetime, dead—betrayed out of his own mouth. From the dead man's pocket-book he had retrieved the ill-omened draft treaty, and then and there, in the presence of the other three, it had been reduced to ashes... England was saved!

And now, on the evening of the 30th, in a private room at the Savoy, Mr Julius P. Hersheimmer was receiving his guests.

Mr Carter was the first to arrive. With him was a choleric-looking old gentleman, at sight of whom Tommy flushed up to the roots of his hair. He came forward.

'Ha!' said the old gentleman surveying him apoplectically. 'So you're my nephew, are you? Not much to look at—but you've done good work, it seems. Your mother must have brought you up well after all. Shall we let bygones be bygones, eh? You're my heir, you know; and in future I propose to make you an allowance—and you can look upon Chalmers Park as your home.'

'Thank you, sir, it's awfully decent of you.'

'Where's this young lady I've been hearing such a lot about?' Tommy introduced Tuppence.

'Ha!' said Sir William, eyeing her. 'Girls aren't what they used to be in my young days.'

'Yes, they are,' said Tuppence. 'Their clothes are different, perhaps, but they themselves are just the same.'

'Well, perhaps you're right. Minxes then—minxes now!'

'That's it,' said Tuppence. 'I'm a frightful minx myself.'

'I believe you,' said the old gentleman, chuckling, and pinched her ear in high good-humour. Most young women were terrified of the 'old bear,' as they termed him. Tuppence's pertness delighted the old misogynist.

Then came the timid archdeacon, a little bewildered by the company in which he found himself, glad that his daughter was considered to have distinguished herself, but unable to help glancing at her from time to time with nervous apprehension. But Tuppence behaved admirably. She forbore to cross her legs, set a guard upon her tongue, and steadfastly refused to smoke.

Dr Hall came next, and he was followed by the American Ambassador.

'We might as well sit down,' said Julius, when he had introduced all his guests to each other. 'Tuppence, will you—'

Agatha Christie

He indicated the place of honour with a wave of his hand. But Tuppence shook her head.

'No—that's Jane's place! When one thinks of how she's held out all these years, she ought to be made the queen of the feast tonight.'

Julius flung her a grateful glance, and Jane came forward shyly to the allotted seat. Beautiful as she had seemed before, it was as nothing to the loveliness that now went fully adorned. Tuppence had performed her part faithfully. The model gown supplied by a famous dressmaker had been entitled 'A tiger lily'. It was all golds and reds and browns, and out of it rose the pure column of the girl's white throat, and the bronze masses of hair that crowned her lovely head. There was admiration in every eye, as she took her seat.

Soon the supper party was in full swing, and with one accord Tommy was called upon for a full and complete explanation.

'You've been too darned close about the whole business,' Julius accused him. 'You let on to me that you were off to the Argentine—though I guess you had your reasons for that. The idea of both you and Tuppence casting me for the part of Mr Brown just tickles me to death!'

'The idea was not original to them,' said Mr Carter gravely. 'It was suggested, and the poison very carefully instilled, by a past-master in the art. The paragraph in the New York paper suggested the plan to him, and by means of it he wove a web that nearly enmeshed you fatally.'

'I never liked him,' said Julius. 'I felt from the first that there was something wrong about him, and I always suspected that it was he who silenced Mrs Vandemeyer

312

so appositely. But it wasn't till I heard that the order for Tommy's execution came right on the heels of our interview with him that Sunday that I began to tumble to the fact that he was the big bug himself.'

'I never suspected it at all,' lamented Tuppence. 'I've always thought I was so much cleverer than Tommy—but he's undoubtedly scored over me handsomely.'

Julius agreed.

'Tommy's been the goods this trip! And, instead of sitting there as dumb as a fish, let him banish his blushes, and tell us all about it.'

'Hear! hear!'

'There's nothing to tell,' said Tommy, acutely uncomfortable. 'I was an awful mug—right up to the time I found that photograph of Annette, and realized that she was Jane Finn. Then I remembered how persistently she had shouted out that word "Marguerite"—and I thought of the pictures, and—well, that's that. Then of course I went over the whole thing to see where I'd made an ass of myself.'

'Go on,' said Mr Carter, as Tommy showed signs of taking refuge in silence once more.

'That business about Mrs Vandemeyer had worried me when Julius told me about it. On the face of it, it seemed that he or Sir James must have done the trick. But I didn't know which. Finding that photograph in the drawer, after that story of how it had been got from him by Inspector Brown, made me suspect Julius. Then I remembered that it was Sir James who had discovered the false Jane Finn. In the end, I couldn't make up my mind—and just decided to take no chances either way. I left a note for Julius, in case he was Mr Brown, saying I was off to the Argentine, and I dropped Sir James's letter with the offer of the job by the desk so that he would see it was a genuine stunt. Then I wrote my letter to Mr Carter and rang up Sir James. Taking him into my confidence would be the best thing either way, so I told him everything except where I believed the papers to be hidden. The way he helped me to get on the track of Tuppence and Annette almost disarmed me, but not quite. I kept my mind open between the two of them. And then I got a bogus note from Tuppence—and then I knew!'

'But how?'

Tommy took the note in question from his pocket and passed it round the table.

'It's her handwriting all right, but I knew it wasn't from her because of the signature. She'd never spell her name "Twopence," but anyone who'd never seen it written might quite easily do so. Julius *had* seen it—he showed me a note of hers to him once—but *Sir James hadn't*! After that everything was plain sailing. I sent off Albert post-haste to Mr Carter. I pretended to go away, but doubled back again. When Julius came bursting up in his car, I felt it wasn't part of Mr Brown's plan—and that there would probably be trouble. Unless Sir James was actually caught in the act, so to speak, I knew Mr Carter would never believe it of him on my bare word—'

'I didn't,' interposed Mr Carter ruefully.

'That's why I sent the girls off to Sir James. I was sure they'd fetch up at the house in Soho sooner or later.

314

I threatened Julius with the revolver, because I wanted Tuppence to repeat that to Sir James, so that he wouldn't worry about us. The moment the girls were out of sight I told Julius to drive like hell for London, and as we went along I told him the whole story. We got to the Soho house in plenty of time and met Mr Carter outside. After arranging things with him we went in and hid behind the curtain in the recess. The policemen had orders to say, if they were asked, that no one had gone into the house. That's all.'

And Tommy came to an abrupt halt.

There was silence for a moment.

'By the way,' said Julius suddenly, 'you're all wrong about that photograph of Jane. It *was* taken from me, but I found it again.'

'Where?' cried Tuppence.

'In that little safe on the wall in Mrs Vandermeyer's bedroom.'

'I knew you found something,' said Tuppence reproachfully. 'To tell you the truth, that's what started me off suspecting you. Why didn't you say?'

'I guess I was a mite suspicious too. It had been got away from me once, and I determined I wouldn't let on I'd got it until a photographer had made a dozen copies of it!'

'We all kept back something or other,' said Tuppence thoughtfully. 'I suppose secret service work makes you like that!'

In the pause that ensued, Mr Carter took from his pocket a small shabby brown book.

'Beresford has just said that I would not have believed Sir James Peel Edgerton to be guilty unless, so to speak, he was caught in the act. That is so. Indeed, not until I read the entries in this little book could I bring myself fully to credit the amazing truth. This book will pass into the possession of Scotland Yard, but it will never be publicly exhibited. Sir James's long association with the law would make it undesirable. But to you, who know the truth, I propose to read certain passages which will throw some light on the extraordinary mentality of this great man.'

He opened the book, and turned the thin pages.

'...It is madness to keep this book. I know that. It is documentary evidence against me. But I have never shrunk from taking risks. And I feel an urgent need for self-expression... The book will only be taken from my dead body...

'...From an early age I realized that I had exceptional abilities. Only a fool underestimates his capabilities. My brain power was greatly above the average. I know that I was born to succeed. My appearance was the only thing against me. I was quiet and insignificant—utterly nondescript...

'...When I was a boy I heard a famous murder trial. I was deeply impressed by the power and eloquence of the counsel for the defence. For the first time I entertained the idea of taking my talents to that particular market... Then I studied the criminal in the dock... The man was a fool—he had been incredibly, unbelievably stupid. Even the eloquence of his counsel was hardly likely to save him... I felt an immeasurable contempt for him... Then it occurred to me that the criminal standard was a low one. It was the wastrels, the failures, the general riff-raff of civilization who drifted into crime... Strange that men of brains had never realized its extraordinary opportunities... I played with the idea... What a magnificent field—what unlimited possibilities! It made my brain reel...

'...I read standard works on crime and criminals. They all confirmed my opinion. Degeneracy, disease—never the deliberate embracing of a career by a far-seeing man. Then I considered. Supposing my utmost ambitions were realized—that I was called to the bar, and rose to the height of my profession? That I entered politics—say, even, that I became Prime Minister of England? What then? Was that power? Hampered at every turn by my colleagues, fettered by the democratic system of which I should be the mere figurehead! No—the power I dreamed of was absolute! An autocrat! A dictator! And such power could only be obtained by working outside the law. To play on the weaknesses of human nature, then on the weaknesses of nations—to get together and control a vast organization, and finally to overthrow the existing order, and rule! The thought intoxicated me...

'...I saw that I must lead two lives. A man like myself is bound to attract notice. I must have a successful career which would mask my true activities... Also I must cultivate a personality. I modelled myself upon famous K.C.'s. I reproduced their mannerisms, their magnetism. If I had chosen to be an actor, I should have been the greatest actor living! No disguises—no grease paint—no false beards! Personality! I put it on like a glove! When I shed it, I was myself, quiet, unobtrusive, a man like every other man. I called myself Mr Brown. There are hundreds of men called Brown—there are hundreds of men looking just like me...

'...I succeeded in my false career. I was bound to succeed. I shall succeed in the other. A man like me cannot fail...

'...I have been reading a life of Napoleon. He and I have much in common...

'...I make a practice of defending criminals. A man should look after his own people...

'...Once or twice I have felt afraid. The first time was in Italy. There was a dinner given. Professor D——, the great alienist, was present. The talk fell on insanity. He said, "A great many men are mad, and no one knows it. They do not know it themselves." I do not understand why he looked at me when he said that. His glance was strange... I did not like it...

'...The war has disturbed me... I thought it would further my plans. The Germans are so efficient. Their spy system, too, was excellent. The streets are full of these boys in khaki. All empty-headed young fools... Yet I do not know... They won the war... It disturbs me...

'...My plans are going well... A girl butted in—I do not think she really knew anything... But we must give up the Esthonia... No risks now...

'...All goes well. The loss of memory is vexing. It cannot be a fake. No girl could deceive ME!...

'...The 29th... That is very soon...' Mr Carter paused.

'I will not read the details of the *coup* that was planned. But there are just two small entries that refer to the three of you. In the light of what happened they are interesting.

'...By inducing the girl to come to me of her own accord, I have succeeded in disarming her. But she has intuitive flashes that might be dangerous... She must be got out of the way... I can do nothing with the American. He suspects and dislikes me. But he cannot know. I fancy my armour is impregnable... Sometimes I fear I have underestimated the other boy. He is not clever, but it is hard to blind his eyes to facts...'

Mr Carter shut the book.

'A great man,' he said. 'Genius, or insanity, who can say?'

There was silence.

Then Mr Carter rose to his feet.

'I will give you a toast. The Joint Venture which has so amply justified itself by success!'

It was drunk with acclamation.

'There's something more we want to hear,' continued Mr Carter. He looked at the American Ambassador. 'I speak for you also, I know. We'll ask Miss Jane Finn to tell us the story that only Miss Tuppence has heard so far—but before we do so we'll drink her health. The health of one of the bravest of America's daughters, to whom is due the thanks and gratitude of two great countries!'

And After

'That was a mighty good toast, Jane,' said Mr Hersheimmer, as he and his cousin were being driven back in the Rolls-Royce to the Ritz.

'The one to the joint venture?'

'No—the one to you. There isn't another girl in the world who could have carried it through as you did. You were just wonderful!'

Jane shook her head.

'I don't feel wonderful. At heart I'm just tired and lonesome—and longing for my own country.'

'That brings me to something I wanted to say. I heard the Ambassador telling you his wife hoped you would come to them at the Embassy right away. That's good enough, but I've got another plan. Jane—I want you to marry me! Don't get scared and say no at once. You can't love me right away, of course, that's impossible. But I've loved you from the very moment I set eyes on your photo—and now I've seen you I'm simply crazy about you! If you'll only marry me, I won't worry you any—you shall take your own time. Maybe you'll never come to love me, and if that's the case I'll manage to set you free. But I want the right to look after you, and take care of you.'

'That's what I want,' said the girl wistfully. 'Someone who'll be good to me. Oh, you don't know how lonesome I feel!'

'Sure thing I do. Then I guess that's all fixed up, and I'll see the archbishop about a special licence tomorrow morning.'

'Oh, Julius!'

'Well, I don't want to hustle you any, Jane, but there's no sense in waiting about. Don't be scared—I shan't expect you to love me all at once.'

But a small hand was slipped into his.

'I love you now, Julius,' said Jane Finn. 'I loved you that first moment in the car when the bullet grazed your cheek...'

Five minutes later Jane murmured softly:

'I don't know London very well, Julius, but is it such a very long way from the Savoy to the Ritz?'

'It depends how you go,' explained Julius unblushingly. 'We're going by way of Regent's Park!'

'Oh, Julius—what will the chauffeur think?'

'At the wages I pay him, he knows better than to do any independent thinking. Why, Jane, the only reason I had the supper at the Savoy was so that I could drive you home. I didn't see how I was ever going to get hold of you alone. You and Tuppence have been sticking together like Siamese twins. I guess another day of it would have driven me and Beresford stark staring mad!'

'Oh. Is he—?'

'Of course he is. Head over ears.'

'I thought so,' said Jane thoughtfully.

'Why?'

'From all the things Tuppence didn't say!'

'There you have me beat,' said Mr Hersheimmer.

But Jane only laughed.

In the meantime, the Young Adventurers were sitting bolt upright, very stiff and ill at ease, in a taxi which, with a singular lack of originality, was also returning to the Ritz via Regent's Park.

A terrible constraint seemed to have settled down between them. Without quite knowing what had happened, everything seemed changed. They were tongue-tied—paralysed. All the old *cameraderie* was gone.

Tuppence could think of nothing to say.

Tommy was equally afflicted.

They sat very straight and forbore to look at each other.

At last Tuppence made a desperate effort.

'Rather fun, wasn't it?'

'Rather.'

Another silence.

'I like Julius,' essayed Tuppence again.

Tommy was suddenly galvanized into life.

'You're not going to marry him, do you hear?' he said dictatorially. 'I forbid it.'

'Oh!' said Tuppence meekly.

'Absolutely, you understand.'

'He doesn't want to marry me—he really only asked me out of kindness.'

'That's not very likely,' scoffed Tommy.

'It's quite true. He's head over ears in love with Jane. I expect he's proposing to her now.'

'She'll do for him very nicely,' said Tommy condescendingly.

'Don't you think she's the most lovely creature you've ever seen?'

'Oh, I dare say.'

'But I suppose you prefer sterling worth,' said Tuppence demurely.

'I—oh, dash it all, Tuppence, you know!'

'I like your uncle, Tommy,' said Tuppence, hastily creating a diversion. 'By the way, what are you going to do, accept Mr Carter's offer of a Government job, or accept Julius's invitation and take a richly remunerated post in America on his ranch?'

'I shall stick to the old ship, I think, though it's awfully good of Hersheimmer. But I feel you'd be more at home in London.'

'I don't see where I come in.'

'I do,' said Tommy positively.

Tuppence stole a glance at him sideways.

'There's the money, too,' she observed thoughtfully.

'What money?'

'We're going to get a cheque each. Mr Carter told me so.'

'Did you ask how much?' inquired Tommy sarcastically.

'Yes,' said Tuppence triumphantly. 'But I shan't tell you.'

'Tuppence, you are the limit!'

'It has been fun, hasn't it, Tommy? I do hope we shall have lots more adventures.'

'You're insatiable, Tuppence. I've had quite enough adventures for the present.'

'Well, shopping is almost as good,' said Tuppence dreamily. 'Thinking of buying old furniture, and bright carpets, and futurist silk curtains, and a polished dining-table, and a divan with lots of cushions—'

'Hold hard,' said Tommy. 'What's all this for?'

'Possibly a house—but I think a flat.'

'Whose flat?'

'You think I mind saying it, but I don't in the least! *Ours*, so there!'

'You darling!' cried Tommy, his arms tightly round her. 'I was determined to make you say it. I owe you something for the relentless way you've squashed me whenever I've tried to be sentimental.'

Tuppence raised her face to his. The taxi proceeded on its course round the north side of Regent's Park.

'You haven't really proposed now,' pointed out Tuppence. 'Not what our grandmothers would call a proposal. But after listening to a rotten one like Julius's, I'm inclined to let you off.'

'You won't be able to get out of marrying me, so don't you think it.'

'What fun it will be,' responded Tuppence. 'Marriage is called all sorts of things, a haven, a refuge, and a crowning glory, and a state of bondage, and lots more. But do you know what I think it is?'

'What?'

'A sport!'

'And a damned good sport too,' said Tommy.

324

Agatha Christie

Short stories for your E-reader

TOMMY & TUPPENCE

The Affair of the Pink Pearl

The Adventure of the Sinister Stranger

Finessing the King/The Gentleman Dressed in Newspaper

The Case of the Missing Lady

Blindman's Buff

The Man in the Mist

The Crackler

The Sunningdale Mystery

The House of Lurking Death

The Unbreakable Alibi

The Clergyman's Daughter/ The Red House

The Ambassador's Boots

The Man Who Was No. 16

HARLEY QUIN

The Coming of Mr Quin

The Shadow on the Glass

At the 'Bells and Motley'

The Sign in the Sky

The Soul of the Croupier

The Man from the Sea

The Dead Harlequin

The Love Detectives

The Harlequin Tea Set

PARKER PYNE

The Case of the Middle-Aged Wife

The Case of the Discontented Soldier

The Case of the Distressed Lady

The Case of the Discontented Husband

The Gate of Baghdad

The House at Shiraz

The Pearl of Price

A Death on the Nile

The Oracle at Delphi

Problem at Pollensa Bay